Gaia's Temptation

Elizabeth Salo

Copyright © 2026 by Elizabeth Salo

All rights reserved.

No part of this publication may be reproduced, distributed, or transmitted in any form or by any means, including photocopying, recording, or other electronic or mechanical methods, without the prior written permission of the publisher, except as permitted by U.S. copyright law.

The story, all names, characters, and incidents portrayed in this production are fictitious. No identification with actual persons (living or deceased), places, buildings, and products is intended or should be inferred.

Book Cover by Graphicsoul Art

First edition 2026

EBOOK ISBN: 978-1-962460-09-5

PAPERBACK ISBN: 978-1-962460-10-1

HARDCOVER ISBN: 978-1-962460-11-8

Contents

Prophecy

The day shall come when storms will rise,

Evil comes in friendship's guise.

Chaos reigns to ill effect,

Giving rise to an Architect.

While lives are lost and costs incurred,

He shall raise the harbinger.

Yet hope remains while bonds stay strong,

Friendship rules and all belong.

Fire, Air, Earth and Water,

Must stand against the endless slaughter.

Prologue

A BALL OF FLAMES whooshed into existence, cupped carefully in Roderick's hand. The heat was intense, but he remained rock steady. He slowly built the intensity, coaxing it higher and hotter into a miniature inferno.

Sweat beaded on his forehead as he poured his power into the tiny blaze. His fire magic protected his skin from the damaging side effects of his gift, but even that only went so far. Just as his skin started to crack, he pulled his magic back inside himself. The flames died and a silence fell on the warehouse.

Yet there it was, the small piece of metal still resting in his open palm. The witch's-knot talisman reflected the warehouse's overhead lights, winking at him—mocking him. His magic hadn't even made a dent in the metal. Who would have thought that such a tiny thing would have caused him so much frustration?

"Haven't you tried that already?" Danika asked, not even glancing up from the magazine she was reading.

Of course he had, but he wasn't willing to admit to her exactly how desperate he was. He'd had the talisman in his possession for almost three months, and yet he was no closer to getting his hands on the magic that the talisman's rightful owner—his former student Jenna—could wield with it. The amount of power at Jenna's fingertips was astonishing, and Roderick wanted it for himself. Using her power was the only way he could carry out his sworn mission.

He just needed to figure out how to access it.

Roderick had been planning for a long time. He still remembered the shock he'd felt thirty years ago when he heard the Elementa had been reborn. Four elemental witches—born on the same day, at the same hour, in the same place. Jenna Hastings commanded water. Sierra Dalton shaped the earth. Aura Burton ruled the air. Brigit Westlake wielded fire.

The Elementa were orders of magnitude more powerful than other witches, even those with the same elemental affinities. His own fire magic was a tiny match compared to the raging inferno Brigit could wield.

Roderick knew, even when the girls were young, that they would be the key to his destiny. He'd studied magic like a man obsessed, learning new spells that steadily grew his power. Learning magic the *right* way only took him so far, so he'd moved on to studying the darker side of his powers. Dark magic granted him gifts that he could only have dreamed of. Roderick maneuvered his way up the ranks and positioned himself so that by the time the Elementa had come of age at sixteen, he was the logical choice to be their mentor.

He had carefully crafted four identical talismans in the shape of a quaternary knot—a witch's knot—and on each one he placed a binding spell. On the day of their sixteenth birthday, Roderick presented each girl with her own talisman to use as he taught them and honed their skills. A witch's relationship with their talisman was a symbiotic, living one. The witch's powers imbued themselves into the talisman, and it, in turn, helped the witch's magic reach its full potential. The binding spell Roderick had placed on each talisman was designed to grant him access to that power.

And then he waited. For years.

Then three months ago, it finally happened. He convinced Jenna to surrender her talisman to him voluntarily. He even convinced her it was for her own protection. *Naïve idiot.*

What he hadn't counted on was that his binding spell was nowhere to be found. The very thing he'd been expecting to grant him easy access to Jenna's magic ... gone. He was so close to being able to siphon the magic he needed to raise his sovereign, the Harbinger, and yet still so far. If he could incorporate even a fraction of each of the girls' magic into his own, he would be unstoppable. Prophecy be damned.

Unfortunately, no matter what spell, potion, or magic he tried on Jenna's talisman, he was still unable to tap into the power it held. Luckily, he had a backup plan.

He glanced at the waif-like woman sitting across from him looking bored. "It's time for phase two."

Chapter One

THE PETAL PATCH WAS, in Sierra's mind, perfect. The floor was a warm brick, and the walls were a complementary wood tone. There were coolers of individual cut flowers and arrangements off to one side. Shelves covered with potted plants lined the walls. Baskets hung from the ceiling, spilling greenery toward the floor, and small tables were crammed everywhere filled with plants, candles and tchotchkes of all varieties. In honor of the fall season, painted pumpkins sat cheerily on her counter, giant bundles of dried cornstalks leaned up against the outside of the store, and a wreath made from dried wheat hung from the door. The Petal Patch was Sierra's happy place.

Except when Tansy Sandoval darkened her doorstep.

A black cloud descended on Sierra Dalton's mood the moment Tansy walked through the door. The bride from hell. This time, she'd brought reinforcements in the form of her mother, Cassondra. Too bad she hadn't brought her father, Eric, instead. He was the only reasonable one in the family. Sierra had commiserated with him a lot over the last few months about the stress that went into planning a wedding, especially for the pretentious blonde woman currently assaulting a display of daisies. How a caring local school administrator wound up marrying one of the richest, and most obnoxious women in Boston and having a child together was a mystery for the ages.

Tansy glanced around the small flower shop with the same disdain she always showed when she deigned to set foot in Sierra's domain. Like most bridezillas, Tansy insisted her wedding had to be perfect, but she also didn't think much of the people she paid to make that happen. Cassondra's nose turned up in a perfect imitation of her daughter's as she inspected the space.

Sierra's shop did excellent business, but she still couldn't turn down a wedding with the price tag that Tansy and Cassondra had. This single event could pay for Sierra's expenses for months, so she did what she always did. She smiled sweetly and braced herself for whatever shitstorm was about to come her way.

Tansy carefully picked her way around the tables, ensuring that her impeccable clothing—which probably cost more than Sierra made in a month—didn't so much as brush up against anything. She dragged her mother to where Sierra stood at the rear of the shop.

"Sarah, we need to talk about the flowers for the arch on the altar. They're all wrong."

Sierra clenched her jaw. She had been working on this event for months and they'd met dozens of times to discuss the flower arrangements. Yet, no matter how many times Sierra corrected her, Tansy always got her name wrong. It had to be deliberate at this point. Nevertheless, she tried again. "It's Sierra."

Tansy waved her hand dismissively. "Roses are completely wrong for the aesthetic we're going for."

This was the third time that Tansy had changed her mind about what flowers she wanted covering the arch. "What did you have in mind, this time?" Sierra asked, her voice carefully neutral.

Tansy and her mother shared a look. "I'm thinking peonies. Pale pink, obviously, but as many of them as you can possibly fit."

Sierra clenched her fists behind the counter where the other women couldn't see them. "Your wedding is in less than a week."

Tansy stared at her blankly.

"And?" Cassondra asked, her perfectly manicured eyebrows lifting.

Sierra closed her eyes and took a deep breath. Opening her eyes again, she said, "I can call around to my suppliers, but I'm not sure if I'll be able to get enough peonies to cover the arch you have picked out. If I'd had more notice I could have placed a special order, but with the wedding only a few days away, it might not be possible. Even if I can find them, it's going to cost extra for a rush order."

Tansy let out an irritated huff that dug under Sierra's skin even further. "I don't care what you have to do to get them. Flowers are your thing, not mine. Just get me my peonies." Tansy reached for her phone, already done with the conversation.

"I'll do my best," Sierra said through gritted teeth.

Cassondra turned up her nose and brushed invisible lint off her perfect Chanel dress. "You'd better. The governor is going to be at this wedding, and you will not embarrass us. You know who I am, and you know the circles I run in. I can have your tiny shop shut down by morning."

A rough, scratching sensation started from the tips of Sierra's fingers and ran under her skin to her chest, head, and feet. The feeling wasn't new, but it had been a long time since she'd experienced it. Sierra felt threatened, and her long-dormant magic was responding accordingly. The small, closed buds in the vase at the end of the counter began to bloom, transforming into full, luscious blossoms. Vines of ivy and hoya crept out of their hanging baskets and lengthened, stretching toward the ungrateful customers.

Sierra started panting, her eyes widening as the plants in her shop slowly reacted to her distress and came alive. "No, no, no ..." Sierra whispered under her breath as she willed her powers back under her control.

"What was that?" Cassondra asked sharply.

A vine from a creeping fig had almost reached Tansy's Louboutins before Sierra finally unfroze enough to move. She stepped around her counter and gestured for the women to head toward the door. "Ladies, it has been a pleasure as always. I'll get to work right this instant on finding you those peonies. You can count on me."

Sierra got one last look as Tansy delicately seated herself in the back of their ridiculously expensive vehicle before one of the vines finally reached the shop door and slammed it shut. Sierra—frantic—flipped the lock and turned off the open sign.

She spun until her back hit the door and slowly sank down to the brick floor. The plants all seemed to take a collective sigh of relief. Most of the flowers and greenery settled down, maybe a little brighter or larger than they'd been before, but basically the same. One lone ivy vine inched its way across the shelf next to her until it brushed her shoulder gently then retreated.

What. The. Hell.

Sierra didn't know what to make of it. Yes, she was an earth witch. But she also hadn't practiced magic in more than ten years. That part of her was locked down and there was no reason it should have come out now, especially not in front of ordinaries. There were rules and codes to stop exactly that from happening, something her best friend, Jenna, had dealt with just a few months ago. Sierra had no desire to duplicate her experience.

But why had it happened?

She glanced at her hands like they would tell her anything. She hadn't called her magic, it had just sort of happened. Yes, she'd been upset by the snotty and entitled Bostonians. That alone shouldn't have been enough to trigger anything. Being in a customer-facing profession meant that Sierra had dealt with plenty of horrible people, especially when it came to weddings. Perfectly normal people seemed to go a little batty when it came to getting married—not that Tansy Sandoval was normal by any stretch of the imagination. But Sierra didn't have time to think about her magic right now. She needed to get on the phone with every supplier she had and see what she could do to salvage the biggest event of her career.

Her cell phone started ringing just as she rose to her feet. Sierra hurried across the floor to grab it. One look at the screen had her sagging in defeat. It was the elementary school. Again.

"Hello?" She braced herself as she answered the phone. It was the middle of the day. There was almost no way this call was a good thing.

"Mrs. Dalton, this is Andrew Knight. I'm Lucas's teacher at Rock Cove Elementary School."

She knew who Andrew Knight was by name, even if she hadn't had a chance to meet him yet. "Yes, Mr. Knight. What can I do for you today?"

"I'm afraid we have a little situation with Lucas. I'd like to speak to you or your husband this afternoon, if possible."

Her heart skipped a beat then slammed into double time. "What's this about? Did something happen to Lucas? Is he hurt?" If Lucas was injured his teacher would have led with that, right?

"No, Lucas is fine. I'm sorry to have scared you." The man's voice softened slightly. "It's just a behavioral situation that needs to be addressed."

Sigh. It was the second week of first grade and Lucas was already having behavioral issues. Sierra loved Lucas like crazy, but single parenting wasn't for the faint of heart, and Lucas seemed to take that to a whole different level. Not that he was a bad kid. He was a normal six-year-old. Well, *normal* might be a stretch for a pint-sized witch, but what else could she say? It wasn't like she could tell that to his first-grade teacher.

She resigned herself for yet another conversation where she could only explain half the story. "What time should I be there?"

Chapter Two

Andrew Knight had been an elementary school teacher for ten years, but he'd never come across a situation like this one. He watched the sullen six-year-old from across the room. Lucas scuffed the bottom of his well-worn sneakers against the floor while he rested his head on his arms on top of the empty desk in front of him. That sort of behavior was normal for a kid his age.

It was Lucas's bizarre behavior at recess that had concerned him.

Andrew gave a cursory look at the assignments on his desk that he was supposed to be grading. It was only the second week of school, so they hadn't covered a lot of material yet, but he had pages and pages of simple addition problems. He picked up the pile and tapped it neatly into a stack and then glanced at the top assignment. Coincidentally, it was from Lucas Dalton.

Keeping half of his attention on Lucas, Andrew grabbed his blue pen to correct whatever mistakes he'd made. Except he hadn't made any.

Lucas's math homework was flawless. Andrew wrote a big "10/10" on the top of the page and circled it.

Glancing back at where Lucas was now tapping his fingers against his arms, Andrew said, "Your mom should be here any minute." He peeked at the clock. It was already ten past three. Mrs. Dalton had confirmed she would be at the school at three o'clock. Hopefully she wasn't one of those absentee mothers that couldn't pull her head out of her own life long enough to care about her son.

"Okay." Lucas's lack of reaction was hard to interpret. Was he used to waiting on his mother or was this atypical?

Andrew was almost through his stack of assignments when an attractive brunette woman burst into his classroom. He stood to meet her, but she went straight to Lucas and crouched by his desk, ignoring Andrew entirely.

"Hey, bud. How are you?" Lucas lifted his head off his hands, and the woman ran her hand through his floppy brown locks.

"Hi, Mom. I'm okay." That seemed to be Lucas's favorite word. "I didn't do anything, I swear."

She smiled at her son. "Don't worry, baby. Everything is fine. I just need to talk to your teacher for a few minutes. Is that all right?"

"Okay."

Mrs. Dalton stood and grabbed her son's backpack with one hand while gesturing with the other arm for Lucas to join her. "Why don't you take this and go sit in the hall for me? I'll only be a few minutes."

Lucas left without complaint. His mother turned to face Andrew, and he finally got his first real look at her. *Holy crap.* She was a knockout. She was trim and toned, but not in a forced gym body way, more like she had a naturally slim build. Her wavy brown hair perfectly framed her oval face and tumbled past her shoulders in a riot of curls. She wore a snug pair of jeans and a slim-cut T-shirt with a bunch of flowers on it and the words "The Petal Patch." Unfortunately, her warm brown eyes looked nervous now that they were alone.

Andrew wrenched his gaze away from her too-tempting form and back to her face. He should *not* be checking out his student's mother. Besides, she was likely happily married and definitely off-limits.

"I'm sorry I'm late, Mr. Knight. I had to wait for Zachary, my employee, to arrive to cover the store."

"Store?" Not that he needed to know the details of her life. They weren't pertinent to why he'd asked her to come.

She nodded. "Yes, I own a flower shop downtown called the Petal Patch."

That explained her shirt and maybe some of what he'd been noticing with Lucas. Her job might be more relevant to the situation than he'd realized.

"Why did you want to see me, Mr. Knight? Did something happen with Lucas?" She worried her lower lip with her teeth.

"You can call me Andrew." It was important that his students used his last name, but he was rarely that formal with their parents. He found being on a first name basis generally put them more at ease.

"Okay, Andrew. I'm Sierra. Now, why did you want to talk to me?"

Right to the point. He liked that. "I've been noticing some interesting behaviors in Lucas. Nothing dangerous or anything, but he sometimes upsets the other children."

A worried vee appeared between her eyebrows. "He's bullying them? That doesn't sound like him at all. Did something happen?"

Andrew shook his head. "It's not bullying, but he did get angry at a few of the other students."

Her eyes narrowed. "Angry about what?"

"During recess, a few of the students were playing in the grass and picking dandelions. They started tying them in knots and throwing them around." She winced, but when she didn't say anything, he kept talking. "Lucas came over and yelled at them. He told them they were hurting the plants and that they needed to stop or he was going to call his mom." He lifted one eyebrow.

She let out an uncomfortable chuckle before she stifled it and schooled her face. "Lucas is a sensitive kid. He's always had an affinity for plants." Her gaze darted around the classroom as if trying to avoid his.

"With a mother who's a florist, I guess I can understand that."

Her eyes flew back to him, and a look of relief washed across her face. "Yes, that's it. He spends a lot of his free time in my shop after school. He loves flowers and gets upset when he thinks others are mistreating them."

"While I can understand where he's coming from, it's affecting other students. Today wasn't the first time this happened. Can you and your husband work out a different after school arrangement for him?"

Sierra's spine straightened. The sheepish expression slid off her face and was replaced with one of determination and anger. "His father left us when Lucas was three, so unless you'd like to call him back from wherever he lives these days to complain about a handful of dandelions, then you're stuck dealing with me. And since I happen to enjoy having a job that keeps a roof over our heads and food on our table, I try to balance that with looking out for my son. I'll talk to Lucas. Good day, Mr. Knight."

Sierra stormed out of his classroom. He'd really put his foot in it. Not only had he meddled in something that he should have stayed out of, but he'd insulted the most attractive woman he'd met in a long time. A woman who, as it turned out, wasn't married—not that he was thinking about that right now. His focus needed to be on Lucas and the rest of his students.

Damn it. He knew better than to make assumptions on any kid's home life. Families came in all shapes and sizes, and it was unacceptable that he'd presumed that Sierra was not only married, but in a relationship with a man.

With a groan, he sat down and leaned back in his chair. He rubbed his hands over his face and squeezed the bridge of his nose to stave off a forming headache.

This was his first year teaching at this school, and he got the impression that his principal didn't like him for some reason. He was a good teacher, but he couldn't afford to piss off parents. That was the death knell in a small town like Rock Cove. If he got in trouble here he would always be employable elsewhere, but he didn't want to work elsewhere. He'd moved to Rock Cove for a reason, so he needed to make this work.

The drive from the elementary school back to the Petal Patch was short. Rock Cove was small, and you could pretty much get anywhere in less than ten minutes. It didn't give her a lot of time to talk to Lucas, but hopefully it would be enough. Sierra glanced in the rearview mirror and saw him sullenly staring out the window.

"How was school today?" Sierra asked, trying to lure Lucas out of his mood.

"Fine."

One-word answers. Great. Lucas was normally a talkative kid, so it was a good indication he was upset about something, almost assuredly what had happened at school today. "What did you learn about?"

"Nothing."

"Nothing? I find that hard to believe. Weren't you studying addition and practicing your word flashcards?"

"I guess."

If Lucas stared any harder out the window, he might make something explode with his mind—not that he had that kind of power. Not yet, anyway. Time to try a new tactic. "Was Cameron at school today?"

"Yeah, he was." Lucas's tone got angrier.

"Did you get to hang out with him today? Maybe at recess?" She broached the subject of recess carefully, not wanting him to think he was in trouble. Nothing Andrew—*Mr. Knight* she silently corrected herself—had told her was a surprise, nor was it something to punish Lucas for.

"No. He was too busy hanging out with Lila and Jason." Lucas crossed his arms and kicked the back of the passenger's seat.

Ooh, she'd hit a sore spot. "And you didn't want to hang out with Lila and Jason too?" she asked as she pulled her minivan into the alley behind her shop and cut the engine. She stayed where she was but cranked herself around as much as she could to see Lucas in the back seat.

"No. They're mean."

"They were being mean to you?" If that was true, it was definitely something she would mention to Mr. Knight. Maybe the recess situation hadn't gone exactly like he'd thought it had.

"No. Not me." He kicked the back of her seat again and she gave his leg a pointed stare. "Sorry." He mumbled under his breath.

"So if it wasn't you they were being mean to, was it Cameron?" If Lucas was defending his best friend, his anger at the other kids was more logical.

"It was the flowers!" Lucas practically screamed. "They were pulling the dandelions and tearing them up and I could hear them yelling."

"Lila and Jason were yelling?" she asked tentatively.

Lucas leaned forward and gave her a mutinous expression, like he knew she wouldn't believe him. "No. The flowers were yelling."

Sierra blinked back her shock. She knew that Lucas was an earth witch too, but that's not how her magic worked. She didn't actually *speak* to plants, and they didn't talk back to her. "Maybe you heard some of the other kids yelling?" she asked.

He threw himself back against his seat, crossed his arms again, and went back to staring out the window. "It was the plants, Mom. They were in pain. And Cameron was doing it too. I had to stop them."

She had no idea what to make of what Lucas was telling her. Sierra hadn't practiced magic since her eighteenth birthday, but even during her years of studying she'd never heard of someone who could hear plants. However, if Cameron was involved, she could see why Lucas had reacted the way he had. Cameron knew that Lucas had a soft spot for plants, and if he'd hurt them anyway, it would have upset Lucas.

She needed to process Lucas's magical abilities another time. Right now, she had to deal with the behavior. She reached around and tugged on his jeans to get his attention. "Hey, bud. I'm sorry the kids at school were hurting the plants, and I'm especially sorry that Cameron was involved. But what have we talked about when it comes to our magic?"

He sighed then turned to face her. "We need to keep it hidden because not everyone likes magic."

She nodded. "Exactly. You can talk to plants when you're in the shop with me, but you need to keep it just between us. It's our special secret."

He sighed again. "Okay, Mom. It's our secret."

Sierra held out her pinky and Lucas wrapped his smaller one around it. "Pinky swear."

"Pinky swear."

She smiled. "How about a snack to tide you over until dinner? Maybe apple slices and peanut butter?" The answering smile on her son's face said it all.

They hopped out of the car and Sierra unlocked the back door of the shop, letting them into the storeroom. Lucas barreled ahead of her and raced up the stairs to the apartment above the shop, stopping only to let her unlock the apartment's door before he took off toward his bedroom.

"Don't forget to wash your hands!" she called after him.

His indistinct shout told her he'd at least heard her, which she called a win, so she headed to their tiny kitchen to make food and think about the very yummy, if slightly uptight, Andrew Knight.

Chapter Three

S IERRA BROUGHT THE CRISP fall air with her as she walked into Cinder & Spice—the café her friend Brigit owned. She was on a mission to talk to Jenna about the situation with Lucas. It was common for kids to start displaying their powers young, though usually not quite as young as Lucas had. Most kids start developing their gifts between eight and ten. With Lucas, however, it had been obvious by the time he was three that he'd inherited her gifts. She'd also received more than one call last year from the kindergarten teachers who were concerned that Lucas spent too much time on his own hanging out in the grass or near the school gardens. Sierra had put them off each time by using the same excuse she'd given Andrew the day before: "Lucas has an affinity for plants." One day it was going to stop working, so she needed to figure out how to handle what was going on.

Hence asking Jenna for coffee, and if Sierra happened to get a lemon poppyseed muffin to go with it, who could blame her? Brigit was an amazing chef and baker. The extra calories were worth it.

Jenna was sitting exactly where Sierra expected her to be, in the last booth in the back corner of the shop. It was their favorite table since it was so close to the over-sized fireplace, though it wasn't lit at the moment. Jenna was already sipping something out of a stoneware mug and had a gooey-looking pecan roll on a plate next to her.

"Thanks for meeting me," Sierra said as she sat down across from Jenna.

"If it was important enough to leave the new guy in charge of the Petal Patch, it must be pretty dire." She took a sip of her drink. "How's he doing by the way? Dropped anything precious yet?"

Sierra rolled her eyes. "Yeah, yeah, Killian warned me about how clumsy he was, but so far he hasn't done any irreparable damage." The server stopped by and Sierra ordered a pumpkin spice latte and the muffin she'd been craving then turned back to her friend. "But yeah, it's something all right. I got called into Lucas's school yesterday."

Jenna tried—and failed—to stop a laugh. "Already? Isn't it only week two or something?"

Sierra rolled her eyes. "Exactly. This doesn't bode well for the rest of the year if things keep going the way they're going. But that's why I wanted to talk to you."

Jenna's eyebrows rose as she carved off a small piece of her pecan roll and ate it. "What can I do? You realize I have zero experience with six-year-olds, right?"

Sierra glanced surreptitiously around the café making sure no one could overhear her. "Yeah, Lucas's problem is bigger than those of a normal six-year-old." She told Jenna about her trip to see Lucas's teacher and what he'd said about the other kids and the dandelions. "Afterward, in the car, Lucas told me he could *hear* the plants. That the flowers were yelling as the other kids were picking them."

Jenna slowly set down the coffee mug she'd been sipping from. "He can *hear* them?"

Sierra shrugged. "That's what he claims." Sierra slammed her mouth closed as the server returned with her order and nodded to the younger woman in thanks. As soon as the server had returned to her spot behind the counter, Sierra hissed, "What does that mean?"

Jenna took another bite of her roll and chewed in thought. "Honestly, I'm not sure. I've never heard of anything like this happening before, but that doesn't mean it hasn't. I can try to dig through my mom's books and see if they mention anything about it." Jenna's mom had been a very powerful witch in her own right, and when she'd passed away several months prior, Jenna had inherited all her belongings, including her spell books and magic supplies.

Sierra sagged with relief. "I would be forever grateful." She didn't want to be a burden on her friend, especially with respect to magic.

"I told Lucas not to use or talk about his magic unless it was just the two of us, but I wonder if I need to get him some training or something. I can't have him doing anything suspicious in front of Andrew, I mean Mr. Knight." Sierra tried to quickly correct herself but something about the way she'd stuttered out his name caught Jenna's attention.

She smiled like a cat that got the canary. "Which is it, Andrew or Mr. Knight?" She took a slow sip of her drink but didn't break eye contact with Sierra.

Nothing like being put on the spot. She tucked a strand of hair behind her ear. "He told me I could call him Andrew, but he's Lucas's teacher. It's probably best to call him by his last name. It's more professional."

"And is Andrew an older gentleman? Someone of our parent's generation perhaps? I can see someone like that wanting to be addressed more formally." Jenna took another bite of her pecan roll.

Visions of Andrew's attractive face and blonde hair swam to the front of her memory. His hazel eyes and blonde goatee with a trimmed beard had practically screamed for her attention. Not that she'd been focused on his looks, obviously. He was Lucas's teacher and that was all he would ever be. "No, he's probably pretty close to our age."

Jenna smirked. "Ah, so based on your current expression, he's not only our age, but he's also the hottest thing on two legs. On the bright side, if Lucas keeps getting in trouble at school you and *Andrew* will get to spend a lot of quality time together."

"Have you heard anything from Roderick?" Sierra asked then immediately regretted the change of topic.

Jenna's teasing smile shut down, and she leaned back heavily against the booth. She dropped her fork and crossed her arms. "No, but then again, I'm not expecting to. I've told you, he's up to something. Even the Circle of Thirteen thinks so."

The Circle of Thirteen was the governing body for all witches in the United States. It was made up of the thirteen most powerful witches in the country, and they were not only the rule makers but also the enforcers if someone stepped out of line. If they thought Roderick was up to something, it was hard to overlook.

"Maybe him taking your talisman was a mistake somehow?" Sierra asked. It was hard for Sierra to mesh her memories of the man who had been her mentor for two years with the person Jenna was describing. Jenna had never liked Roderick, but she'd put up with him anyway. Sierra, on the other hand, had never had anything against him. Sure, he'd been tough on them, especially her, but it was for a purpose. His role in their lives was to train them to use their magic safely and effectively. It was his job to correct them when they were doing something wrong and ensure they were as skilled as they could possibly be. He'd done that job with remarkable success. Even if she hadn't always been a fan of Roderick's methods, they'd certainly been effective.

"Are you talking about Roderick *again*? When are you going to get over your weird obsession with him?" a new voice asked.

Sierra startled out of the memories of her teenage years by the unexpected appearance of a willowy blonde woman in a trim pale-pink suit. Aura Burton always looked immaculate and made Sierra feel slightly inferior in her often dirt-smudge jeans. Though since Aura was raised in a lifestyle most could only dream about, and since her life revolved around getting up in front of a television camera as a meteorologist, looking perfect was just part of the gig. Thankfully, her warm and accepting personality offset what otherwise could have made her unapproachable.

Jenna rolled her eyes. "And that's my cue to leave." She grabbed her belongings and stood. "Sierra, I'll be in touch with whatever I find about Lucas." She sped out of the café.

Sierra huffed. "Did you have to say that?"

Aura shrugged and took Jenna's spot across the table. "You know I'm right. She's never liked Roderick. She's been trying to convince us there was something wrong with him since we were sixteen years old. It's time to drop it already."

Brigit walked up, carefully placed two black coffees on the table, then plopped down on the bench next to Aura. "Aura isn't wrong. I have no idea what Jenna has against Roderick, but he's not evil. He's not up to something. He's the same man that helped us learn magic when we were teenagers. He's done nothing but help us. It's Jenna that needs to stop, not us. I don't know what she gets out of constantly trying to prove that there's something wrong with Roderick, but I'm over it."

Sierra narrowed her eyes as she stared at the two women across from her. "What about her talisman? She said that Roderick asked her to hand it over and said he would deliver it to the Circle, but the Circle never got it."

Brigit shrugged, her red ponytail bouncing. "She probably lost it and just doesn't want to admit it."

As reluctant as Sierra was to admit that Roderick might be doing something that wasn't in their best interests, that was still easier to believe than Jenna lying to her. "Jenna is my best friend. Regardless of whatever animosity the three of you have—for reasons that no one ever felt like explaining to me when we were eighteen—I believe Jenna. You can believe whatever you want about Roderick. I choose to believe our friend. She's like a sister to me, and she used to be one to you too."

"Some sister," Brigit bit out. "She couldn't wait to escape this town and leave us behind."

Sierra gave her a pointed glare. "Gee, I wonder why that could be, Brigit?"

Brigit's eyes narrowed and she opened her mouth to reply but Aura beat her to it. "So, what's this Jenna was saying about Lucas?" She smoothly changed the topic as she took a careful sip of her piping hot coffee.

Sierra went with the change in the topic, happy to move away from the weirdness between her friends. Jenna hadn't been friends with Aura and Brigit since they graduated from high school, but Sierra had maintained friendships with all of them. It often put her in the middle of arguments she was tired of mediating, but the alternative was that she would have to give up one or more of her closest friends, and that just wasn't an option.

"Lucas can apparently hear plants screaming." Now that she'd talked it over with Jenna, she was feeling slightly calmer about the situation and was able to see the amusement in it. She could just see her sensitive son striking up a conversation with a daisy in someone's garden.

"Well, that's certainly a new one," Brigit said as she sipped her own mug of coffee.

"Yeah, it's definitely out of my depth to deal with, but Jenna said she'd help me look into it with her mom's books."

"Of course she will. Ms. Perfect has access to everything," Brigit snarked.

"Brigit, lay off. If Jenna has resources that can help Sierra with Lucas, that's the important thing." Aura didn't often play mediator, but whenever she did, Brigit seemed to listen.

"Fine. Good luck searching through dusty spell books. I have to get back to work." Brigit left her coffee behind and made her way back into the kitchen.

"God, she can be so exhausting at times," Sierra said as she finished the last of her lemon poppyseed muffin.

Aura nodded. "Her magical affinity for fire certainly does match her temper."

"What does that make you? Someone who blows hot air?" Sierra teased.

Aura crumpled up a paper napkin and threw it at her. "Better than someone who plays in the mud all day."

"Really? You couldn't come up with something better than that? Someone with a dirty mind perhaps? Or someone with rocky relationships? Of all the earth-related puns, and that's the best you could come up with?"

Aura laughed. "You got me there. Go hug your emotional support ficus and leave me alone."

Chapter Four

ANDREW WAS ON RECESS monitor duty, which he fully believed was better than lunch monitor duty. At least at recess the kids could run around and get out some of their energy. If there was a disagreement at lunch, food tended to get involved, and that got sticky and messy fast. No thank you.

He was hiding in the shade, leaning against the brick exterior of the school, watching over his charges. Their playground had surprisingly nice equipment for such a small town: a large climbing structure with ladders, tire swings, hanging bars, and swings all painted a cheerful red, yellow, and blue. A separate swing set and a short climbing wall catered to some of the more adventurous of the bunch. Most of the kids seem to be having a blast, with several of them screaming out their excitement as they chased their friends around the enclosed area.

Then there was Lucas Dalton. Andrew sighed and monitored the kid out of the corner of his eye as he scanned the rest of the playground for trouble. Lucas was sitting all by himself in the corner of the fenced-in playground, though he did occasionally throw his friend Cameron looks that were half angry and half longing. Cameron was having a ball with the rest of the kids, climbing the structures and zipping down the slides. Lucas, on the other hand, kept to himself, unless you counted the grass and crisp fall leaves he seemed to be talking to.

"That boy is just strange."

Andrew jumped and spun around to see his boss, Principal Bodrock, standing just behind him. The woman was shorter than him by at least a head, but that didn't make her any less intimidating. She had short white hair that she kept perfectly curled and reading glasses perpetually perched either on the tip of her nose or hanging from a decorative chain around her neck. Right now, they were dangling as she squinted her eyes to get a better look at Lucas. Andrew was still trying to make a good impression on his new principal, but he couldn't let her insult one of the children, especially not where one of the kids could potentially overhear them. "I'm not sure it's appropriate to call one of our students strange. Besides, Lucas is six. All kids that age are a little different."

Bodrock's eyes narrowed and she bristled. "Mr. Knight, I'm not sure if you're aware of this or not, but I knew your grandmother, Madelyn Healy."

The change of topic threw him for a loop, and he stood up straighter, wondering where she was going with this. "I wasn't aware, but I'm not surprised. She taught at this school for several decades."

Bodrock nodded. "Yes, she did. She started here before I did, but I was the principal during her final years here."

"Okay." He really wasn't sure how to respond to that, since he wasn't sure what her point was.

Bodrock crossed her arms as she glared at him. "I knew your grandmother for a long time. Many people labeled her as *different* too."

Whoa, what on earth was she getting at? Andrew knew exactly why everyone in town thought his grandmother was odd, but he wasn't about to share personal information about his late grandmother with his boss. "I'm not sure what you're implying, Principal Bodrock."

She sniffed and straightened her posture. "I don't tolerate strange behavior in my school. We have a responsibility to these students and their parents to see to it that every student in our care is kept safe. I was never able to convince the school board that your grandmother was enough of a threat to get her removed from her position, but I took it upon myself to keep a close eye on her. I don't want any funny business at Rock Cove Elementary."

Andrew was stunned silent for a moment. He couldn't believe the woman standing in front of him had hated his grandmother enough to try to get her fired from her teaching job. Yes, his grandmother had been a bit eccentric. He had to imagine *most* witches were a bit different from the average person. But she would never have put a child's safety at risk. His grandmother had loved kids and would have done anything for them.

He chose his words carefully, trying not to give her any more reasons to dislike him than she already seemed to have. "Principal Bodrock, I can assure you, I do not intend to engage in any *funny business* while teaching at this school. Teaching is my passion, and I love kids. I wouldn't do anything to jeopardize that."

She nodded sharply. "See that you don't."

He almost left it at that, but he couldn't let her go without knowing one more thing. "If you had something against my grandmother, then why did you hire me?"

Her narrowed eyes clued him in that he shouldn't have asked. "We needed a first-grade teacher, and you were the most qualified candidate who applied. However, don't think I'm not willing to fire you if anything untoward happens." She gave him a sharp glare. "Now, I have a task for you. Each fall the elementary school hosts the local first responders. They bring a police car and a fire truck to the school parking lot, and we host an assembly so the kids can learn about public safety and what to do in case of an emergency. It's always a big hit with the children."

Andrew was nodding along. They had done something like this at his old school, too, so he was familiar with the idea. "What do you need me to do?"

"Run it, of course. My administrative assistant can get you the contact information. I believe the point of contact on their side is Holden Kay."

Great. He'd lived in town for less than a month, and he was now responsible for putting together an event while he was still trying to get his feet under him. She was testing him. He couldn't afford to screw up. "Got it. I'll take care of it."

Bodrock sent one last suspicious look at Lucas before heading back inside.

The rest of the day went quickly and soon enough he was wrapping up and heading home. He'd run his students through sight word practice with flashcards, read them stories, and then asked them questions about the stories. They continued practicing their basic addition, and some students were still struggling with the concept. Not Lucas though. He continued to knock it out of the park. And so far, there hadn't been any additional outbursts.

That was both a good thing and a bad thing. It was great for Lucas but bad for Andrew, because it meant he hadn't gotten to see the lovely Sierra again. Not that he thought about her much. Only, you know, multiple times a day. It didn't seem to matter what he told himself or how often he reminded himself that it wasn't appropriate for him to get involved with or want to get involved with his student's mom, his brain wasn't listening. Neither was his libido.

Andrew let himself into his small bungalow that had once belonged to his grandmother. With a resigned sigh, he walked the dozen or so feet from the front door through the living room, to the kitchen and dropped his messenger bag onto the table. The kitchen was barely big enough to turn around in, and the living room fit a couch, a chair, a TV stand, and that was it. There were two bedrooms on the other side of the house and a minuscule bathroom. It was small, but it was cozy, and it felt like home.

Granny had passed away the year before and left the house to him in her will. She could have left it to any of her children, including Andrew's mother, or left it jointly to Andrew and his two older sisters, but she hadn't. He and his siblings often spent summers with Granny when they were kids, but as they got older, Amber and Anya stopped coming. Like most people in Rock Cove, they'd decided that she was an eccentric old woman who was slightly off her rocker.

He knew the truth. She'd told them when they were little kids that she was a witch, and she had even entertained them with some magic. She never did anything extensive or dangerous, but she could make pebbles float and bend wire into intricate shapes without using her hands. He'd always been fascinated by her gifts and sad that he hadn't inherited her abilities. His sisters, on the other hand, had reached puberty and no longer believed that Granny had gifts. Instead, they'd listened to their mother when she'd told them that they were all just parlor tricks and there was nothing magical about it.

Granny Madelyn had been one of Andrew's favorite people in the world. He'd continued to visit her for years after he became an adult. He'd gone into teaching because of her, and he loved it. It felt good to carry on his grandmother's legacy, at least in some small way. Even if his principal was making him jump through hoops.

It wasn't quite dinnertime yet, so he was hoping he still had time to get started on Emergency Services Day before he called it quits. He had gotten what information he could out of the school's administrative assistant. The biggest saving grace was that this event was an annual occurrence, and it basically never changed, so there shouldn't be much to plan. Either way, he needed to get started.

He grabbed his cell phone and dialed the number he'd been given.

"Rock Cove Police Department."

"Hi, I'm looking for Holden Kay." Andrew pulled out a piece of paper to take notes.

"You've found him."

"My name is Andrew Knight, and I teach first grade at Rock Cove Elementary School. I was told to get in touch with you about scheduling the annual Emergency Services Day."

Holden laughed. "Bodrock roped in the new guy, huh? Don't worry, this will be a piece of cake."

Andrew sincerely hoped Holden was right. He could use a quick win.

Chapter Five

"**L**UCAS, DINNERTIME!" SIERRA CALLED as she finished squeezing a package of cheese sauce onto warm macaroni and stirred it in. She grabbed two bowls out of the cabinet and scooped some into each, then grabbed two forks. With a flourish, she set both bowls on the table.

"Lucas, come on bud. Dinner." She normally didn't have to call twice. Her son was nothing if not food-motivated, yet she still didn't hear the pounding of his feet coming down the hall from his bedroom. She made sure the stove was turned off, then went to look for him. Maybe he had headphones on and couldn't hear her.

She glanced in the living room as she passed but didn't see him, so she kept going to his bedroom. The door was shut, so she pushed it open and was greeted by an explosion of boy paraphernalia. Legos on the floor next to toy robots, trains mixed with stuffed monsters. His sheets and blankets were halfway spilling off his twin bed onto the floor. But there was no sign of Lucas.

Her heart skipped a beat. Where could he be?

"Lucas? Buddy?" She quickly checked the bathroom—empty—and her room, which looked exactly like she'd left it that morning. Still no Lucas.

Her pulse skyrocketed, fear squeezing her throat.

"Lucas!" She screamed as she checked every room a second time. She opened closets, checked under the beds, opened cupboards, and looked behind every door.

He was nowhere to be found.

She flew to the apartment door. Lucas knew better than to leave the apartment without her, but there was always a chance he'd gone downstairs to the flower shop. The apartment door was unlocked, which was even more terrifying. She always double- and triple-checked the locks every night. There was no way it could have been unlocked unless Lucas had let himself out.

She flew down the steps. "LUCAS!" The stairs ended in the back room of the flower shop, and she searched high and low around all the backstock of flowers, the coolers, tables, everything. When she had no luck there, she raced through the curtained opening into the store front, winding her way around all the plants looking high and low for her small son.

Was it her, or did the plants somehow look more menacing today? She could have sworn that those creeping vines had been significantly smaller the day before, and they definitely hadn't been wrapped around the handle of the front door of the shop.

She grabbed the handle and tugged. The door didn't budge. Neither did the vines that were holding it in place. The lock was stuck, and the door wouldn't move an inch no matter how hard she pulled. She raced back through the curtain to the rear exit of the store and tried that door. It was also stuck.

She was trapped, and Lucas was missing.

Her mind went blank. What was she supposed to do? Where was her son?

She needed to call for help. She desperately patted her pockets but didn't find her cell phone. She darted into the small office in the corner of the storeroom where she had her computer and video surveillance equipment set up. There, on the desk, was the shop phone. Practically sobbing in relief, she grabbed it and tried to dial 911.

There was no dial tone. She burst into tears.

Sierra sank to the cement floor. She pulled her knees into her chest and wrapped her arms around them, sobbing into her jeans. Bands of pressure closed around her chest, making it hard to breathe.

She'd failed. She'd lost Lucas. She was trapped inside her building, and she couldn't save him. She would lose him, just like she lost everyone else. Her most important role in life was being a mother to her son, and she'd failed at it. She wasn't good enough.

She was never good enough. Roderick had taught her that lesson a long time ago.

"I can help you," a silky voice purred in her ear.

Sierra's head whipped up as she frantically looked around, but didn't see anyone. "Who are you? How did you get in my shop? Where's my son?" She jumped to her feet and searched for the source of the voice. She didn't recognize it.

"I did not take your son. You lost him through your own incompetence. You said it yourself. You're not good enough. Not yet anyway." The whisper seemed to come from everywhere and nowhere at once.

Sierra was positive she hadn't said that out loud, so how could this person know she'd thought that? "Who are you? What do you want with me, and where the hell is Lucas?" She made her way back through the shop, trying to pinpoint the source of the voice.

"I can help you, you know. You might not be good enough or strong enough now, but together we can fix that." The voice tempted and taunted her.

"Where. Is. My. Son?" She grabbed a pair of pruning shears off her counter.

"I'll be seeing you again, Sierra ..." the voice faded to nothing.

"Mom!" Lucas screamed.

Sierra whipped her head up, but instead of the shop overflowing with flowers and vines, she was shocked to see her bedroom. She was lying in bed, her floral-printed duvet wrapped around her like she was a burrito. Lucas was standing next to her bed, a look of terror on his face and fat tears rolling down his cheeks.

"Lucas?" Sierra untangled herself from her bedding and grabbed her son in the tightest hug she could manage without suffocating him.

"You were yelling, and you wouldn't wake up. I tried to wake you, but you wouldn't do it." Lucas was full-on sobbing now, and she pulled him into her bed and tugged the covers over both of them.

"Shh, it's okay, baby. It's okay. Mommy's fine now, it was just a bad dream. Thank you for waking me up." She rubbed her hand up and down his back as he shuddered through a few more minutes' worth of sobs and trembles before he relaxed and fell asleep in her arms.

Her pulse slowed, but unlike her son, she was wide awake. Unfortunately, she knew from experience that there was no way she was going to be able to sleep after that nightmare. While she'd never had this exact nightmare before, it was just one of many along the same lines. She'd had them on and off for years, but they had gotten much worse over the last several months.

Being a single parent was the scariest thing she'd ever done in her life. Opening her own business was the second most frightening thing, but in the grand scheme of things, there was no comparison. Lucas was fully reliant on her to keep him safe, warm, fed, clothed, and sheltered. Her asshole of an ex, Todd, had left when Lucas was three, and she'd been on her own ever since. She had help from family, friends, and neighbors—people who were kind enough to babysit when she needed to get out—but ultimately, the buck stopped with her.

She wasn't sure if she was up to it. Even after six years of raising this precious child in her arms, she wasn't convinced she could keep it up.

In broad daylight she felt like she could tackle anything. Each new disaster was just a small blip on her radar. She dealt with each thing as it came because she didn't have any other option. The choices were survive or collapse under the weight of everything, and she wasn't going to let herself do that.

It was when night fell that the doubt started to creep in, and she wondered when it would all be too much for her. How much weight could fall on her shoulders before she could no longer stand under the crushing force?

She lay in bed, Lucas snuggled up next to her, and wished she had someone she could reach out to for comfort. Someone to share the burden with. She thought about calling Jenna, but not only was it the middle of the night, but she wouldn't understand. Oh, she would try to understand how Sierra felt, but there was no way for Jenna to really get it. She wasn't a mother. That wasn't a knock on her either, but someone who had never been fully responsible for another human being, a helpless child, could never understand the terror of what it was like to screw it up.

Of the four of them—her, Aura, Brigit, and Jenna—Jenna was the strongest. She had the strongest magic, and she had an ancestral tie to her family's land that only strengthened her gift. It wasn't like Sierra's great-grandparents had lived in this small apartment above a flower shop over a hundred years ago.

Brigit and Aura were more like her than Jenna, but even they had more magical power than Sierra did. Roderick used to tell her that she was going to have to work harder than the others to be anywhere near as good. He'd offered her extra tutoring, and yet somehow, she'd never seemed to measure up to whatever expectations he'd had for her.

Even at sixteen she hadn't been good enough.

She'd done whatever she could to be a good mother to her son and raise him well. She worked her tail off at her flower shop and made a decent living. She wasn't ready to retire to Tahiti or anything, but Lucas would never want for anything, or at least not the essentials. And if she had to say no more often than she would like—especially when they happened to walk past Whimsy & Wonder, the toy shop directly across the street—that was just a part of life.

Maybe someday she would find a new partner, someone to share the burdens with. Todd Dalton had clearly not been the right person for that, but there was still a chance, however slim, that she would find someone else. Someone who wouldn't mind the fact that she had a kid and, most importantly, someone who wouldn't run away when he figured out that both she and Lucas were witches.

Unbidden, the far-too-attractive face of a certain first-grade teacher swam into her mind. Obviously, Andrew liked kids. He probably wouldn't teach elementary school if he didn't. She had no idea where he stood on the idea of magic being real, but she would never find out. Andrew Knight was her son's teacher. Even without the whole "Hey, I'm a witch. What do you think of that?" of it all, it wasn't appropriate for her to think of him like that. Plus, she didn't even know if he was single. Not that she wanted to know, of course. He would probably never go for someone like her anyway. Not with her history. Her focus needed to be on Lucas, not his instructor.

Sadly, her brain didn't cooperate, and she finally nodded off while still picturing a particular head of sandy hair and warm hazel eyes that had the crinkles of a smile just forming at the corners.

Chapter Six

T HE COPPER LANTERN LOOKED like a typical Irish pub. The outside was painted green with gold trim around the windows and the sign, which was written in a traditional block font. Out front, planters overflowed with flowers and greenery, even this late in the year.

Andrew wasn't sure why Holden asked to meet here rather than the school or the police station, but he couldn't say he was sad about it. He'd lived in town for just over a month, and he hadn't had a chance to check out the pub yet. With any luck they had good brew on tap and hearty food he could grab for dinner.

The interior was nicely done with slate floors, a mixture of brick and drywall on the walls, and wooden beams crisscrossing the ceiling. The overall effect was warm and dark, but in a comfortable way. Someplace to get cozy with a partner, or warm up by the oversize fireplace during the colder months.

Andrew had no idea where to look for Holden. They'd been texting back and forth for the last few days, but the place was packed tonight, and Holden hadn't given him any way to recognize him amid the crowd. He was just about to give up and go ask the man with reddish-brown hair behind the bar if he could point him in the right direction when a man stopped right next to him.

"Andrew Knight?"

Andrew took in the closely cut brown hair, the muscles that bulged underneath his tight Henley, and the authoritative way he held himself. This had to be Holden. He screamed police officer from his head to his toes. "Is it that obvious?"

Holden chuckled, a warm sound that immediately put Andrew at ease. "To me it is. Rock Cove is a small town, and I'm a detective. I pretty much know everyone already, so when a new face shows up, they tend to stick out."

Andrew stuck out his hand to shake. "Nice to meet you."

Holden gripped his hand firmly for a quick pump. "Same. Come on, join us over here."

Holden turned and led him to a table that had one other person already seated there. "Andrew Knight, meet Denver Wallace. He's lived in Rock Cove his whole life, just like me, and he drives boats for a living. Mostly for the aquarium down in Boston. Denver, this is Andrew. He teaches at Rock Cove Elementary."

Andrew reached out and shook Denver's hand. "Nice to meet you."

"Same."

The same bartender he'd noticed earlier chose that moment to make an appearance, holding a pitcher of beer and three pint glasses, which he placed on the table.

"And this is Killian O'Rourke. He owns the place," Holden said. "Killian, this is Andrew. Play nice. He's new in town."

"Where's the fun in that?" Killian asked with a laugh.

Andrew laughed. "Go easy on me. It's my first time." He smirked.

"Elementary school teacher's got jokes," Denver laughed.

"Only when little ears aren't around to hear them," Andrew responded honestly. He, like most people who spent a lot of time around small kids, had to constantly watch his language. He didn't need a student overhearing him swear and telling their parents about him. He didn't need to add any more reasons for the principal to dislike him.

"If it's your first time at the Copper Lantern, then your first drink is on the house." Killian patted his shoulder.

"That just means he's going to charge you more for all the rest of them." Holden laughed.

"This is a reputable establishment, officer. I take offense that you think I would fleece my customers. At least the sober ones," Killian said. "There are a few drunks at the bar that I should get back to, though. Enjoy your Emerald Crown Lager. Wave me over if I can get you anything else."

Holden grabbed the pitcher and started pouring them drinks. Andrew accepted his and took a sip. It was crisp, clean, and refreshing and perfectly hit the spot on a Friday night. "Not that I'm not grateful for the invitation and the drink, but I thought we were going to plan the Emergency Services Day for the school."

Holden shrugged and took a drink of his own beer. "Can't we do both?"

"Well, when you put it that way ..."

Holden nudged Denver. "Get this, Dragon Lady has the new guy over here doing her grunt work."

Denver was nodding. "That sounds about right."

Andrew laughed. "You call Principal Bodrock the Dragon Lady?"

"Oh, yeah. The number of times she yelled at us when we were growing up. We always said she looked mad enough to breathe fire. It just stuck," Denver said.

At least he wasn't the only one who wasn't on the best of terms with her.

"She's only slightly less scary now that I'm a fully grown adult who carries a badge and a gun," Holden added.

Andrew was glad he'd taken Holden up on his offer to meet at the pub. He could already tell that he was going to enjoy hanging out with these guys, and since his pool of local friends currently stood at exactly one—Jasmine Fell, the only other first-grade teacher whom he'd met on his first day at the school—he could stand to meet all the new people he could.

As the first pitcher of beer slipped into the second, they nailed down the details for the Emergency Services Day. Andrew was finally starting to feel like he knew what he needed to do when Denver's face lit up, his eyes sliding to something or someone behind Andrew.

Holden noticed too and glanced in the same direction. "I don't know why I bothered looking. Only one person puts that look on Denver's face."

"Jenna!" Denver said with a smile as a slim woman with long black hair approached the table and gave Denver a quick kiss.

"He's whipped," Holden whispered to Andrew loud enough for everyone at the surrounding tables to hear.

"You're just jealous," Jenna said as she wrapped her arm around Denver's shoulders.

Holden didn't correct her.

"Do you want to join us?" Andrew asked as he pulled out the last chair at their table.

Jenna shook her head. "I'm meeting someone. Oh, there she is!" Jenna waved at somebody. In a weird twist of fate—or maybe just because Rock Cove was a small town—the woman who walked up was none other than Sierra. She was wearing a pair of slim fitting jeans and a deep purple sweater that hugged her curves nicely. Not that Andrew noticed or anything.

"Hey, Denver. Hi, Holden. Oh," Sierra froze when she finally realized he was sitting at the table with her friends. "Mr. Knight."

"Mr. Knight?" Denver asked curiously. "You can't just call him Andrew like the rest of us?"

Sierra hesitated, so Andrew jumped in to rescue her. "Her son, Lucas, is in my class. I think Ms. Dalton is just trying to keep a professional distance between us." The very same professional distance that Andrew struggled to maintain in his brain every day when she popped into his thoughts.

Jenna glanced from Sierra to Andrew, "Oh, so *you're* Andrew Knight." If he wasn't mistaken, Jenna was smirking.

"Um, yes? Does my reputation precede me?" What had the principal said to people about him? He nervously spun his nearly empty pint glass on the table.

"Only in certain circles," Jenna answered mysteriously.

"Anyway," Sierra interjected. "We should really go grab our own table and leave these boys to themselves." She tugged on Jenna's coat and then headed across the bar to a table that had just opened up on the other side of the room, basically as far away as a person could get from them without going outside.

Jenna's eyebrows rose as she watched her friend. "It was nice to meet you, Andrew." With one last peck on the lips for Denver, Jenna left them and followed Sierra.

"She seems nice," Andrew ventured.

Denver's gaze finally left Jenna to return to their own table. "She's amazing. She's a whale biologist."

Andrew had never met a whale biologist before. "You work together at the aquarium? That's convenient."

Denver laughed. "It's convenient now. Not so much when she first moved back to town. She was a bit standoffish at first." He explained.

"It's amazing what almost dying during a whale rescue will do for your relationship," Holden said. He raised his hand to get Killian's attention. "Can we get some potato skins and onion rings?" Killian nodded his acknowledgment.

Andrew was missing a huge part of a story, but before he could ask for more details, it was Holden's turn to get snared by a newcomer, or in this case, newcomers. A pair of women walked into the pub and snagged the two remaining stools at the end of the bar. One woman was slim with long, wavy red hair, the other a model-perfect blonde with tanned skin and eyes so blue he could see them even in the dim light from across the pub.

"Is one of them *your* girlfriend?" Andrew asked.

Denver smirked. "He only wishes. That's Brigit with the red hair. She owns Cinder & Spice. The one with the blonde hair is Aura. She's a meteorologist for Channel 10 in Boston."

Holden wrenched his gaze away from the two women and back to Andrew. "No, I'm not dating either of them."

Denver rolled his eyes. "Not because he doesn't want to, though."

Holden smacked his friend in the arm and narrowed his eyes. "You said that, not me."

Andrew wasn't about to wade into an old debate between friends, especially since he was the outsider. However, if that longing gaze was anything to go off, Denver was almost surely right about Holden wanting one of them.

Andrew stole a peek at the table across the room with Jenna and Sierra. Sierra was laughing, and it lit up her face. She really was an amazingly beautiful woman. Under different circumstances he might have tried to work up the nerve to approach ask her out on a date. He wouldn't do it, though. She was probably still mad at him. Plus, he had to respect the parent teacher relationship. It wasn't a smart move to try to change that dynamic, at least not while Lucas was in his class. Maybe next year, when Lucas was no longer his student, Andrew could pursue her, but he wasn't ready to think far in advance. A lot could happen in the course of a school year.

"Looks like Holden isn't the only one pining from afar."

Andrew whipped his head around to see Denver's grin. "What?"

Denver nodded Sierra's direction. "She's a beautiful woman. I'm sure you've noticed."

How could he not? He had to fight his instinct to look in the direction Denver was gesturing to. "Of course she is. But she's also a parent whose son is in my classroom every day."

Denver shrugged. "That won't always be the case."

It was like Denver was reading his thoughts. That was unsettling. "I already stepped in it once with her." Andrew winced at the memory. "I asked about her husband."

"Yeah, that's a sore topic for her, but she's doing a kick-ass job raising Lucas on her own. You could just go apologize." Denver shrugged and took a sip of beer like what he was suggesting was easy.

Andrew glanced across the room and saw Sierra's head tilted back in laughter. Apologizing probably was the adult thing to do, even if he was embarrassed. Besides, it gave him an excuse to talk to her again. He guzzled down the last of his beer for some extra fortification and nodded.

"That's the spirit." Holden smacked him on the shoulder and practically shoved him across the room.

Jenna was the first one to see him approach, and she tapped Sierra's arm to get her attention. The smile on Sierra's face dimmed but didn't quite extinguish.

"Andrew, to what do we owe the pleasure of your company?" Jenna asked when neither he nor Sierra said anything. "Do you want to join us?" She gestured to an empty chair.

He grimaced and rubbed his jaw. "I don't want to intrude. I just wanted to apologize."

Jenna's eyebrows rose and she looked at Sierra, who still hadn't said anything. "Fair enough. I'll go hang out with Denver. Take your time."

Once Jenna was gone, Andrew felt like he was awkwardly looming over Sierra, so he quickly perched in Jenna's abandoned chair.

"I'm sorry," Andrew said at the same time Sierra blurted out, "I overreacted."

He held up a hand to forestall her saying anything else. "Just let me say this. I know better than to assume anything about a student's home life, and it was way out of line for me to presume anything about your relationship status. I hope you'll forgive me."

"I'll forgive you if you forgive me for the way I acted." She blew out a breath and sagged back into her seat. "Being a single parent is *hard*. I honestly don't know if it would be easier or harder if Lucas's father was still around, but it doesn't matter because he's not. I'm sensitive about the topic, but that doesn't excuse me from trying to bite your head off. It's far too attractive to lose." She cut herself off abruptly and blushed.

Well, now that was interesting. He smiled as he filed that piece of information away for later. "Forgiven?"

"Forgiven."

Chapter Seven

S IERRA WAS EXHAUSTED BUT elated. The wedding from hell was over and she'd never have to deal with Tansy Sandoval again.

Sierra loved weddings. They were generally happy occasions, with everyone smiling, laughing, and enjoying themselves, and her flower arrangements set the scene and tone for the celebration. It was special to her that she got to partake in other people's joy, even if she wasn't part of the wedding itself. However, she was happy to never have to deal with this particular wedding again.

The bride had insisted on over-the-top flower arrangements. In the church's entryway, Sierra had placed several ostentatious vases overflowing with lilies, orchids, roses, and ranunculus blooms. The vases were so heavy that even with Zachary's help she'd had trouble getting them all inside the venue. Thankfully Eric, the bride's father, had offered to help them haul. He'd been a lifesaver, helping them cart all the arrangements to the correct positions. She and Zachary had decorated each pew in the enormous church with an aisle arrangement of pink and white roses and carefully positioned the arch, where hundreds of pink peonies spilled over in abundance, near the altar. She'd called in more than a few favors and cleaned out her suppliers, but she managed to secure every bloom the bridezilla demanded, despite the short notice.

Not that Tansy had thanked her for the extra effort, but Eric had slipped her a handwritten note.

Sierra,

I know they were a lot. Thanks for putting up with everything. You did an amazing job. If there's ever anything you need, don't hesitate to reach out. I owe you one.

Eric

She shook it off. Tansy no longer mattered. The wedding was done, and the exorbitant fee had been deposited into Sierra's account. Maybe she could take Lucas to the toy store for a special surprise to celebrate.

Thankfully, once the venues were set up, her job was done. She picked up Lucas after he had spent the day with her father, Fred. They had gone to the park while she'd spent the long hours decorating the church and the event center.

It was early evening when she pulled up behind the Petal Patch. She glanced in her rearview mirror. Lucas was passed out in the back seat. He looked so content that she almost didn't want to wake him up, but he was getting heavy enough that it was hard for her to carry him up the stairs. Hopefully once she got him into his own bed, he'd fall right back asleep.

She got out and opened the back door of the van to help him out of his booster seat. She gently shook his shoulder. "Hey, bud, it's time to go inside and head to bed." He muttered something unintelligible but didn't wake up. She tried again. "Lucas, baby, we're home." He reluctantly woke up and stumbled out of the vehicle. She urged him to the back door then unlocked it and let them inside. With her arm on his shoulder, she guided him across the back room, up the stairs, and into the apartment.

Something was *wrong*.

She immediately shoved Lucas behind her and frantically scanned the apartment. Nothing looked out of place, but she was dead certain she was right.

"What is it, Mommy?" Lucas's sleepy voice came from behind her.

"Yes, Mommy, what is it?" An unfamiliar woman's voice came from the direction of the kitchen.

Before Sierra could react, a slim woman in her early twenties strolled into the living room. Sierra had never seen her in person before, but she knew exactly who this wait with mousy-brown hair was. "Danika."

Danika was the witch who attacked Jenna over the summer. They'd caught footage of her in several places around Rock Cove, including sitting on a bench outside the Petal Patch and attacking Jenna outside Cinder & Spice.

Now she was inside Sierra's apartment.

Questions flew through Sierra's mind a mile a minute. What did Danika want? How had she gotten in? Did she intend to harm them? And most importantly, how could Sierra keep Lucas safe?

"Lucas, I need you to run downstairs and hide in the office. Lock the door from the inside." She tried to unwind his small arms from around her waist and shove him back out the door to the apartment and down the stairs. "Go!" she yelled when he didn't move.

"Mommy?" he asked in a terrified voice. His eyes widened with fright and his chin started to tremble.

"Lucas, just go. I'll come find you in a bit, I promise." She tried to keep her tone even and calm even though she was secretly petrified.

Danika smirked as she sauntered across the small living room. "Why don't I help you with that?" She flicked her finger and the apartment door slammed closed and the lock clicked audibly.

Sierra grabbed the knob and tried to twist it, but it was stuck. She fumbled with the lock, but that was also frozen in place. The door rattled uselessly in her hands. Lucas started sobbing, his fingers digging into her waist through the black dress pants she'd worn to the wedding.

She was paralyzed. She had to protect Lucas, no matter what. He was her number one priority. It didn't matter what Danika wanted or why she was there. Sierra had to get both her and her son out of this situation alive.

She lifted her arms behind her and used them to box Lucas in as she shifted them over several feet, always staying between Danika and Lucas. "What do you want?" Her hands hit the walls behind her, and she'd realized that she'd found the corner of the room. She tucked Lucas firmly against her back.

Danika seemed to enjoy Sierra's discomfort. She casually, too casually, tapped her finger against her lips like some sort of Bond villain. "Would you believe me if I said I just stopped by for a chat?"

"No. If you wanted to talk to me, you could do it at any point when the shop is open. Plus, talking doesn't necessitate breaking into my house and ambushing us in the dark." She grasped one of Lucas's hands in her own and clenched tightly. With her free hand, she fumbled without looking, aiming for the bookshelf next to her. She grabbed the thick candleholder sitting on the shelf and brandished it in front of her like a weapon.

Danika let out a delighted laugh. "You're bringing a candlestick to a magic fight? I knew you would be unprepared, but this is ridiculous." She casually twirled her fingers and a gray mist flowed across the floor. The mist solidified into a handful of crabs, which scuttled across the floor and started snapping at their feet. Sierra stomped on the conjured crabs, which dissolved into smoke. Danika chuckled again, clearly not surprised or upset that her creatures had been destroyed.

It was disconcerting how at ease Danika appeared to be. She had no fear whatsoever, which was troublesome and a little insulting. Okay, yes, Sierra hadn't used her magic in more than ten years—on purpose at least—but that didn't mean she couldn't use it. "What do you want?" she asked again through gritted teeth, her hand flexing on her poor choice of a weapon. This confrontation needed to be over before anyone got hurt.

"I was curious how weak you really were," Danika said with a shrug.

Sierra tried not to let the barb sting. "And you're so strong? What, are you just going to stand there and talk me to death?" Taunting the psychotic witch probably wasn't the smartest thing she'd ever done.

"Of course not." With another casual hand wave Danika conjured a snake and sent it slithering in their direction. She then conjured a rope and flung it through the air.

Sierra ducked as the rope flew at her head and she heard it hit the wall behind her. Before she could take a step or try throw her candleholder at the other woman, the rope wrapped around her torso, circling her several times and pinning her arms to her sides and binding her legs together.

Lucas whimpered and shrank back as the snake coiled up and prepared to strike, its fangs dripping with venom. With a hiss, it lunged at Lucas, who screamed as the fangs sank into his leg.

Oh, *hell* no. No one attacked her son.

Power rose within Sierra and burst outward. The rope around her exploded into dust. The snake shriveled and collapsed. Sierra lifted her newly freed hands and dug deep. She searched within for the power that used to be just beneath her fingertips, but it didn't want to respond. Panic gripped her by the throat.

Danika conjured a long, slim blade and used her magic to send it flying at Sierra. Seconds before the blade sliced through her neck, Sierra's magic sluggishly responded and created a protective barrier in front of her and Lucas. The blade hit the barrier with a clang, and Sierra tried to redirect it back toward its creator, but her magic sputtered and died. The blade moved less than a foot before it dropped like a stone and hit the floor with a thump.

Danika laughed as she watched Sierra's pitiful attempt to use her magic. "Well, as much fun as this has been, I have what I needed." She turned around and walked straight through the exterior wall of the building as if it didn't even exist.

Sierra gasped and ran to the window. A full story below, Danika was walking away completely unscathed, as if she hadn't just phased through a solid wall and then fallen twenty feet into an alley.

The sound of Lucas's sobs immediately brought her racing back to where she'd left him in the corner of their apartment. He was clutching his leg and rocking back and forth. She frantically ran her hands over him and found rips in the thigh of his jeans in the shape of two puncture marks. She grabbed the waistband of the pants and yanked them off.

His leg was red and irritated around the two bloody puncture wounds. Apparently, Danika's conjured snake had caused real damage.

"It hurts, Mommy," Lucas whimpered.

She had no idea if the conjured snake had truly been venomous, but she couldn't take any chances. She placed her hand over the wound and once again called to her powers. She was an earth witch. She had a connection with both plants and animals. She should be able to draw the snake's poison out of his body if she was precise enough.

Nothing happened. Her powers didn't respond. She tried again with the same result. She looked at Lucas's tear-streaked cheeks and made a snap decision. She fished her phone out of her pocket and hit one of her speed dial contacts.

"Jenna, I need you at my place immediately. No time to explain." She hit the red button to hang up and then wrapped her arms around Lucas. She hoisted him in her arms and carried him to the couch. She snuggled him on her lap, unwilling to let him go.

The ten minutes she had to wait for Jenna to arrive were agonizing. Sierra's mind kept replaying the fight—if you could call that a fight—over and over again. Lucas had been in danger, and she hadn't been able to protect him. She'd been worthless.

Everything Roderick had told her when she was a teenager came flooding back. She hadn't been as strong as the others back then either, and here she was once again not measuring up. That might have been something she could ignore when it was just her, but she had Lucas to think about now. She was his only parent and his only form of protection. She didn't have the luxury of being useless.

Jenna burst into the apartment. "What happened?"

"Danika showed up. I'll explain later. Right now, I just need you to heal him. He was bitten by a snake. I'm not sure if it was venomous or not." Sierra gestured to the irritated wound on Lucas's leg.

Jenna crouched next to the couch and put her hands on Lucas's leg. He flinched away from her touch, and Sierra ran her fingers through his hair to calm him. "Hey, buddy. I know that probably hurts a lot, but I'm going to fix it. Would that be okay?" Jenna asked gently

Lucas glanced at Sierra and she nodded her approval. "It's okay, baby. Jenna will take good care of you." He nodded shakily, giving his permission for Jenna to proceed.

Jenna closed her eyes and the energy in the room shifted as her powers rose to the surface. Jenna placed her palm over the wound and then slowly pulled it away. A yellow liquid seeped out of the wound and eventually floated into the air in a small ball of self-contained liquid. Sierra grabbed a small decorative dish off the end table and handed it to Jenna, who deposited the venom with a wave of her hand. Jenna returned her palm to the wounds in his leg and chanted under her breath. Seconds later she removed her hand and the marks were gone.

Lucas sagged, his relief obvious. "There you go, bud. All better." Sierra kissed his forehead. "You had a big night, huh?" He nodded but didn't say anything. She let him cling to her as she settled more deeply into the couch. She did her best to rock him back and forth, even though he usually claimed he was too big for that anymore. Tonight, he didn't even pretend to complain.

Jenna rose from her crouch and sat on the other end of the sofa. "I'm staying right here until I get some answers."

Sierra nodded. If anyone could help her, it was Jenna.

It took Lucas less time than expected to pass out in her arms. She thought about moving him to his bedroom down the hall but decided they could both use the extra comfort and put him in her own bed instead. She left the door open a tiny crack, then crept back to the living room to find Jenna staring at her, forehead pinched in concern.

"What really happened?"

Sierra sagged back down onto her somewhat lumpy couch, all the energy leeching from her now that Lucas was settled. "We came home and Danika was already in the apartment. Apparently, she can walk through walls."

Jenna's eyes almost bugged out. "That explains how she keeps breaking into places."

"Exactly. But it wasn't just that." She recounted the fight and how her magic hadn't responded. "It can't happen again, Jenna. Lucas is too important to me. I can't be the weak link that fails to protect him."

Jenna nodded. "Then we train. You're going to be out of practice after taking a hiatus for so long. You need to build up your magical muscles, so to speak. Now where's your talisman? Wearing that would have helped you tap into your gifts a lot easier."

Sierra dragged herself off the couch and across the living room to one of her bookshelves. In the center of the middle shelf was a beautiful wooden box carved with flowers. She opened it and sifted through all the photos and mementos she kept tucked inside. She'd put the necklace in the box years ago, a memory of a time in her life when things had been different. Only her talisman wasn't there.

She yanked the box off the shelf, brought it to the coffee table, and dumped out the contents to see if the charm had gotten stuck between other items in the box. No such luck.

The necklace was gone.

Sierra met Jenna's eyes. "Well, I guess we know what Danika came for."

Chapter Eight

ANDREW CHECKED THE TIME on his phone. It was almost 9:00 a.m., which meant that any minute now the parking lot at the elementary school would be filled with a police car, a fire truck, an ambulance, and a bunch of men and women in uniform. This was it—the culmination of all his preparation for Emergency Services Day. It was also the day that he either showed his boss that he could be relied on or proved to her that he couldn't be trusted.

It needed to go off without a hitch.

Jasmine was watching his students inside the building as he waited for Holden and the rest of the folks to show up. The kids had been talking about the event nonstop for days, and they were all practically vibrating out of their skin with excitement.

Oh, to be that young and full of wonder.

The sound of loud rumbling engines drew his attention to the road where a giant fire truck was turning into the parking lot followed by the ambulance and police cruiser. He heard a muffled cheer go up from inside and glanced back at the school to see a row of eager faces plastered up against the windows.

Andrew waved his arm toward the vehicles in greeting and then gestured for them to make a semi-circle in the parking lot. They came to a stop and firefighters, police officers, and EMTs poured out. Holden led the pack as the crowd slowly gathered around Andrew.

"Holden, nice to see you again." Andrew nodded at him.

Holden smirked. "Look at the first-grade teacher, all formal and shit."

The fire chief standing next to him and wearing a name tag with the last name of Rojas smacked Holden in the chest. "Watch your language, Kay. There are kids around."

Holden stood up straighter. "I'll be on my best behavior, Chief. I promise." He held up three fingers in the Scout salute.

Rojas rolled his eyes. "You were never a Scout."

Holden shrugged. "I thought about it for a day or two when I was twelve."

Andrew smothered a laugh. "Let's get started, shall we? We'll have each of you standing by your vehicles to give your overview of what you all do and your usual precautionary tales of stop, drop, and roll. Then, once the speeches are out of the way, you can show the students around your vehicles to whatever extent you're comfortable letting them climb all over the place. Sound good?" He got a series of head nods in response. "Right. Time to release the Kraken. Krakens? Kraken-lings?"

Holden laughed as he and the rest of the first responders returned to their vehicles. Andrew walked up the short sidewalk to the front door of the school, grabbed two of the doors, and propped them open. He was greeted by the eager faces of columns of children lined up behind their teachers. "Are you all ready?" he asked them. A deafening storm of yesses, yeahs, and uh-huhs nearly damaged his ear drums. "Okay everyone, follow your teachers."

The organized chaos that followed eventually got all the kids outside, lined up by year, with the youngest—and shortest—kids in front and the older kids in the back craning their necks to see around the kids in front of them.

The fire chief kicked things off like the old hand he was, telling the kids about what it was like to be a firefighter and the dangers of house fires. Holden took it from there and talked about what it was like to be a police officer and a detective. Finally, the lead EMT gave her spiel about how they spend their days saving lives and occasionally rushing sick people to the hospital.

"Now who wants to blow the horn on the fire truck?" Chief Rojas asked. Every kid's hand shot in the air. He pointed at a tiny girl with box braids in the third row, who shyly approached him. He walked her over to the cab of the truck and showed her the button to push, which she did with great relish. The loud, low-pitched noise was immediately followed by screams of excitement from the kids.

Andrew met Jasmine's eyes over the kid's heads and shared an amused smile.

"The fire truck's horn might be loud, but I'm pretty sure the siren in my police cruiser is way more fun. Does anyone want to help me show Chief Rojas how it's done?" Holden asked the students. Again, every hand immediately shot in the air. Holden pretended to think about it for a moment before pointing at Lucas.

Lucas yelled, "Yes!" then spun in a circle before racing toward Holden's side.

"Walk!" Andrew felt bad about having to correct him, but safety was important. Even with half of the town's emergency personnel on site.

Lucas gave him a chagrined look and slowed to a fast walk.

Holden winked at Lucas and ushered him over to the police car before showing him how to work the siren. Lucas smashed his finger on the button then danced in the passenger seat as it let out its whooping noise. Another round of cheers went up from the kids.

Finally, the EMTs selected a student to blast their siren to another bout of screaming. After the siren had been silenced, the emergency personnel brought kids closer to the vehicles in small groups so they could look around. Some of the teachers were snapping photos that they could show the parents later.

"The Dragon Lady seems at least mildly less uptight today," Holden commented as he made his way to Andrew's side.

Andrew cast a surreptitious glance at Principal Bodrock out of the corner of his eye. While she didn't exactly appear to be having fun, at least she didn't look angry or upset. He would count it as a win. "She isn't glaring at me or accusing me of *funny business,* so I'll take it."

Holden laughed. "She used those words?"

Andrew had to hold in a laugh. "Yeah. I guess she knew my grandmother—who used to teach here—and didn't like her much. She thought she was suspicious or something."

Holden's eyes lit up. "Who was your grandma? If she taught here, I probably knew her."

"Madelyn Healy."

A wide grin spread across Holden's face. "She was my second-grade teacher. I loved that old lady. In fact, I'm pretty sure we all had her for second grade—even Sierra." Holden nudged him with his elbow, but Andrew ignored it.

It was logical that Sierra, who had grown up in Rock Cove, would have had his granny as a teacher at some point or another, but for some reason it was the first time Andrew had contemplated it. He wondered what Sierra had thought about her. Granny had been one of the most important people in his life, so it would be unfortunate if Sierra—or any of his brand-new friends really—hadn't liked her.

"I guess we're about ready to wrap things up here, right?" Andrew changed the topic. The kids were having so much fun it was hard to pull them away, but they needed to let the first responders get back to their usual jobs and the children needed to head back inside to their classrooms. When he got a nod of agreement from Holden, he said, "Kids, I'd like you to all give a great big thank you to our special guests."

"Thank you!" a hundred students all yelled at once.

Holden sent him a knowing look then waved at the kids before he headed back to his police car. The engine rumbled to life on the enormous fire truck and Chief Rojas turned on the flashing red lights and blew the horn one more time as they pulled out of the parking lot. The ambulance and the cruiser each followed suit, much to the excitement of the kids.

The teachers corralled their students into neat lines to head back into the school. The kids were still babbling excitedly and talking about their favorite parts of the demonstration. The tiny girl with braids who got to sound the horn on the fire truck was now an instant celebrity as her friends crowded around her.

"That was adequately done." Principal Bodrock materialized at his elbow. Her words were at odds with her demeanor, since she somehow managed to look down on him, despite being much shorter than he was.

Andrew bristled but refused to show it. She'd given him a test. He'd passed it. That was what was important. Now it was just about keeping his head down so she didn't *keep* giving him extra crap to do for no reason other than spite. "Thank you, ma'am." He hoped he managed to keep the sarcasm out of his voice. Judging by her irritated sniff, he might not have fully managed it.

"Well then, back to your classroom." She hitched her shoulder as she turned her back on him and headed inside.

Andrew slumped, feeling like he'd been put through the wringer. Sadly, it wasn't even lunchtime yet, and he still had to get through the rest of the school day before he could fully relax. He glanced around the parking lot one last time to make sure he hadn't forgotten anything.

A beam of sunlight glinted off something small where the pavement met the grass. He squinted but couldn't make out what it was, so he walked over to it to inspect it more closely. Laying among a handful of dried leaves was a piece of broken glass. He could picture some kid's tiny hand picking it up out of curiosity and getting seriously injured. He futilely patted his pockets for something he could use to grab it and dispose of it, but he had nothing on him. With a sigh, he gingerly reached out and grabbed it with his bare hands.

"Whatcha doing, Mr. Knight?"

Andrew jumped, and his hand slipped. The sharp piece of glass sliced across his palm and deep red blood instantly welled to the surface. "Mother fudger!" Andrew yelped as he spun around to find Lucas directly behind him. He dropped the piece of glass and used his uninjured hand to press down on the wound and try to stanch the blood that was now dripping on the ground. "Lucas, what are you doing out here? You should be inside with Ms. Fell until I get back." He'd have to talk to Jasmine and figure out how Lucas had managed to disappear on her.

Lucas, to his credit, wasn't squeamish. He stared at Andrew's injured hand and concentrated, almost like he was trying to figure something out. "The ambulance people could help you."

It was cute that Lucas was making the connection to the demonstration they'd all just watched but now wasn't really the time. "That's right. The EMTs could have helped me get better. Unfortunately, they've already left, so I need to go inside and get this cleaned up. Why don't you come with me, and I'll take you back to Ms. Fell."

Andrew tried to herd his wayward charge back inside while also silently freaking out about how deep the cut on his hand really was. He wasn't an expert, but if he had to guess, he needed stitches. He didn't relish the thought of telling the Dragon Lady how he'd screwed up and needed to go to urgent care.

Lucas didn't budge from where he was standing on the sidewalk. "I can fix it."

Now really wasn't the time for a stubborn six-year-old. "It's okay, Lucas. I'll go talk to the school nurse and she'll fix me right up." No need to scare the kid and tell him the nurse probably wouldn't be able to help.

"I can do it," Lucas said again. Without waiting for Andrew's permission, Lucas reached for his hand. He placed his much smaller hand right over the top of Andrew's palm, almost but not quite touching him. He closed his eyes, his whole face scrunching up like he was concentrating.

A tingling warmth spread across Andrew's hand, more than just the body heat of having another person's skin that close to him. It wasn't a comfortable sensation, but neither was it painful. There was a slight tug and then a release. Lucas opened his eyes and dropped his hand back to his side with a small smile.

Andrew stared at his hand in astonishment. The cut was *gone*.

Chapter Nine

The grove in Jenna's woods was somehow exactly like Sierra remembered it and yet different enough that her heart skipped a beat when she first walked into the clearing. It was about thirty feet across, with a soft bed of amber and brown leaves and pine needles on the ground that cushioned her steps. The trees that encircled the grove were as familiar to her as the back of her hand. She remembered each root and every branch, especially the ones that grew overhead to form a canopy, creating a protective dome around the space that made it all the more special.

Like the earth witches who had come before her, Sierra had helped create that dome. She'd poured some of her magic into the trees to help them grow tall and wide and pushed magic into the earth itself to help nourish them. The trees were taller and fuller than the last time she'd been here, which was more a testament to the passage of time than any influence she'd had.

In the center of the grove was a flat circular stone approximately ten feet in diameter. The stone platform was perfectly smooth except for an expertly carved symbol of a quaternary knot. The carving was a single line that twisted over and under itself, creating a series of interlocking half-circles without a beginning or end. The knot had four points, one pointing toward each of the four cardinal directions.

Standing on the westernmost point of the symbol—waiting patiently for Sierra to finish her perusal—was Jenna.

"How long has it been since you've been here?" Jenna asked as Sierra slowly walked across the ground to meet her.

Sierra swallowed thickly, flashing back to the day that was burned into her brain like a cattle brand. She cleared her throat and said, "Not since our eighteenth birthday."

Jenna's eyebrows rose. "You haven't been to the circle since the Trials?"

On their eighteenth birthday, each witch was required to pass a series of tests known as the Trials. Only after passing the Trials was a person considered to be a full-fledged witch. Those that didn't pass had their powers stripped from them by the Circle. The Trials were designed to test the witch's knowledge, skill, and magical ability and ensure they could safely handle the magical gifts they had inherited.

They were also what had nearly broken Sierra and convinced her she shouldn't be doing magic anymore.

"No," she answered Jenna's question. "That day was a lot for me. I couldn't bring myself to come back here when it was over." Jenna was aware that the Trials had been rough on Sierra. They'd discussed it at great length.

Jenna gave her an understanding nod. "Why don't we start with the basics then, just to see where you are. Let's connect to our elements."

Sierra crossed the remaining distance to the stone circle and took her place on the symbol at the northernmost point. Jenna raised her arms palms pointing to the sky. Sierra mirrored the motion. Then Jenna began to chant.

"Mother, maiden, crone divine,"

The familiar words rolled through Sierra as easily as if she was reciting her ABCs. She added her voice to Jenna's and the chant grew louder.

"With your help my gifts align.
I join you in this sacred space,
By your will and with your grace."

A surge of magical energy flowed from the stone circle up through the bottom of her shoes and into her body. It was a feeling unlike any other. Sierra paused her chant and let Jenna say her verse alone.

"Water flows and ebbs through me,
Rain and river, lake and sea."

It began to rain as a blue glow started beneath Jenna's feet and traveled around the carved grooves in the stone—stopping halfway to where Sierra was standing.

It was her turn. Sierra took a deep breath then began her verse of the spell.

"Earth shifts and moves through me,
Dirt and rock, plant and tree."

Flowers instantly sprang up in the grass behind her. The trees circling the grove groaned and creaked as they responded to her magic. A green glow emerged from where she was standing on the stone circle, traveling to meet Jenna's blue glow on one side, and stopping where Aura's magic would have been on the other side of her.

They finished the spell together.

> *"I call upon this ancient land,*
> *Protect me now at my command."*

A surge of energy rushed through Sierra, starting from where her feet met the stone circle and racing through every extremity. Her fingers tingled and her brain felt like she'd guzzled a fizzy bottle of champagne. Long unused synapses in her brain prickled back to life, which wasn't particularly comfortable.

She stayed where she was, unmoving, letting the swirl of the magic do what it was going to do to her, knowing that whatever it was, it wouldn't hurt her. This was *her* magic flowing in her veins. No matter how long it had been since she'd used it regularly, she would recognize it anywhere.

Eventually the sensation subsided into a dull glow inside of her, a warm presence that felt both like a comforting hug and a sharp rebuke for having ignored her gifts for as long as she had.

"How do you feel?" Jenna asked, lowering her hands and stopping the drizzle of rain she had conjured with the spell.

So many words sprang to mind, but the first one off her tongue was, "Whole."

Sierra had very intentionally left her magic behind after the horrifying experience she'd had with the Trials. She'd come very close to breaking, and though she'd overcome and successfully completed her Trials, the cost had been steeper than she'd realized it would be.

But despite her horrible experience, going without her magic hadn't been easy. As a child and a teenager she'd had her gifts available with the flick of her finger or the wave of her arm. It had been a long process of unlearning before magic wasn't her first instinct, even if she hadn't allowed herself to give in to the temptation.

Eventually, she'd met and married Todd, and shortly thereafter they'd had Lucas. By that point, she never even thought about magic anymore. Her family became the most important thing to her, and she'd felt that way ever since. But feeling this sensation washing over her once more, she could admit that she'd missed it. Her magic was a part of her. It was just a part she'd deliberately let atrophy through disuse.

This was better.

Jenna smiled. "It's good to see you like this again, Sierra. You look happy."

She was. As much as she had tried to convince herself that she'd been happy for the twelve years she had avoided using her power—and Lucas had made her very happy—there was nothing quite like the feeling of once again being complete.

The blue and green glow slowly disappeared from the carved symbol beneath their feet, but it couldn't take the sensation from her. "What now?" Sierra asked.

"That depends on you. How fast do you want to dive back in?"

"That bitch attacked my son. I know he has his own gifts, but I'm his mother. I need to be able to defend him. Danika isn't getting anywhere near him again. Sign me up for the *premium* witchcraft subscription, with all the addons and extra packages. Whatever you need to do to whip this witch into fighting shape. Plus, Zachary is watching the shop today, so let's do this."

They stayed in the grove for over an hour, shifting between trying spells and conjuring their elemental gifts. It was harder than she remembered, which was likely both because she was out of practice and because she didn't have her talisman. After all these years it felt odd to wish for it, but what she wouldn't give for that tiny piece of metal that acted as a conduit to her gifts.

Sierra was exhausted by the time they trudged back through the woods to Jenna's house. She inhaled the scents of rotting leaves and distant smoke from someone's chimney or bonfire, the scents of fall.

"There's something I've been meaning to talk to you about," Jenna said as they entered her house through the kitchen. "Well, it's something I need to show you, really."

"That sounds ominous."

Jenna broke eye contact and ran her palms down her jeans. "Maybe? I should have told you sooner, I just didn't want to put any pressure on you."

"Now I'm really nervous." What on earth could Jenna have been keeping from her?

"Follow me." Jenna led the way up two flights of steps and into the attic. It was a room they had spent a decent amount of time in when they'd been training as teenagers. Jenna's mother had also been a powerful water witch, and she had the room fully stocked with spell books, candles, crystals, and other supplies.

"The attic?" Sierra asked skeptically. "I hate to break it to you, but I've seen all this before."

Jenna was already shaking her head. "Not this you haven't." She crossed the floor to one of the many bookcases and pulled down a book of shadows. She carried it over to the altar, set it down, and flipped it open to a page that was marked by a loose slip of paper.

"A spell for guidance? What, do you think I've lost my way between the stone circle and here?"

"Not that. This." Jenna unfolded the slip of paper. In small, untidy handwriting, there was something labeled "The Prophecy."

The day shall come when storms will rise,
Evil comes in friendship's guise.
Chaos reigns to ill effect,
Giving rise to an Architect.
While lives are lost and costs incurred,
He shall raise the Harbinger.
Yet hope remains while bonds stay strong,
Friendship rules and all belong.
Fire, Air, Earth, and Water,
Must stand against the endless slaughter.

"Oh, god. What in the hell?"

Chapter Ten

ANDREW SPENT SEVERAL DAYS contemplating what he should do. He watched Lucas closely at school, but nothing appeared any different about him than it had before Emergency Services Day. Before Lucas had magically healed his hand.

Andrew was still trying to wrap his brain around that one.

Logically, he knew witchcraft was a thing. He couldn't have grown up with his granny without learning to accept at least a bit of the fantastic. Andrew knew the truth. Magic was real. Granny had it, and apparently so did Lucas.

The kids were going a bit stir crazy, as they always did this close to the end of the school day. Knowing better than to fight their natural energy, Andrew had given them paper and markers and assigned them an art project as their final task. It was a low supervision task on his part. Make sure the kids weren't trying to kill one another or draw on each other with marker. Even if they *did* draw on one another, it was washable marker. It would come off.

Andrew sat at his desk and rubbed the center of his palm where the cut had been. There was an extremely faint scar there, so faint someone could be forgiven for assuming he'd gotten the injury years ago rather than less than a week ago.

The real question was what he was going to do about it. Part of his brain wanted to ignore the situation and pretend it had never happened. It wasn't his business if Lucas had powers. Andrew was just his first-grade teacher, not his parent. It wasn't his place to interfere or butt his nose in.

His mind flashed to Principal Bodrock and the narrow-eyed glare she threw at Andrew just because he was related to his grandmother. She was keeping her beady, judgmental eyes on the lookout for anything suspicious, and Lucas healing Andrew's hand was definitely suspicious. She already thought Lucas was strange, and if Lucas wasn't careful, he'd wind up on the Dragon Lady's radar in an even bigger way, and that just wasn't acceptable to Andrew.

As much as he wanted to keep his nose out of it, he couldn't afford to. Not when Lucas's future was on the line. There was no way around it. He was going to have to talk to Sierra, and not in an official parent-teacher conference sort of way. No, this needed to be totally off the record.

He only felt slightly guilty when he logged in to the school's database and looked up Lucas's file. He copied the home address and put it into Google maps. The pin dropped directly on the Petal Patch, Sierra's flower shop. They must live in the same building as the shop.

The bell shrilled loudly across the school's loudspeakers, startling him. "All right everyone, put away your art supplies in your cubbies, and I'll see you all next week." The kids grumbled but did as he asked. He carefully walked his students to the front of the school to be picked up by either the bus or their parents then returned to his classroom to set it to rights before he left for the weekend.

However, as much as he wanted to go home to his cozy bungalow and hibernate for the weekend, he wouldn't be able to relax until he'd talked to Sierra about Lucas. Though it wasn't exactly a hardship to see her or talk to her. Quite the opposite in fact. But bringing her attention to a topic that she'd be uncomfortable about or perhaps even be ignorant of? That, he wasn't looking forward to.

The drive from the school to the Petal Patch wasn't nearly long enough for Andrew to figure out what he was going to say to Sierra. How was he going to broach the topic that her son was likely a witch, but that for the love of god, he needed to keep it under wraps at school? Right. That would go over well.

Nothing brilliant popped into his head by the time he pulled up at the Petal Patch. With a sigh, Andrew threw the car into park and turned it off with more force than necessary. He'd just have to wing it. He took a deep breath and then entered the shop.

The tinkling of the bell attached to the shop door must have startled Sierra. She stared at him, eyes wide and her hand hovering over a wilting rose bloom. Andrew watched in awe as the bloom transitioned from brown and wilted to pink perfection in less than a second.

"Well, I guess that answers question number one. You are aware that magic exists." Duh, Sierra could *also* do magic. He wasn't sure why he hadn't thought about the possibility, but it certainly made things easier.

Sierra dropped the rose on her counter like it had burned her. "What do you mean?" she asked, feigning nonchalance as she tucked her long brown hair behind her ear.

Andrew scoffed. "Nice try, but I do appreciate the effort."

Sierra glanced at the perfect pink rose blossom before sweeping it into the compost bucket at the end of the counter. "I don't know what you're talking about." She cleared her throat. "Can I help you with something? Buying a bouquet for someone special? A girlfriend perhaps?"

Andrew wound his way through the luscious blooms and leaves to where she was standing. It was somewhat encouraging that she was asking—albeit in a roundabout way—if he had a girlfriend. He was happy to burst her bubble.

"No girlfriend—though I'm flattered that you care," he winked at her, "but that's not exactly why I'm here."

"Oh, a funeral perhaps?"

He chuckled at her stubbornness. "Nope, not that either, I'm afraid." Andrew glanced around the shop to double-check that they were alone before he continued. "We need to talk about Lucas."

Sierra straightened, rolling her shoulders and tugging her Petal Patch-branded Polo shirt in the process. "Then you should have called to arrange a parent-teacher conference, not ambushed me in my place of business."

"I'm fairly certain you don't want me telling Principal Bodrock that your son is a witch but correct me if I'm wrong." Andrew leaned against the counter and crossed his arms and waited for her reaction. He didn't have to wait long.

"I don't know what you're talking about." Sierra pulled a rag out from under the register and started quickly wiping off an already spotless counter. "There's no such thing as witches. Anyone who thinks otherwise should have their head examined." She studiously avoided looking at him.

"Look, I get it. We don't know each other well. It's probably weird to talk about this with me, but I can promise you that not only will I believe you, but I need to warn you."

Sierra stopped her frenetic cleaning and glared at him. "Warn me about what?"

"Principal Bodrock."

"What about her?" Sierra tossed the rag aside.

"She's out for blood. Well, blood isn't exactly the right word, but she's super suspicious of anything she considers not normal. She's been riding herd on me since day one because she didn't trust my grandmother."

"Your grandmother? What does your grandmother have to do with anything?"

Andrew shook his head in frustration. He was explaining this all out of order. "Let me start again. My grandmother was Madelyn Healy. She used to teach at the school before Bodrock became the principal."

A genuine smile spread on Sierra's luscious lips. "Mrs. Healy was your grandmother? I loved that lady. She was always so sweet, even if she was a bit of an oddball."

It warmed Andrew's heart that Sierra had liked his granny, but he didn't let himself get distracted. "Right, except she wasn't just an odd-ball. She was a witch."

Sierra inhaled sharply. "What?"

Andrew nodded and picked up his story. "Yep. She didn't flaunt what she was, but she also wasn't great about hiding it. Principal Bodrock was apparently suspicious of her and even wanted to get her fired, but thankfully she didn't succeed. She's been on my case from the beginning though and made sure to warn me against *funny business*."

"If your grandmother was a witch, does that mean you're one too?" Sierra asked neutrally, her eyes searching his face as if he might have the word witch branded on his forehead.

Andrew was already shaking his head. "I wish, but no. None of her powers came to any of the rest of the family as far as we can tell."

"So why are you here talking to me?"

"To warn you that Lucas needs to be more careful. Bodrock already thinks he's an odd kid because of the way he talks to plants and grass, but if anything like what happened on Monday ever happens in front of her, she's going to lose her mind."

Her gaze pierced through him like a lance. "What happened on Monday?" The growl in her voice told him to tread lightly. Her mama bear energy was high.

"As I was cleaning up after Emergency Services Day, I picked up a broken piece of glass from the parking lot. Lucas came up behind me and startled me, and I cut my hand."

"If you're blaming my son ..." She almost lunged across the counter at him.

He held up his hand to stave off her argument. "No, not at all. What I'm inexpertly trying to tell you is that Lucas healed me." He held out his hand and pointed to the faint silver scar running across the palm.

Sierra's mouth dropped open in shock. "That's not possible."

Andrew shrugged. "I assure you it is. I was trying to lead him back inside the school and he reached out to put his hand on top of mine. A few seconds later, the cut was gone. I'm sorry if you don't want to believe it, but your son is a witch."

"Of course, I believe it," Sierra practically shouted before she lowered her voice again. "I know my son. I know he's a witch; he got it from me.

But he's never been shown how to do a healing spell before. There's no way he …" She trailed off. "Oh, my god. Jenna."

The abrupt change of topic threw him for a loop. "What about her? Is she a witch too?"

Sierra flapped her hand like it wasn't important. "Yes, but that's not my point. Lucas was bitten by a snake a week ago. I called Jenna, and she did a healing spell on him. It's probably the only time he's ever seen one."

"Then he's one hell of a quick study."

A mix of emotions flashed across Sierra's face ranging from awe and pride to anxiety and a tiny flash of fear. Her shoulders slumped. "Thanks for coming to talk to me and letting me know what happened. I've told him many times that he's not supposed to do magic around other people. In fact after the incident with the dandelions at the school I made him promise me he would keep it a secret between the two of us."

"I get it. Six-year-olds can have a notoriously difficult time keeping a secret. I can't imagine having to keep one as big as the fact that he has magic from everyone, including his friends. It's a tough thing for a kid to live with."

The sound of footsteps pounding down steps reached them seconds before a loud "Mooommmm? Can I have a snack?" Lucas shoved his way out of a curtained doorway that led to the back of the shop. He stopped abruptly when he saw Andrew. "Hi, Mr. Knight! Are you here for some flowers?"

Andrew grinned. Like mother like son apparently. "You know? I just might grab some. Which one's are your favorites?"

Lucas launched into a winding explanation of the benefits of roses, tulips, and orchids before saying, "But I like sunflowers the best."

Sierra gave her son a fond smile before a customer entered the shop and she helped him pick out a bouquet.

Andrew leaned down close to Lucas's ear. "I have this friend, and she's a lot like your mom. I think she'd like the same sorts of flowers that your mom likes, so what's her favorite?"

Lucas answered in the same conspiratorial way. "She likes Gerbera daisies." He pointed to a bucket containing bright orange, yellow, and pink blooms.

The tinkling of the bell above the door jerked Andrew back to the present. He immediately stood back up and backed away from where he'd been huddled with Lucas.

Sierra's eyes narrowed slightly, but she didn't address him. Instead, she spoke to her son. "You can have a piece of fruit if you want a snack, but don't eat too much because I'm going to start dinner in a little bit."

"Yes!" Lucas cheered and then took off running for the back room. Seconds later he went pounding back up the staircase.

"I wish I had the energy of a six-year-old," Sierra said with a sigh.

"Try attempting to manage fifteen of them at the same time." Andrew laughed at himself. "I thought this job was going to keep me young, but instead I think it just makes me feel older." He grabbed a handful of the Gerbera daisies Lucas had pointed to and a few sunflowers and clumped them into an awkward handful. He strode back over to the counter and thrust his bundle at Sierra.

She reluctantly accepted it. "You really don't have to buy anything just because you told Lucas you were going to." She fiddled with the blooms, trimming a few and arranging them until they were just so.

"Maybe I do have someone I want to buy flowers for after all," he said as he handed his credit card over so she would ring him up.

Sierra's face went blank as she finished wrapping his bouquet in plastic and tied it off with ribbon. "Then I'm sure she's a lucky girl." She handed him the flowers and his credit card.

"I guess you'll have to let me know." He said with a wink as he handed the flowers right back to her and strode out of the shop.

Chapter Eleven

SIERRA STARED AT THE cheerful bouquet of yellow, orange, and pink flowers next to her cash register. It had been a week since Andrew had handed them to her and left her speechless. She kept telling herself that she was going to bring them upstairs and put them in her kitchen, but she never did. They would ordinarily have started to wilt by now, so she *may* have been giving them a bit of a boost with her magic. She liked looking at them while she worked, so sue her. It wasn't every day that a hot man gave her presents.

Gerberas were her favorite. Sunflowers were Lucas's. What were the odds he grabbed those exact flowers? Based on the way Andrew and Lucas had been whispering back and forth, she assumed Lucas had snitched.

Which was another thing. Andrew had not only hung out with her son but had subtly pumped him for information on her favorite blooms. That had to mean something, right? She'd been endlessly running it over in her head since it happened, a constant push and pull on her mind.

Was he interested in her as more than Lucas's mother? Did she *want* him to be? Her last relationship had been with her ex-husband and that hadn't exactly gone in her favor. She wasn't sure she trusted her own judgement when it came to men anymore. Besides, most men her age weren't interested in getting involved with a single mom. It was a burden they just weren't willing to take on. And she was even more of a mess than most single moms. If life had taught her anything, it was that she was never quite enough.

Andrew was great with kids. But as tempting as he was, getting involved with him was probably a bad idea. Not that she had any proof he was interested in her.

She'd been thinking herself in circles for days and needed to get out of her own head. She was excited for a distraction when the shop door opened, except the man she'd been low-key obsessing about was the one who strolled through the door with a smile on his face. Sierra's eyes darted around the shop as if she was expecting it to be a mess—it wasn't—and her eyes landed on the flowers. She picked them up and spun in place, trying to find somewhere she could hide them so he wouldn't realize she'd been fawning over them. Unfortunately, the Petal Patch just wasn't that big, and there was no place to hide them before he saw her, so instead of acting normal, she wound up standing awkwardly behind the counter holding the vase in front of her like a shield.

Andrew made his way to where she was standing and leaned against her counter. Glancing down at the daisies and sunflowers, his smile widened. "Someone has excellent taste in flowers."

Sierra wasn't sure if he was talking about himself or her, so she let out a small, "Hmm," which just made him chuckle. "Coming to admire your handiwork?" She set the vase back on the counter, shifting it and turning it until it was perfect.

"Just stopping by to see my favorite florist." He winked at her.

Her heart fluttered. "Do you know a lot of florists?" Her voice was more breathless than she would like.

"No, but the point still stands." A grin split is face.

"I can't say I've known all that many first-grade teachers, either." She leaned against the counter, unconsciously swaying closer to him.

"Then, by default, I'm your favorite too." His hazel eyes twinkled with amusement.

She couldn't deny it, but before she could think of a proper response, the bell jingled once more and Holden pushed through the door, his long stride eating up the distance between them. He stopped short when he noticed Andrew.

"Hey there, Holden. What can I do for you? Looking for some flowers to brighten up the police station?" she teased him as she straightened back up.

He rubbed his hand over the back of his neck, which made his biceps bulge and stretch the seams of his sport coat. He glanced at Andrew as if he was uncertain about something. "Um, no. Not exactly. But I do think you might be able to help me. Well, Rock Cove really. Hey there, Andrew," he tacked on, almost as an afterthought.

Andrew straightened from where he'd also been leaning against the counter. "Morning, Holden."

"Always happy to help. Do you have a major plant emergency that only I can solve?" While she'd meant the comment as a joke, the way his face tightened let her know she hit the nail pretty close to the head.

"The fact that you're a florist is only part of the reason why I'm here talking to you." He said as he shifted uncomfortably from one foot to the other. His meaningful glances and uncomfortable body language hinted that he was there about something he didn't want on the official police records.

"So why don't you just tell me what the rest of the reason is?" She arched her eyebrow at him. Andrew glanced back and forth between the two of them with interest.

He glanced at Andrew with unease. "It's probably better if I just show you. Any chance you can sneak away from the shop for a while? I know it's the middle of the day, so if we need to wait until after you close, we can do that too."

There was no way she was saying no. Holden was a friend. Plus, he'd helped Jenna a few months ago, so anything Sierra could do to help pay him back she would. "Of course. I can ask Zachary to cover the shop."

Holden sagged with relief. "Thanks. I appreciate it." He looked at Andrew.

Andrew looked disappointed but held his hands up palms out. "I can make myself scarce. I was just stopping by to check on ... my flowers." He gave Sierra another wink that made her butterflies take off again. "Sierra, I'll see you soon."

Trying not to sigh like a lovesick teenager, Sierra called Zachary—who promised to be right over—and followed Holden to his black SUV. "No police vehicle today?" she asked lightly as she climbed in the passenger's seat.

"I'm trying to keep a low profile."

She almost laughed out loud but managed to stifle it at the last minute. "Got it." Holden was at least 6 feet, 3 inches and attractive in that bad boy sort of way that drew some women like catnip. Holden couldn't keep a low profile if he tried. Plus, everyone in town knew who he was.

He slowly drove down main street, just barely kissing the speed limit, as his head swiveled for pedestrians. He pulled into the small lot reserved for the city park and stopped the vehicle.

"We're going to the park?" Sierra asked skeptically as she unbuckled her seatbelt and followed Holden out of the SUV. They set off across the grass, passing by the dog park and the pavilions with picnic tables.

"It's this way," Holden said with a wave of his hand as he trekked into a small clump of trees.

Sierra followed him, even more intrigued than she had been back in the shop. A few minutes later he stopped so abruptly that she almost ran into his back. She couldn't see what he was looking at from behind his massive shoulders, so she stepped around him. What she saw drew her up short.

"Here it is," he said unnecessarily as he gestured in front of him.

All the trees, plants, and even the dead leaves were shriveled and black. There was no scent of fire or smoke, and no obvious signs of what had caused it. Her first thought was that a campfire or burning cigarette had started a small blaze, but there didn't appear to be a leftover pile of burned firewood or ash, and an out-of-control fire would have spread far wider than the extent of this damage. Her second thought was a lightning strike, but none of the nearby trees showed telltale signs of that, and that also would have likely caused a wildfire under these dry conditions.

She glanced at Holden. "You brought me here to look at the aftermath of a fire that was probably set by some kids messing around? Why not call in the fire department?" It didn't make much sense. She had no idea what Holden thought she could do or how she could help.

"The fire department has already been here and couldn't find any cause for why it started. They also didn't know what put it out. Plus, it didn't exactly measure very high on their level of give-a-crap. The fire is out, no one got hurt. Case closed."

"Okay, but I'm still not sure what you want from me. How exactly do you think I can help?"

"Look at it again. Do you see anything unusual?" He edged closer to the damage.

She narrowed her eyes and squinted at the black spot again. This time, however, she noticed something odd. The burn pattern seemed to form an exact circle. From the center of the circle, there was a perfect ring of damage approximately ten feet across. "I'll admit it's a bit odd that the shape is perfectly circular, but maybe it's a coincidence?" Even as she said it, the words felt wrong on her tongue. It was too perfect. Too neat.

"You're an earth witch, right?" Holden finally asked. "Does anything else feel *off* about this to you? Because it sure is pinging my weird-o-me-ter."

Sierra had been trying her best to brush up on her powers, but it still wasn't second nature to use them and was a bit embarrassed that she hadn't thought about it earlier. Even so, she was tempted to call Jenna. She had so much more experience, and she hadn't neglected her powers the same way Sierra had.

She shook off her insecurities. She had told Jenna that she wanted to get stronger with her magic, and this problem was right up her alley. Besides, all she had to do was make a simple connection to the earth and report her findings. A perfect low-key spell for her to practice with.

She nodded at Holden. "I can take a look. No promises."

She walked right to the edge of the black, charred area but didn't step on it. Whatever had caused the blackness, natural or otherwise, she didn't want to touch it. She closed her eyes and took several deep breaths, trying to find her center. When she was in the grove behind

Jenna's house, it was so much easier because she had the stone circle as a conduit. It took her much longer than she would like to find her magical equilibrium without the stone—or her talisman—but she eventually got there. Then she started to chant.

> *"Mother Earth, now hear my cry,*
> *Sacred Gaia don't deny.*
> *Dirt and stone I call to thee,*
> *Flowers, leaves, plants, and trees.*
> *Where life once grew now only dark,*
> *What did leave death's angry mark?"*

A trickle of energy slowly climbed from the bottom of her feet, along her nerves, up her legs, into her torso, down her arms, and up into her mind. With a swish of her arm, she gestured for the power to spread around the damaged area. Her green magic—invisible to the eyes of ordinaries like Holden—slowly swirled and coated the blackened circle. She let it gather and grow then, when it felt like she had enough, she shoved the magic into the damaged earth, trees, and plants.

Normally, she could feel the life forces around her, be they animals or plants. She could also feel the energy resonance that traveled through earth and stone. Even dead plants had their own signature as their energy broke down and fed the earth once more. Everything was part of the cycle of life, and her power could sense that and tap into it.

Not here. Her magic found absolutely nothing. It was the darkest feeling she had ever touched. This was nothing that could have been caused by fire or a lightning strike. This was the absolute absence of life—beyond death. Something, or more accurately *someone*, had drained this entire area of whatever energy it once had. Only one type of person could have done that. A witch.

Sierra closed her eyes and drew her power back into herself, slowly retreating from the magical carnage left behind by whoever had cast the spell. The caster had been strong enough and smart enough to clean up after themselves. There hadn't been a single trace of a magical signature left for her to find. Which pretty much ruled out Sierra's most likely suspect, Danika. Danika had a decent amount of power at her fingertips, but from what Jenna had said and what Sierra had experienced, she wasn't very good at masking her tracks. With one final tug, Sierra pulled the last of her magic back and closed the spell.

"What on earth is that?" Holden's question had her wrenching her eyes open and staring at the circle.

Before she'd cast her spell, the spot on the ground was blackened and dead, but nothing looked out of the ordinary and the damage could have passed for a fire. Not anymore. Now there was slightly glittery and barely visible shape of a witch's knot hovering about an inch off the ground and taking up most of the circle. The black symbol almost blended into the destruction below. It didn't escape her attention that the circle and the symbol made an almost perfect replica of the stone circle in Jenna's woods.

"We need to call Jenna. She needs to see this right away."

"Care to tell me what I'm looking at?" Holden said as he pulled out his phone and tapped the screen.

She knew that Holden was far more in the know about witch matters than he should be as an ordinary but still wasn't sure how much he'd been told. She gave him something to tide him over until she could talk to Jenna about what it was safe to say. "The symbol is called a witch's knot."

"And it's nothing you did?" he asked.

"Nope. Not me. But it definitely means another witch did this."

"Damn it. Sometimes I hate it when I'm right," Holden said before he wandered away to talk to Jenna.

No more than fifteen minutes later, Jenna showed up with Denver in tow. The symbol on the ground was starting to fade, but it was still just barely visible. Denver let out a low whistle. He'd been to the grove in the woods and knew exactly what he was seeing.

Jenna glanced from the fading symbol to Sierra. "What happened?"

Sierra explained how Holden had brought her there and the spell she'd cast. "Nothing I did would have left that symbol behind. It was more like ..." She paused to think about what she was trying to say. "Like my magic somehow interacted with the magic of whoever caused this, and that's what created the symbol."

Jenna chewed on that for a minute. "That makes me wonder if it was intentional or not. Did the witch cast the spell this way on purpose, leaving us an Easter egg to find?"

"I don't really understand how something like this could have happened on accident," Sierra said.

"I'm sure you're right. Who do you think caused it? Danika? Roderick?" Jenna walked around the black spot and looked at it from every angle.

"I didn't recognize the magic, but I'd hate to think we had yet *another* rogue witch running around Rock Cove. It's like we're becoming the rogue witch capital of the world or something."

Jenna tried several different spells to see if she could figure out anything else about the spell or who cast it. Nothing worked. It was like the other witch had been prepared for them.

"What do you think the purpose of it is?" Denver asked.

"What do you mean?" Holden chimed in. He had mostly been quiet while they worked, but his curiosity must have gotten the best of him.

"I mean if someone left this symbol for one of the girls to find, why leave it out in the middle of the woods where they would likely never come across it? There has to be another purpose to this circle other than simply leaving a witchy breadcrumb."

Denver was right. Thinking back on what she'd learned through her spell, Sierra tried to puzzle through it. "They sucked the energy out of the earth. It's not that they killed everything, I mean they literally sucked the life force out of the plants, trees, and even the dirt. There's nothing left."

"Trying to give themselves a little magical power up?" Jenna asked. "It makes about as much sense as any of this. We shouldn't leave the park this way though. Sierra, any chance you can try to heal the plants or regrow new vegetation?"

"Only one way to find out," Sierra said.

They stayed for another hour. Sierra tried every spell and magical trick she knew and some that Jenna had up her sleeves. She and Jenna even did a few joint spells hoping that the extra power would help. Nothing changed. The destruction was so complete that not even Sierra's earth magic could touch it.

With a frustrated sigh, Sierra gave up. She looked at her watch. "Crap. I have to go pick up Lucas from his friend's house." She glanced at Holden. "I'm not sure what you have the authority to do, but I wouldn't let anyone touch this area if you can help it. Who knows what magic is still lurking that we haven't found yet."

"I'll do my best. In the meantime, I'll drive you back to your shop so you can grab your car."

"Thanks. I'll keep trying to think of something to heal this spot. Maybe if I come back another day I'll have better luck."

She fought the niggling voice in the back of her mind that said she wasn't good enough and that she wouldn't be able to help. Her friends were counting on her the same way her son was. She needed to come through for them.

The earth was her power, damn it. She had to figure this out.

Chapter Twelve

S TOPPING BY THE PETAL Patch during business hours the day before—on a Saturday no less—had been a risk, and unfortunately it backfired on him. He'd barely gotten to spend any time with her, something he was hoping to rectify immediately. He had hoped that if he approached her in her own environment, someplace she felt safe, she wouldn't shut him down when he finally got around to what he had intended to offer her.

Too bad Holden had shown up and whisked her away on some secretive police mission.

Either way, he knew for a fact that the Petal Patch was closed on Sundays. That made it perfect for what he wanted to do, but only if he could get Sierra to agree. He still didn't have her phone number, otherwise he'd just text her. He knew she lived by the shop, however, so he got back in his car and drove over there. He didn't bother trying the front door, since the shop was closed, but walked around the building to see if there was another entrance.

Bingo. There was a back door, and it had a doorbell. He hit the buzzer and waited. There was an older model minivan parked near the door, so he had high hopes that she was inside. A minute or so later, Sierra answered the door looking a little frazzled, her clothing covered in a fine dusting of white powder—flour at a guess. A strong waft of floral-scented air hit him in the face, and he could just catch a glimpse behind her of bucket after bucket of blooms in a riot of colors all waiting for her nimble hands to craft them into something even more beautiful.

Sierra drew up short when she saw him at the door. She glanced down at herself with a helpless looking sigh and then brushed her long brown locks behind her ear, getting even more flour on herself in the process.

Andrew tried his best to hide a smile. She wouldn't appreciate him laughing at her, but it was quite an endearing look on her. He wondered what she was up to. Making cookies with Lucas? Baking bread? Did she like to bake? He realized he wanted to know a lot more about her.

"Back again so soon?" she asked after she finally gave up on trying to brush the flour off her clothes.

Was this a stupid idea? Maybe he shouldn't have come. Ah, screw it. "Holden interrupted us yesterday before I could get a chance to ask you what I came by to ask."

She sucked in a quick breath and rubbed her palms down the sides of her pants. "Oh?"

"I inherited my house from my granny," Andrew said. "I got rid of a lot of her things, but I couldn't bring myself to get rid of any of her witch supplies. I knew I couldn't use them, but they reminded me too much of her to part with. I was wondering if you'd want to come over and rummage through them. You might find something useful."

Sierra took a small step back and brought her hand to her chest, smearing the flour even further. "You want to share your grandmother's possessions with me? You barely know me. Why would you do that?"

Andrew rubbed the back of his neck and leaned against the pink stucco exterior of the building. "I get good vibes from you. I think you'd treat her belongings with the respect they deserve, and they'll do you a lot more good than they'll do me." Plus, he wanted to make Sierra happy. She needed something in her life that was just for her. Something that brought her joy. Maybe he could give her that.

Her eyes softened and a small smile spread on her lips. "That's a very generous offer, but I can't today. Unlike yesterday, Lucas isn't at his friend's house. We were trying to clean up after making pancakes." She gestured to herself with a rueful smile. "Somewhat unsuccessfully I might add."

A leaden lump sank in Andrew's stomach. Something was telling him that if he let her go right now, she would continue to find excuses to put him off. "Bring him with you." The offer was out of his mouth before he even thought about it.

Sierra's eyes widened and she scuffed her foot against the cement floor. "I don't know ..."

"Lucas is awesome. He and I can hang out together while you sift through and see if there's anything worth saving." He wasn't entirely sure why it was so important to him that Sierra took him up on his offer. She was nice—though a little prickly when it came to her son—and obviously she was attractive. He liked her, or at least he liked what he knew about her.

He could see she was on the fence still, so he tried to sweeten the pot. Something inside of him just sort of knew that *she* was meant to have his granny's things. "She was an earth witch just like you and Lucas. She might have some spell books that would be of interest."

She gave a small nod like she'd come to a decision then glanced down at her flour-covered clothes again and said, "I'll need to change. I'll get Lucas to pack a bag of stuff so he can keep himself entertained. I wouldn't expect you to babysit him. You probably get enough of that during the week."

Andrew had to stop himself from doing a fist pump. He was excited she had agreed to come, but he didn't want her to know exactly how happy he was—he wouldn't want to scare her off. He also wasn't going to argue with her about babysitting Lucas. He was a great kid, and he was looking forward to spending time with him when he wasn't in a classroom. "Can I do anything to help?"

"Thanks, but we're good. We've got it down to a science by now."

"Take whatever time you need. Once you're ready, you can follow me back to my place. I'm parked just around the corner." He figured it was safer to give her an easy out. If she took her own car, she and Lucas could leave whenever she felt like it.

"It might take a while. Everything seems to take longer with a six-year-old."

He smiled. "I've got nothing but time."

Sierra acknowledged him then shut the door. Andrew wandered away, taking in the cute downtown. He'd always loved this town, even when he was a little boy. He remembered Granny taking them for ice cream and then to Whimsy & Wonder to pick out a special toy to play with. He wondered if Lucas would enjoy that. Then again, what little kid wouldn't?

About twenty minutes later, Sierra emerged looking freshly showered and dressed in flour-free clothes. Lucas stood next to her holding a backpack bursting full of what Andrew was certain were absolute essentials for any little boy. He could just barely make out the head of a stuffed alien sticking out of the zipper where it didn't fully close.

"Ready?" he asked.

"As we'll ever be," Sierra responded.

Andrew climbed behind the steering wheel of his car and slowly pulled out of his spot, making sure that Sierra was right behind him on the road. He didn't want to lose her at a traffic light or anything. Sierra's shop was at the south end of town, and he lived in a neighborhood of cute bungalow houses on the north side. He pulled in the driveway and waited for her to pull in next to him before he got out of the car.

Lucas was out the back door of the van in a flash. "Is this where you live, Mr. Knight?" he asked as he took in the small slate-blue house.

"Lucas! You know you're supposed to wait for me," Sierra said in the exasperated voice all moms seem to have perfected.

Lucas scuffed the bottom of his shoe against the driveway and said, "Sorry, Mom." His contrition didn't last long, though, because he immediately turned back to Andrew and asked again. "Is this your house?"

Andrew reached out and ruffled Lucas's hair. "It sure is, buddy. You want to look inside?"

Lucas practically yelled "Yeah!" Sierra rolled her eyes and smiled fondly at her son.

The house wasn't huge, but it was neat and tidy. It was basically a small square box, with clean blue siding and a short porch that took up half the front of the house—just big enough for two rocking chairs. Granny had lived in the house for decades and had taken excellent care of it. Unfortunately, in her golden years, she'd had a harder time keeping up with the maintenance, so the lush bushes and plants Andrew remembered from when he was a kid had died or gotten completely overgrown. The house needed a little bit of TLC, but overall, it was in great shape, and he was happy to have it.

They started walking up the short sidewalk from the driveway to the front door, but Lucas stopped abruptly and gave Andrew's house a critical eye. "You need gardens. With lots of flowers. Your house is sad without flowers."

Andrew swallowed down a smile. "I'll have to remember that in the springtime. Maybe I can plant some flowerbeds then. I don't think they would grow that well in the fall."

"That's true." Lucas seemed to take his explanation in stride as if there was no doubt in his mind that Andrew would plant flowers in the spring.

Andrew unlocked the front door and let Sierra and Lucas enter the house before him. Even though he knew the space was immaculate—he'd made sure of it before he'd left that morning—he was still nervous. He wanted Sierra to like his place, even if he'd only lived there for a month. The small house was still a mishmash of his own belongings and his granny's, but he was slowly working to make it more his own.

The door entered right into the cozy living room where he had a plush green couch and a large TV on a stand against the wall. The walls were a warm beige that he'd accented with various nature photographs he'd collected over the years. There was a small eat-in kitchen in the back left corner that was open to the living room. He wasn't much of a cook, but he could hold his own, so he made sure his kitchen was in tiptop shape. Off to the right of the living area was a small hallway that led to a bathroom and two bedrooms, one on either side of the bathroom.

Sierra looked around his space with interest, her eyes tracing over the fluffy pillows on the couch and lingering a bit longer on the photos of trees, streams, and mountains he'd selected to put on display.

When he couldn't take the silence any longer, Andrew cleared his throat and ran his hand through his hair. "It's not much."

Sierra turned and smiled. "It's wonderful. It feels very well loved."

Andrew wasn't sure he'd ever heard of a place referred to as well loved before, but since it was true, he couldn't argue with her. "Hey, Lucas, what do you think about watching some television?" he said with a raised eyebrow at Sierra, who nodded her agreement.

"Do you have Bluey?" Lucas asked as he tossed his bag on the couch and plopped down next to it.

Andrew grabbed the remote and flicked on the TV but then froze. For as much as he spent all day with small kids, he had no idea where to find their favorite shows.

The panic must have been obvious on his face, because Sierra smiled and gestured to his remote control. "Do you mind?"

He gestured for her to proceed, and she navigated to one of the popular streaming services and located the show within seconds. Lucas was immediately entranced. Andrew found himself getting caught up in the lessons and adventures of the dog family on the screen.

"New to Bluey?"

Sierra's voice startled Andrew out of his trance. He could feel a blush creeping up his cheeks. "Um, yes? I mean, I've heard about it from the kids, obviously, but I've never actually watched it."

"It's surprisingly entertaining, even for adults." Sierra crossed her arms.

Andrew found himself simply enjoying spending time with her. She looked fresh faced and relaxed, and he wished he could help her feel that way all the time. He wondered what it would take to convince her to spend more time with him.

"Do I have something on my face?" she asked lightly as she self-consciously wiped her cheek.

Andrew realized he'd been staring at her. He shook his head, trying to clear his thoughts. Right. He'd brought her here for a reason, not just to hang out with her and Lucas. "Sorry. This way." He gestured to the short hallway that led to the other half of the house. His bedroom was at the back of the house, but he turned away from it and led her to the front bedroom.

The room was cram-packed full of stuff. One entire wall was full of bookshelves that held spell books, herbal medicine reference texts, and journals. Another wall had a series of drawers, each containing a different dried plant, candle, stone, or charm. In the center of the room was a round table covered in a black tablecloth. In the middle of the table was a metal bowl that was currently empty but was surrounded by fat green candles.

Sierra took in the space with wide eyes. "I can see why you didn't want to get rid of her things. This space is amazing." She walked around the room reverently, her hands not quite touching anything, but dancing in the air above them as if she could just barely feel them.

"I'll leave you to it," Andrew said as he left her, though honestly he wasn't sure she even knew he was gone. If possible, Sierra looked even more at peace than she had before, and Andrew was glad he'd been able to give that to her. Now he got to hang out with Lucas, who was rapidly becoming one of his favorite people.

Chapter Thirteen

T HE SPACE SIGHED WITH relief as it welcomed Sierra through the door. She was already itching to dig through the plethora of books and supplies in front of her.

The altar in the center of the room was fairly standard. The metal bowl, which appeared to be made from pewter, was clean except for a very fine layer of dust. The fat green candles weren't brand new, yet still relatively fresh, as though they hadn't been burned for long.

She ran her hand along the drawers of an antique hutch and opened each one. Several held large quantities of sage—both loose leaves and bundles for smudging and burning. Lavender blooms practically spilled out of another drawer, the sweet floral scent instantly calming her. There was a live rosemary bush in the corner of the room that Andrew must have been watering, since it still looked vibrant and green rather than dried and dead. Drawer after drawer, she found mugwort, basil, eucalyptus, and cinnamon.

After the plants, she moved on to the stones and minerals. She found every color of quartz one could possibly imagine—amethyst in a range of shades of purple, pale pink rose quartz, and grayish smoky quartz. She found bright yellow-orange citrine, opaque green malachite, and striped agates in several different colors. Yet another drawer contained a deep red and green bloodstone, while the last one contained a large chunk of shiny black onyx. Almost every gem or mineral she could name off the top of her head was represented, some pieces as small as a fingernail, others as large as a softball.

Sierra couldn't imagine the care it would have taken to assemble such a varied collection. It would have taken years to collect them all. Madelyn had clearly been dedicated to her craft, even though Andrew claimed she wasn't super powerful. She had everything an earth witch could want right at her fingertips.

Once Sierra had gone through all the supplies—much of which she didn't have herself, since she was rebuilding her practice—she turned her sights to the endless rows of books. Sierra crossed the warm hardwood floor and stood in front of the bookshelves, but she was reluctant to touch them. A witch's spell book was a very personal thing. Reading another witch's book of shadows was akin to reading someone's diary.

She started with the reference books. There was nothing personal about a plant identification guide or a book that explained the magical properties of the various stones and gems.

Sierra wound up sitting on the rug and pulling books off the shelf almost at random. Reference books went into one pile. Those were something Andrew almost assuredly would be okay parting with. They probably didn't hold a lot in the way of sentimental value. Spell books went into a second pile. Those books had plenty of handwritten notes and scribbles in them that Andrew might want to look at.

Halfway down the second bookshelf, Sierra stumbled across something that wasn't related to witchcraft at all. It appeared to be an old family photo album. She gently pulled the book onto her lap, careful not to harm the cracking black cover and spine.

The oldest pictures in the book were of a middle-aged woman who looked exactly like the elementary school teacher Sierra remembered from the second grade. In various photos, she stood among groups of people who looked to be in their twenties, presumably her children. As she flipped through the book, the faces aged and changed, and younger kids started to appear. Sometimes there were more, sometimes fewer, but Madelyn was always there and always smiling.

Sierra smiled as she realized she was watching Andrew grow up. She barely recognized him when he was young, but as he grew up, she saw more of the man she knew today. He was usually surrounded by two girls with equally blonde hair, who were, at a guess, his sisters.

By the time she'd flipped to the back of the album, Andrew and his sisters were probably high-school-aged. But one photo caught her eye. There was a fourth teenager in the photo, and it was a face she knew all too well.

Todd Dalton. Her ex-husband.

"Andrew?" She tried to get his attention, but her voice came out more of a croak than a shout. She tried again. "Andrew?" Her voice was much louder the second time, with an edge of panic that she valiantly fought back.

Seconds later, Andrew popped his head into the room and seemed surprised to find her on the floor surrounded by books. "Hey, do you need something?" he asked as he picked his way around her neatly stacked piles.

Now that he was here, she was reluctant to ask what she desperately needed to know. Just because being confronted by her ex—even in picture form—made her stomach sink to somewhere around her toes, didn't mean that Andrew was guilty of anything. Knowing someone, even an asshole like Todd, wasn't a crime.

She swallowed a few times trying to clear the lump from her throat. "I think I found one of Madelyn's family photo albums." She held the book in his direction until he was forced to take it or let it fall.

A soft smile settled on his mouth as he flipped through the pages. "I don't think I've seen these before. Thanks for finding this."

She slowly got to her feet. "Um," she hemmed and hawed, then finally flipped to the page she'd been staring at when he came in. "Can you explain this one?" She tapped her finger on the photo with Todd.

Andrew squinted at it, then appeared to think for a minute. "I think it might have been my sixteenth birthday? I always insisted on celebrating with Granny, long after my sisters no longer wanted to spend time with her."

That didn't tell Sierra what she wanted to know. "Who's this? He's obviously not one of your siblings." She tapped Todd's face.

The confused cloud seemed to clear from Andrew's face. "Oh, that's my cousin, Todd."

For the second time in five minutes, her stomach dropped out from underneath her. "You're related to Todd Dalton?"

Andrew froze. "You know Todd?" he asked carefully.

She swallowed down a hysterical laugh. "You could say that. He's my ex-husband. Lucas's father. The man who walked out on us when Lucas was three because he couldn't handle that his son and wife were both witches."

Andrew tried to reach for her, but his hand stopped short of making contact. He opened his mouth, but nothing came out.

She waved her hand to forestall any more attempts to talk. "I need to go. Now."

His shoulders slumped, but he rallied. "Of course. Whatever you need."

Sierra barreled out of the bedroom and back into the living room, where she found Lucas happily smashing trucks together as he drove them around a makeshift racetrack made of plates, bowls, and kitchen utensils. A tiny fraction of her brain processed that Andrew must have helped him build the elaborate structure before she barked out, "Lucas, we need to leave."

Instant heartbreak raced across Lucas's face. "Can't I have ten more minutes?" He begged as he gestured to the construction wonder in front of him.

"I'm sorry, not today. Pack your things and thank Mr. Knight for his hospitality."

With a small grumble, Lucas grabbed his trucks, his stuffed alien, and his books—which appeared to be scattered from one end of the couch to the other—and shoved them back into his backpack. "Thank you, Mr. Knight," Lucas mumbled.

"You're very welcome, Lucas. It was great hanging out with you."

Sierra almost jumped when Andrew's soft voice came from behind her shoulder. She knew she should thank him for watching Lucas while she'd been digging into Madelyn's things, but her brain just couldn't process things like social niceties at the moment.

As soon as Lucas had shoved his belongings hap haphazardly into his bag, Sierra put her hand on his shoulder and steered him to the door. She glanced over her shoulder and gave Andrew a tiny nod, then fled.

Chapter Fourteen

F UCKING TODD. OF ALL the assholes in the world, why did Sierra's ex-husband have to be his cousin Todd? He'd noticed that they had the same last name, of course, but it wasn't like Dalton was an uncommon name. Of all the luck.

Andrew knew that he was the only one in his family who was willing to accept his granny in all her witchy glory. Madelyn had been somewhat philosophical about the fact that even her own children—of which she had three, two daughters and a son—hadn't believed in and supported her. Most of her grandchildren had taken after their parents and agreed that there was no such thing as magic.

But that was nothing compared to Todd's side of the family. Todd's mother, Susan, was ten years older than Andrew's mom, and she was the strictest, most puritanical person Andrew had ever met. She'd moved out of her parents' house when she was eighteen and had very rarely visited. She moved to California, got married, and did everything in her power to keep her distance from the rest of the family. She'd had Todd later in life, so he was only two years older than Andrew, who was the baby of his family. However, even while they'd been growing up, it was rare that Todd was anywhere to be seen. Honestly, Andrew couldn't even remember what chain of events had led him to be at Andrew's sixteenth birthday. It wasn't a normal occurrence.

Todd had taken on all his mother's worst tendencies and inherited none of the warmth that Madelyn showered on everyone she met. Andrew could vividly remember one instance where Todd had openly scoffed in Granny's face when she performed a small spell in front of them. It hadn't been anything earth-shattering or pivotal—she'd handed them each a perfect rose blossom—but Todd had rolled his eyes and said that "any cheesy stage magician could pull a flower out of their sleeve."

"Earth to Andrew. Come in, Andrew." Andrew jerked out of his own thoughts. Jasmine had just taken a seat across from him at a table in the teacher's lounge. "You okay over there?" she asked.

"Of course. Why wouldn't I be?"

Jasmine threw a baby carrot at him. "Liar."

The carrot bounced off his chest, but he grabbed it before it hit the table. With a shrug, he ate it. "Just personal stuff," he said as he glanced around. The last thing he needed was the Dragon Lady hearing anything about the fact that he'd been spending time socially with one of his students' parents.

Jasmine waggled her eyebrows. "That's the best kind of stuff. Does this have anything to do with a certain flower shop owner?"

Andrew suddenly regretted confessing his attraction to Sierra to Jasmine. They were friends, so she wasn't afraid to call him out on his crap. "Shh, keep your voice down," he hissed as he glanced around nervously again.

Jasmine waved him off. "Don't worry about it. Our least favorite overseer is busy keeping her eagle eyes on one of the student teachers. The poor woman might crack under Bodrock's glare."

Andrew went back to munching on his ham and cheddar sandwich and studiously avoiding Jasmine's eyes.

"Well?" She drew the word out like it had several extra syllables than it actually did.

He finished his bite and slowly lowered his sandwich. "All right, if you must know. Yes. It does have to do with Sierra."

Jasmine wiggled excitedly in her seat. "I knew it! Give me all the dirty details. Did you two knock boots?"

Andrew waved his hands to shush her. "Seriously. How are you an elementary school teacher? And who says knock boots?"

"One of the many mysteries of life. So, did you?" She happily munched on a carrot.

He sighed. He was going to have to give her something, or she would never leave him alone. "No, we didn't ... do that," he said primly, "but I did invite her to my house on Sunday. Lucas was there too." He cut off the question he could practically see brewing in her eyes.

"Okay, so you had a six-year-old for a babysitter. That sucks. Is that what has you so bummed out?" She moved on to a prepackaged container of sushi.

Andrew took the time to bite into his apple and chew before responding. "No. I enjoy spending time with Lucas. He's a great kid."

"Okay, so then what's the issue? You can tell Dr. Jasmine. I've seen all the talk shows, and I'm here to help."

He rolled his eyes at her. "It turns out that we have history."

She immediately stopped eating her California roll. "You slept with her and didn't remember her? Dick move, man."

Andrew practically spit out his next bite of apple. "What? No. That's not what I meant."

She glared at him. "It better not be." She shoved another roll in her mouth and chewed.

Feeling off balance, Andrew finally just blurted it out. "She used to be married to my cousin, Todd—Lucas's father. Todd left her when Lucas was three." He wasn't about to share the reason for Todd leaving Sierra.

Her mouth dropped open, and she leaned closer. "Now that is some messy family drama right there. And you had no idea?"

Andrew rubbed the back of his neck. "No. Todd and I aren't close. Needless to say, I didn't attend the wedding."

Jasmine leaned back in her chair and rubbed her chin. "So where does that leave you?"

Boom. That was the million-dollar question, and Andrew had no idea what the answer was. It wasn't like he and Sierra were dating, at least not yet. They had a connection of some sort, and obviously he found her devastatingly beautiful, but at every turn it seemed like something was getting in their way. If it wasn't his job, or the fact that she was a single mother, it was that her ex-husband was a class-A jerk, and Andrew was related to him. He wanted more with her, but wasn't sure how to take it to the next level.

"Honestly, your guess is as good as mine." He'd suddenly lost his appetite. He carefully wrapped up the rest of his apple and tossed it into the trash, then tucked his untouched chips back in his insulated lunch bag.

Jasmine's eyes narrowed as she studied him. "How did she react when you figured it out?"

Just the memory of her frozen expression haunted him. "Not great. And she's the one that figured it out. She saw a family photo of us from high school. She basically freaked out and left." He rubbed the base of his skull where he could feel his muscles starting to tighten.

Jasmine dipped her sushi in some soy sauce and then popped it into her mouth, her gaze thoughtful. "Well, that's not great," she said when she'd finished chewing. "It's not the end of the world either. Have you talked to her since then?"

"No."

Jasmine stared at him. "You let her stew on this information for four days?" Her eyebrows shot up.

Andrew shrugged. "That's not exactly how I would put it. It seemed like a pretty heavy piece of information. My cousin ..." He paused to think about how he wanted to describe Todd. "He's not a great human being. I figured I would let her deal with the fact that I was related to him on her own terms."

Jasmine was already shaking her head. She pointed at him with her chopsticks. "Are you like Todd? Are you a 'not great human being'?" she asked while doing her best attempt at air quotes while holding her utensils.

Andrew bristled. "Of course not."

She gave him an exaggerated nod. "Exactly. You are not your cousin—who I automatically hate, by the way, even if I've never met him. You need to talk to Sierra. Remind her that you are not, in fact, Todd, and that unlike him, you're awesome."

He wasn't sure if that was the right move. He didn't want to be pushy. Sierra had probably had enough of that in her life. "Yeah, maybe."

"No. No maybe. Dr. Jasmine only gives good advice. Trust me on this." She went back to eating her lunch as if the matter was settled.

Chapter Fifteen

"WE HAVE A PROBLEM." Jenna's voice sent a wave of dread coursing through Sierra.

It had been a week since Sierra had learned that Andrew was related to her asshole ex-husband, and her feelings were finally evening out again, so hearing the worried tone in Jenna's voice flooded Sierra with more anxiety. She gripped her phone tighter and held it harder against her ear. "What happened?"

"That black spot that appeared in the park? One of them showed up in the grove."

"Damn it." Sierra did a quick check around her kitchen to make sure Lucas wasn't around.

It was Sunday afternoon, which was normally her time to hang out with Lucas. Sometimes they built Lego structures, other times they went to the playground in the park. When she was feeling particularly flush with cash, they went to Whimsy & Wonder across the street.

Today was one of their more low-key days. They'd been watching whatever Lucas wanted on TV and coloring at the coffee table in their living room. As much as she relished having time to just hang out and be silly with her son, the grove situation needed her attention. They didn't know for sure who was causing the energy drains or what their intention was. Doing some strange magic in the woods in the public park was one thing, but sneaking onto Jenna's property and into her woods felt personal.

"I'll drop Lucas off with my dad and be there as soon as I can." Sierra hit the button to end the call. Her shoulders, which had been somewhere up near her ears, slowly slumped. She couldn't help feeling like this was all somehow her fault. Maybe if she hadn't missed out on twelve years of training and used her magic more often, she would have been able to fix the damage in the park. Or maybe she would have been able to somehow prevent it from happening.

She texted her dad to make sure it was okay to drop Lucas off at his house. After she got a thumbs-up emoji, she called out, "Lucas, pack a bag. I need to go see Aunt Jenna, so you're going to go visit Grandpa." Jenna wasn't really his aunt, but Sierra had encouraged Lucas to think of her that way, especially since he didn't have any actual aunts or uncles floating around.

A loud "Yes!" from the other room made her smile. Lucas loved spending time with her father. Her dad wasn't a witch—that had been her mom, who had died when she was five—but he was the only stable male influence in Lucas's life. He happily trailed after her father, no matter what he was doing. Thankfully, her dad loved hanging out with Lucas just as much, and the two of them had a blast together. Her dad loved to garden, which was right up Lucas's alley, but also loved to do things like build bird houses and bat houses, which also tickled Lucas's fancy.

Lucas was back with his bag full of essentials in less than five minutes, which was practically a record. He was even wearing shoes and had grabbed a jacket. She almost wanted to snap a photograph to commemorate the moment.

Her dad only lived a few blocks away, and Lucas was out of the car and halfway up the sidewalk before Sierra even got out of the driver's seat. She thought about scolding him for running off without her—*again*—but gave up as soon as her dad opened the door and accepted the little-boy-shaped missile that flew at him in a huge hug.

"Thanks again, Dad," Sierra said as she finally caught up to them.

"Always. You know that," he said as he finally unwrapped his arms from around his grandson. "Go set yourself up in the den. I'll be right there."

Lucas took off like a shot, his never-ending energy on full display. They watched him go, then her dad pinned her with the concerned eyes that only a parent could send to their child. "What's wrong?"

Sierra had no idea how he always knew when something was bothering her. If she didn't know for a fact that her father was an ordinary, she would have assumed he had a little mind magic of his own.

He knew she was a witch, but she was still reluctant to draw him into whatever was brewing magically around Rock Cove. The more he knew, the more of a target he was, and she had no intention of painting a bullseye on her own father. "Just," she waved her hand, "witch stuff."

His eyes narrowed. "Are you practicing again?"

He wasn't anti-magic, but he'd supported her decision to stop practicing, even if she'd never fully explained why she'd done so. He knew that it involved something that happened during her Trials, and he knew how badly Todd had reacted when he'd found out that she and Lucas had powers. Her father wanted her happy, no matter what it took, so he supported whatever decision she made with respect to her magic. "Yeah, I am. There are reasons ..."

He held up his hand to stop her. "You don't need to explain your reasons to me. If it's something you felt you had to do or wanted to do, then I support you."

She glanced over his shoulder in the direction that Lucas had gone. "I need you both to be safe."

Her dad nodded. "Then we will be. Lucas and I will be fine. You do what you have to do. And say hi to Jenna for me."

Sierra gave her dad a quick hug, called out a loud "Bye!" to Lucas, and hopped back in her minivan.

Jenna lived on the outskirts of town. She had a huge property with dozens of acres that her family had been collecting for generations. The back of her property was mostly wooded, though it also contained a decently sized lake that they'd gone swimming in as kids. Beyond the edge of the property was state-owned forest, so it was relatively isolated.

Sierra didn't even bother stopping by the house itself. If the grove was in danger, then that's where Jenna would be. Sierra hiked through the woods that she'd spent so much time in as a kid. The bright orange and yellow forest hummed with energy, the trees slowly going dormant to hibernate until the spring, the animals rummaging for the last remaining nuts and berries of the season. Everything felt perfect—right up until she got to the grove.

"Holy shit." The words practically fell out of her mouth before she could stop them. Just as Jenna had said, there was a charred black spot in the clearing just like the one from the park.

"I know, right?" Jenna said as Sierra approached. They stared at the black mark in mutual shock.

Sierra glanced from the dead ground in front of her to the nearby stone circle. They were exactly the same size. "What, or should I say who, could even do this? I can't imagine how much magical mojo this would take."

Jenna only shrugged. "I have no idea. Roderick? Danika? But almost more important than the who is the why. What are they after? What's the purpose here?"

Sierra paced around the outside of the dead spot, occasionally running her hands along the invisible boundary. On one side, she could feel the life force of the forest pushing at her skin. On the other side, a complete lack of anything. "It's like it's trying to feed on my energy."

Jenna nodded. "Yeah, but why? What spell are they trying to cast that would need that much energy? I've never seen a spell in any of my spell books that would cause this."

Sierra completed her circle around the dead spot and stopped next to her friend again. "What if the point of the spell *is* the energy?" It was something she'd been thinking about over the last week or so. She was still working on her theory, but maybe it was time to run it by Jenna.

"What do you mean?" Jenna cocked her head.

"What if whoever caused this," she waved vaguely at the dead circle, "is trying to do something big. Something they don't have the magical juice to accomplish on their own. Then, when they figured out they couldn't do it by themselves, they went in search of a bit more oomph to help them get there."

Jenna's lips pursed. "I guess it's possible, but how did you come up with that idea?"

"From the Prophecy you showed me. When you were fighting Danika in this very spot, didn't you say she mentioned the Architect?" Sierra started pacing as her brain picked up speed and she needed an outlet for her energy.

"Yes, she did," Jenna said.

"Right," Sierra said, pointing a finger in Jenna's direction. "And the Prophecy stated that this Architect person—"

"Roderick," Jenna said his name matter-of-factly.

Sierra's eyes narrowed. "We don't know that for sure. And before you interrupt me again," Sierra said when it looked like Jenna was going to do exactly that, "Yes, the Circle of Thirteen said they were tracking him, but they didn't actually say he was this prophesied Architect, right?"

"Well, no, but—"

"Exactly. So anyway. This Architect person is trying raise the Harbinger, the super evil creature bent on death and destruction, blah, blah, blah, right?" Sierra sent Jenna a piercing gaze.

"Right, or at least according to the Circle it's right." Jenna crossed her arms as she watched Sierra walk in circles.

"Well if you ask me, raising a soulless creature bent on destroying the world sounds like something that would take a lot of magical mojo." She stopped walking and stared at Jenna, hoping Jenna would believe her. It all made sense in Sierra's head, but she was still feeling insecure when it came to magic, and everything about this situation was saturated in the stuff.

"Okay, let's say that's true. If this Architect person is trying to raise some big bad, like it says in the Prophecy, then what else do we know? What else did the Prophecy say?" Jenna rubbed her forehead for a moment. "I think it was, chaos reigns to ill effect, giving rise to an Architect. While lives are lost and costs incurred, he shall raise the harbinger."

Sierra's stomach sank. "Chaos doesn't sound good. Neither does losing lives and incurring cost."

"And don't forget the part where the four of us working together is the only thing that can defeat it. You know, the four of us that can barely be in the same place at the same time."

"Have you ever ..." As much as she wanted to know, Sierra had tried her best to stay out of the mess between Jenna and Brigit. "Never mind. Ignore me."

"Sierra, just say what you wanted to say. You're my best friend. I won't be mad at you, I promise."

Sierra wandered over to the stone circle and sat down. She patted the spot next to her, and Jenna joined her, leaning against her side. "I know something big happened between you and Brigit, but it was twelve years ago. Have you talked to her about it at all since you've been back?"

Jenna stiffened. "I've *tried* talking to her. You know I have. She's always such a bitch to me."

Sierra put her arm around Jenna's shoulder and tugged her back against her side. After a second's hesitation, Jenna laid her head on Sierra's shoulder with a sigh. "Don't take this the wrong way, but I mean *talk* to her. Not yell at her. Not throw magic at each other in the forest. Not be snide to each other, but actually have a bidirectional conversation," Sierra said.

Jenna let out a huff. "We almost did. I thought there was a moment a few months ago when we might have made some progress. When she came to see me to clear up some stuff about Denver, we briefly touched on what happened when we were eighteen. She accused me of putting myself first and somehow costing her everything, then stormed off." She sighed. "I still have no idea what that means or what I'm supposed to have cost her."

Sierra squeezed her friend. "Maybe it's time to try again. If this," she gestured to the giant black spot in the clearing, "is anything to go by, then this possibly apocalyptic confrontation is coming sooner rather than later. We need to be whole again. Don't you miss it?" she asked wistfully.

"Of course, I miss it. I miss everything about it. I loved being part of our coven. You were my sisters in all but blood, and we spilled enough of that over the years that sometimes it felt like that way too. But Brigit was the one who broke us apart. Why should I have to be the one to mend us?"

Sierra chuckled. "Water is the healing element, which basically means it's your job to fix things. Blame magic, not me. Besides, you know how she is. If we have to wait until Brigit admits she did something wrong, we could be waiting until the Rapture."

Jenna shoved her lightly with her shoulder. "Depending on what happens with this Harbinger creature, the Rapture might be here before we know it."

"We're joking about the end of the world now? Is that what we've come to?"

"Better to laugh than have a panic attack, crawl into a hole, and wait for the end of time, right?" Jenna took a deep breath. "I'll see what I can do."

"That's all I ask. Well, that and for you to help me try to clean up this mess." Sierra gestured to the giant dead spot in the grove.

They spent several hours trying every spell they could, but it all had the exact same effect as it did in the park, which is to say none. They tried healing it, regrowing the plants, cleansing it, and nothing worked. They tried just channeling a bunch of energy into the black spot, which seemed to work for a time as the grass started to regrow, but even that was short-lived. The grass immediately withered and died again. As dark fell they finally admitted defeat, at least for the day.

As they headed back to Jenna's house, Sierra stopped for one more look at the dark smear. "I don't know what it's going to take, but I will fix this."

Chapter Sixteen

S IERRA WAS FRUSTRATED BEYOND belief.

It was Monday afternoon. She'd been stewing over the problem with the grove and the park ever since she'd left Jenna's house the night before. As soon as she'd gotten back to her apartment, she'd immediately pulled out every book she had stashed in her closet about earth magic. She'd even brought them down to the store that morning and read them between customers. Nothing she'd seen even hinted at what the problem was or how to fix it.

Her mind flashed to the front bedroom of Andrew's house, to the place that Madelyn Healy had considered her sacred space. Those bookshelves had been filled to the brim with research tomes and spell books that Sierra had never seen before. She couldn't help wondering if there was anything in any of those books that would help her with her current problem, but that would mean approaching Andrew again, and she wasn't sure if she could do that.

She was embarrassed about how she'd reacted. She'd freaked out over nothing. It was obvious, in retrospect, that Andrew and Todd weren't close. She and Todd had a very small wedding, with only immediate family and a few friends there to support them and celebrate with them. At the time she hadn't thought it was all that strange. They'd been trying to keep costs down by not inviting everyone and their brother. But looking back on it, it now seemed strange that she hadn't known that Todd even had cousins. He'd never mentioned them. Just one more thing about their marriage that they hadn't been honest about. No wonder she had trust issues.

Sierra slammed the book she was reading closed just as the bell above the door to her shop tinkled merrily. She quickly shoved the spell book under her counter and out of sight before glancing up to greet the customer.

She froze in her tracks. "Roderick." She swallowed thickly. She hadn't seen or heard from Roderick in months, not since before the showdown in Jenna's woods with Danika and the Circle of Thirteen.

Roderick Mccann was in his mid-fifties, with a head of closely cropped hair and a severe widow's peak. His skin had the weathered appearance of someone who had spent far too many hours out in the sun during his life, his face tight and slightly leathery. He was wearing a worn pair of jeans with a white T-shirt under a black leather jacket, which suited him well, even if it did make him look like he belonged on the back of a motorcycle.

"Sierra, how have you been?" He stopped in front of her and leaned on the counter like he was planning on getting comfortable.

She wasn't sure how to answer. She'd never had the same grudge against Roderick that Jenna had, but she had to admit he'd done some questionable things—namely, when it came to Jenna's talisman. He'd asked Jenna to give it to him with the promise to give it to the Circle. Did that make Roderick a liar? Or was the Circle withholding the truth for some reason? Jenna was also convinced that Roderick was the prophesied Architect, but that was just a theory. They had no proof of that. Still, it would be silly of her to trust him with too much, just in case there was any truth to Jenna's accusations.

"The same as usual, really. Running the shop and keeping Lucas out of trouble as much as I can."

He nodded like he'd expected that answer. "So nothing strange or unusual has come up lately?" He arched an eyebrow as he ran his thick index finger along the delicate petals of a sunflower in the vase on the counter.

Why would he be asking about strange and unusual? Did he know something about what was going on in the park and in Jenna's woods? If so, was it possible he knew because he'd caused it? Sierra's stomach sank as she tried to keep her expression neutral. "What sort of strange or unusual?" She pushed the question back on him.

He tsked his tongue. "Come now, Sierra. We both know what I'm talking about. The magical dead spot in the park?"

She shifted uncomfortably under his scrutiny. Should she press him for more information? Or pretend like she had no idea what he was talking about? "I've seen it." She settled on a semi-neutral answer. "How do you know about it?" She couldn't help asking.

He gave her a look that spoke volumes. "Sierra. We've known each other long enough that you're aware of my reach and my connections. I know everything magical that goes on around Rock Cove. How else would I look out for my girls?"

He made the question sound so innocent, like of course he had their best interests at heart. She wanted to believe him, but she just wasn't sure if she could or not. "What have you been able to figure out about it?" If he wanted to talk about the marks, it couldn't hurt to see what he knew.

He shrugged. "Not much, at least not yet. Someone cast some sort of spell on the spot. Clearly it went very wrong."

"Hm," Sierra made a noncommittal noise. She wasn't planning to share her theory with him that the spell had actually gone very right.

"I assume you've tried to do something to repair it?"

"What makes you think that?"

"Once upon a time, Sierra, I knew you four almost as well as you knew each other. I know what makes you tick and what gets under your skin. A problem like this—where it's clear that someone has been messing with magic that's affecting the very earth itself—is the type of thing that would have offended your younger self right down to her bones." He raised his eyebrows at her. "Somehow, I doubt that grown-up Sierra is all that different. Let me guess. You've been training with Jenna."

It really was uncanny how well he knew them. He wasn't wrong that her younger self would have been full of indignation about the situation. He'd also correctly guessed that she and Jenna had been working together. "I've tried a few things." She finally conceded.

"And let me guess. None of them have worked."

Now it was Sierra's turn to raise her eyebrow. "If they had, the scar wouldn't be there anymore."

Roderick raised his hands like he was surrendering. "Fair enough."

"Have you tried to fix it?" she prompted him.

He waved his hand back and forth in a so-so gesture. "I tried one or two things. But you know, I was never as gifted at earth magic as you were."

Roderick's affinity was fire magic, which is one of the many reasons he got along so well with Brigit. Sierra also noticed that he referred to her power in the past tense. While it was true that she hadn't practiced in a while, it still stung that he was pointing out that she'd lost some of her power over the years. "Look, I'm trying, okay? I realize that by stopping practicing, I tied my hands, metaphorically and magically speaking. I've been working with Jenna to rebuild what I've lost, but it just hasn't been enough."

He gave her a sympathetic look. "I understand, my dear. But that's why I'm here. I'm offering my services as your mentor once again. My own power has grown through the years, and I have resources you girls just simply don't have access to. I may even have figured out a way that allows me to share magic with you and give you a boost. I can help you. More than Jenna can, at any rate. Together we can fix this."

Sierra had to admit his offer was tempting, especially the part about extra magic. Even though she was getting stronger every day, she still felt inadequate. As much as she'd hated some of Roderick's methods, she couldn't deny he'd made them better witches.

But she couldn't get Jenna's nagging suspicions out of the back of her head. If she had to pick between Roderick and Jenna, she was going to choose Jenna every time.

"Thanks for the offer, but I think I'm good for now."

Roderick pushed off her counter, an annoyed look flashing across his face before he masked it. "Well, the offer stands. If you change your mind, just let me know." He strolled out of the shop and left her to stew in her own thoughts.

She was out of ideas. For the rest of the day, she tried to come up with her next steps, and only two options came to mind. She could reach out to Roderick and take him up on his offer, which she wasn't comfortable doing, or she could swallow her embarrassment over how she treated Andrew and ask him to look at his grandmother's books.

She knew what she needed to do.

Chapter Seventeen

A KNOCK ON THE door startled Andrew out of his staring contest with his rather empty refrigerator. He'd been trying to conjure up something that resembled food that could pass for dinner, but he wasn't in the mood to cook, so nothing was jumping out at him.

Rock Cove may be a small town, but it still wasn't normal to have neighbors knocking on his door at night. He padded across his wood floor, opened the door, and was pleasantly surprised to see Sierra standing on the other side, holding a bouquet of colorful blooms in one hand and a pizza that smelled amazing in the other. Despite his conversation with Jasmine, he still hadn't figured out how to approach Sierra in a way that wouldn't make the situation worse. It looked like Sierra had beaten him to the punch.

"Well, if it isn't my favorite florist. I'm glad you stopped by." He quickly glanced behind her, but there was a distinct lack of six-year-old behind her. "Lucas isn't with you?" He asked as he stepped back and ushered her inside his house.

She shook her head. "No, Jenna is watching him for me. I wanted a chance to talk to you without him overhearing." They stood awkwardly in the entryway for a few moments, staring at each other, before she seemed to remember what she was doing. She thrust out the hand holding the flowers and said, "These are for you."

He accepted them with an eyebrow raise. "You brought me flowers?" he asked as he gestured with his head toward the kitchen. He went in search of a vase to put the blooms in, and she followed a few steps behind.

"They're an apology peace offering. I'm so sorry for freaking out on you last week. Todd and I didn't part on the best of terms, so figuring out that you were related to him caught me off guard. I honestly didn't even know that Todd had cousins, much less that you were one of them. He never mentioned any other family apart from his parents."

Andrew couldn't find a vase, so he settled for a collector's beer stein he'd gotten on vacation several years before. He filled it with water and placed the flowers inside, which instantly brightened up his kitchen. "That doesn't surprise me. Todd's mother, my aunt, distanced herself from the rest of the family a long time ago. She didn't approve of magic and did everything she could to forget that her mother was a witch. She moved to California and never looked back. How did you even meet Todd, anyway? If that's okay to ask?" He didn't want to push her into talking about anything she wasn't comfortable discussing, but he'd been dying to know.

She placed the pizza on his kitchen table and tucked a lock of her long, wavy hair behind her ear. "We met when he was at Harvard. I was visiting Aura at Boston College, and we went out to a bar. Todd had been hanging out with his friends, and we hit it off and started talking. Things sort of progressed from there."

He nodded. "I didn't even know he went to Harvard, but it makes sense. He was always a stuck-up snob. Nothing less than an Ivy League school would have met his exacting standards."

Sierra let out a quick burst of laughter before she reined it in. "God, you're so right. Nothing against Harvard or anything, but Todd always did think he was better than everyone else. I much prefer the down-to-earth type."

Was it his imagination or was Sierra giving him some serious side eye? "If the flowers were an apology—which is totally unnecessary, by the way. I get that Todd is a total jerk—then what's with the pizza? Not that I'm not grateful. I had just been contemplating a sad lunch meat sandwich, so pizza is a step up."

She bit her lower lip briefly before letting it go. "The pizza is a bribe. I was hoping you would let me look at your grandmother's books."

Andrew was dumbfounded. "You don't need to bribe me to look at her books. You're welcome to take any of them that you find useful. I don't have a drop of magical blood in me, so they won't do me any good. I'd much rather they go to someone who can make use of them." He had a brilliant idea. "Tell you what. I'll eat the pizza, but only if you share it with me."

"Oh, I really should be getting back. Lucas is waiting for me." Her words didn't match her actions though. Instead of heading toward the door, she lingered in the kitchen.

"You said he was hanging out with Jenna. Don't you trust her to watch him?"

"Of course I trust her. She's my best friend." She seemed offended at the thought.

"Then maybe you can stay for an hour or so and enjoy this delicious-smelling dinner?" he asked lightly. He flipped the pizza box open. "Pepperoni. My favorite."

She sat down and reached for a slice. "Isn't it everybody's favorite?"

With a smile of triumph, Andrew turned to his cupboards and grabbed two plates and some paper towels. Based on the pools of grease, he could already tell the pizza was going to be delicious.

They chatted about anything and everything, as long as it didn't venture into anything too serious, favorite books, must-see movies, and the highs and lows of being a florist.

"Even after I stopped practicing magic, it was like I couldn't pull myself away completely. Earth magic is an intrinsic part of who I am, so despite choosing to stop practicing, I couldn't give up nature entirely. I love plants. I've always had a connection with them, much like Lucas does. Being a florist was a way to balance that for me. I still get to be around the plants I love, but I didn't have to give so much of myself to keep that connection alive."

Andrew held his breath. This was the first time she'd mentioned that she had given up her magic. "You stopped practicing?"

She suddenly looked shy. "Um, yeah. I only recently picked it back up again."

"Why did you give it up?" he asked gently.

She sighed, the crusts of her pizza slices long since forgotten on her plate. "I've gone over that decision thousands of times in my life, wondering if I made the right call. It felt like the right move at the time, but now, with everything going on, it feels like such a foolhardy decision."

With everything going on? He didn't know what she was talking about, but he didn't want to interrupt and get her off topic. "What tipped the scales?"

She leaned back in her chair and chewed her lip for a moment. "When an apprentice witch turns eighteen, they have to pass a series of Trials before they're considered a full-fledged witch. It's a series of grueling tests that not only prove that you know how to use and control your magic, but that you know when to use it and when not to. There's a skills trial, where you have to capture a controlled version of your power in a glass bottle without destroying the container. It proves that you can not only sufficiently wield your powers but also control them.

"There's a physical trial, which is sort of like an obstacle course where they're constantly putting stuff in your way and attacking you. It's up to you to know when it's appropriate to use your magic and when it's not, and to not let your magic get the best of you." Sierra shifted in her seat, her eyes blurring like she was no longer seeing Andrew's tiny kitchen, but something else entirely. "The one that almost broke me was the mental trial. The witch is trapped in a room and forced to face their greatest fear." Her voice broke and she swallowed thickly.

When Sierra didn't immediately continue, he grabbed her hand gently. Her fingers were like icicles next to his. He placed his other hand on top of hers, cocooning her frigid digits in the warmth from his body. "It's okay. You don't have to tell me anything you're not comfortable talking about."

She shook her head. "I think I need to get it out."

Andrew nodded at her and squeezed her hand but didn't say anything else.

"I was five years old when my mother died."

The change of topic threw Andrew for a loop, but he wasn't about to interrupt with questions.

Sierra's gaze was focused on her lap, the index finger of her free hand tracing nonsense patterns on her jeans. "My mom and I had been in the basement of our house. She'd been doing laundry, and I'd been following around after her like little kids do. Without any warning, she collapsed. The laundry basket in her arms crashed to the tile floor, spilling the freshly washed clothes all over the place. I screamed for her and shook her shoulder, trying to wake her up, but she wouldn't respond to me. She just lay there, her eyes still open but her gaze sightless." Sierra took a shuddering breath. "I remember thinking that she would be so irritated when she woke up because she was going to have to rewash all the laundry."

"What happened?" he asked gently.

Sierra took a deep breath and lifted her gaze but still didn't meet his eyes. "She had a brain aneurysm, though I didn't know what that meant at the time. She died almost instantly. I knew something was wrong, but I didn't know what to do about it. My dad was at a job site—he used to be a carpenter—and I had no way of getting ahold of him. I didn't want to leave my mom alone. She wouldn't have left me alone, so I refused to leave her side. I sat there on the cold tile floor, holding my mother's hand just wishing she would come back to me. Eventually I could see through the basement windows it had gotten dark outside. I heard the slam of my father's car door as he came home from work. I could hear him calling my mother's name and mine as he wandered through the house looking for us. He eventually found me curled up in the basement next to her. I had been there for hours. He rushed to her side to help her, but it was too late by then. He called 911 and an ambulance came and took her away, but her body was already cold. She was long gone."

Andrew's heart broke for that little girl. Not only had her mother died when she'd been a kid, but she'd watched it happen. That had to be traumatic for anyone, not to mention a five-year-old. He wished he could take away her pain, but there was nothing he could do to heal twenty-five-year-old pain. "I'm so sorry, Sierra." It felt so inadequate, but it was the only thing he had to offer.

Sierra sniffled once as moisture gathered at the corners of her eyes, but the tears never fell. "My dad tried to get me out of that basement, but it was like I was stuck. It was the last place I saw my mom alive, and I felt like if I left that room and went back upstairs something horrible would happen, or maybe that I would forget her forever. None of what I was afraid of was logical, just the inner workings of a kid's brain who had just witnessed something traumatic. I know that now, looking back on it logically, but at the time, it felt like I was betraying her by leaving." Sierra sighed. "Eventually I did leave the basement, but I never went back into that room again. At least not until the day of my eighteenth birthday."

"Oh, no." He was afraid he knew what was coming.

She nodded at him. "Exactly. As soon as the trial started, I was thrown back through time—mentally, not literally—into the body and mind of that girl. I watched my mother die over and over again. Each time I tried to save her, I failed." Her breath hitched and she took a moment before she continued. "I tried to catch her before she hit the ground. I tried to heal her using my magic. I tried to invent a way to stop or reverse time, despite knowing it couldn't be done." Tears started flowing down her cheeks, but she made no move to wipe them away. "Sometimes it was my dad dying in the basement instead of my mom. The outcome was always the same. They died. Every time. I was powerless to stop it."

He couldn't even imagine the torment that would have caused, ripping open her old wounds again and again and forcing her to relive the single worst moment of her life. He grabbed a paper napkin from his kitchen table and handed it to her so she could wipe her eyes. "Holy shit. Sierra that's awful. I can't believe you had to go through that. How did you finally escape?"

She sighed, and her shoulders slumped, the napkin crumpled in her fist. "It took me a long time to complete that trial. I was only able to move on once I accepted that there was nothing I could do. Nothing I could have done, physically or magically, would have prevented my mother's death. Once I realized that, I was able to use my magic to pull myself out of the illusion. But it was too late by that point. I had already decided I was done with magic. It had failed me, and therefore I wasn't giving it any more of myself. I finished the Trials almost on autopilot and then told my mentor, Roderick, that I was done practicing magic. I took off my talisman and didn't use my gifts again until a few weeks ago."

He didn't want to push her anymore, but there was one last piece of the puzzle that was missing. "If you stopped practicing magic when you were eighteen, how did Todd find out about it?" He braced for her anger, but the opposite happened.

A huge grin split her face, even as a few remaining tears slid down her cheeks. "That's Lucas's fault. Most kids don't start showing magical abilities until they're around ten years old. I figured I had some time before it became an issue. But for whatever reason, Lucas seems to defy all the odds. When he was three, he picked up a maple seed—you know those things that drop from the trees like helicopters every fall—tucked it into his tight little fist, and just went, 'Look, Mom!' and then handed me a sprouted tree. I was astonished at his abilities. Todd was, too, though for totally different reasons."

Andrew could practically picture it. A tiny version of the boy he knew so well and his surprised but proud momma. Not to mention his cousin Todd, who would have, to put it politely, flipped the fuck out. Andrew grinned. "I would have paid to see that."

Sierra's smile dimmed slightly. "Well, you know Todd. It went over about as well as you would expect, which is to say not well at all. He started ranting and raving about how we had to squash it out of him, that there was no such thing as magic, and even if there was, there was no way that *his* son could be a witch." Sierra took a deep breath. "I'd finally had my limit with Todd's prejudiced behavior and asked why he thought Lucas couldn't possibly be a witch when I was one too."

"Oh, shit."

She nodded. "Yeah. As far as mic drop moments, that one was a doozy. He looked at me as if I'd sprouted horns and a tail and then told me in no uncertain terms that he wouldn't associate himself with people *like that* and stormed out. Divorce papers showed up in the mail the next week."

A sense of fierce protectiveness surged through him. "Good." Sierra blanched and Andrew realized what he'd said. He rushed to clarify. "I just meant good that you're no longer with him. He's not good enough for you. And if he couldn't see the magic that you and Lucas share as a beautiful gift, then he's the asshole in this situation. You're better off without him."

Before he could even blink, his arms were full of Sierra as her mouth descended on his.

Chapter Eighteen

S IERRA HAD NO IDEA what she was doing, but it felt right. One minute she'd been confessing her sob story to Andrew, the next she'd literally thrown herself at him. She had one fraction of a second where she was worried that she screwed up, but then Andrew's arms closed around her and tugged her close.

The angle was slightly awkward since they were still sitting at his kitchen table, but Andrew solved that by tugging her until she was straddling his lap. The chair creaked ominously with both of their weight, but she ignored it. Instead, she wrapped her arms around his neck and tugged his mouth even closer to her.

Andrew's lips were soft, and he knew exactly how to use them. Even though she'd been the one to initiate the kiss, he quickly took over, owning her mouth as he gently sipped at her lips before sweeping his tongue inside her mouth. Their tongues danced and darted around one another in a game as old as time.

His arms had landed on her hips after he tugged her onto his lap, but now they roamed everywhere, caressing her neck and jaw, down her shoulder and to her side. When he reached her waist, he detoured to her back, gently rubbing up and down her shoulders and lower back. He pulled her so close to him that not even a breath of air could fit between them.

It wasn't close enough. Sierra made a frustrated moan, and Andrew tore his mouth off hers. "What's wrong? Do you want to stop?" he asked through gasping pants.

She shook her head. "Exactly the opposite. I want everything." She planted a peck on his lips, then moved to his ear, where she traced the tip of her tongue around the shell before tugging on his earlobe with her teeth.

"Sierra." He groaned. "What are you doing to me?"

He let out an almost painful grunt and stood. Sierra flailed wildly, feeling like she was going to get dumped on the kitchen floor, but she should have known better. Andrew's arms banded around her waist to hold her steady. He waited until she had her feet solidly beneath her before he unwound his arms from around her torso and grabbed her hand. "This way," he said as he tugged her down the short hall that led to his bedroom.

Sierra got a quick look at a room that was simply decorated in blues and greens before she felt the soft cushion of a thick mattress behind her legs. She let herself be laid down on the thick, cloud-like duvet as she stared up at Andrew's molten gaze. There was nothing particularly sexy about the jeans and sweater she was wearing, but you couldn't tell that from the intense look in his eyes. It was like she was wearing the sexiest lingerie from an expensive store in Paris.

Andrew joined her on the mattress and hovered above her. "You are so astonishingly beautiful. I can't believe I'm here with you right now."

Sierra wasn't normally shy, but his compliment made her blush. "You're not so bad yourself." Her gaze raked over him, enjoying the way his Henley lovingly hugged his muscles. She tugged on the shirt until he finally lay on top of her, pressing her into the mattress with his body weight. She spread her knees slightly, allowing him to drop between her legs.

He swooped down and planted a kiss on her mouth, the heat of his lips almost searing. They fought for dominance for a few moments before Sierra gave herself over to the feelings that coursed through her. It had been so long since she'd been with a man, since she didn't have a lot of free nights to date. Tingles crawled up her body until she felt like she was buzzing with electricity.

Her hands found their way under the bottom of his shirt, and she traced the muscles of his back, bringing the shirt with her until there was nothing left to do but rip it over his head and toss it away.

Andrew trailed kisses along her jaw and down her neck, then let out a frustrated growl when he was stymied by her sweater. "Off. This needs to come off." They broke apart just long enough to get naked then came back together in the middle of the bed.

His hands delicately traced her body, lingering on any spot that made her gasp or moan. It felt amazing, but it also felt like he was holding himself back. "You're not going to break me. I'm tougher than I look."

It was like her words were the permission he needed. His mouth latched onto her nipple and sucked hard, drawing a moan out of Sierra that she couldn't have stopped even if she wanted to, which she didn't. His hands grabbed her hips and held her in place as he rocked against her, driving her out of her mind.

The crinkle of foil packaging hinted that Andrew had somehow managed to grab a condom, but he rolled it down his dick before she had time to figure out where it had come from. His fingers sank between her legs, slowly tracing from front to back, slipping between her slick folds. He traced her entrance in mind-drugging circles before plunging deep inside.

Sierra's hips bucked, almost forcing him off her. He took her movement in stride, using his hips to pin her in place as his fingers moved to trace her clit. He rubbed and tugged and flicked the sensitive bud until she was moaning uncontrollably. Just when she thought she was going to come without ever knowing what it was like to have him inside her, he shifted his weight, lined himself up, and plunged to the hilt.

Andrew froze, his eyes rolled back in his head, and his head dropped until it was next to hers on the pillow.

The momentary pause allowed Sierra to catch her breath and pull herself away from the brink. When she was no longer on the verge of coming instantly, she finally asked, "Andrew?"

"Just give me a minute. You feel too good. I'm worried I'm going to embarrass myself if I move to soon," he said somewhere in the vicinity of her ear.

She smiled into his hair. "Take your time. Though, you know ... not too long."

Andrew lifted his head and glanced at her as he chuckled. "Oh, no? Are you saying you want me to move?" Without warning, he pulled out, thrust back into her, and made them both groan with pleasure.

She wanted to tease him some more, but she couldn't. She wanted him too much. "Yeah, just like that." She raked her fingers through his damp hair as he moved in and out of her.

Andrew's pace slowly picked up until he was pounding in and out of her. She wrapped her legs around him, hooking her feet together at the base of his spine to anchor him to her. Pressure was once again building inside her, as if she was going to explode at any moment. The electric tingles were back, racing underneath her skin. His hands on her arms were a caress that felt as soft as flower petals.

Tension built until she could barely tell up from down. Her orgasm exploded out of her, catching her off guard and shaking her to her core. Andrew's euphoric shout told her he was right behind her in falling over the edge. She felt like she was floating, the bed moving around her as her world realigned itself.

"What the hell?" Andrew's groggy voice was the first clue that something was going on beyond just soul-shattering sex. "Is that an earthquake?" His voice was suddenly a lot more alert. "Come on, we have to get under cover." He tried to tug her from her blissed-out state on the mattress toward the door frame. Photos were rattling in their frames on the walls, and she heard glass shatter in the other room.

Sierra's brain finally clicked online. While it wasn't impossible for Rock Cove to experience earthquakes, it wasn't typical either. Which meant either they were experiencing a unique anomaly, or she was *causing* the anomaly.

She searched inside herself and realized that there was a low level of magical energy rumbling through her. She wouldn't have thought she'd be able to cause such a huge effect without her talisman, but that didn't matter right now. Right now, she just needed to shut it down before someone got hurt. She reached for that sensation deep within her and switched it off, smothering the energy racing through her.

The quake stopped instantly.

"That was intense." Andrew was still hovering above her on the bed, with one foot on the ground as if uncertain he still needed to run for cover.

"Um, yeah, sorry about that." Sierra suddenly felt very exposed, vulnerable. Not because she was naked, but because her magic had gotten away from her. She tried to sit up and make her way to wherever her clothes had wound up, but Andrew didn't move from his position.

His eyes widened. "You're sorry about that?" He asked incredulously. "Does that mean you caused the quake?" His eyes swept slowly over her as if he'd never seen her before.

Sierra rolled off the opposite side of the bed. "Um, yes?" It came out like a question even though it was anything but. She found her clothes and started tugging them on.

"Holy crap." Andrew plopped into a seated position on the bed as if his nakedness didn't bother him at all. "I had no idea that much power was even possible. Granny couldn't do anything like that, at least not that I ever saw."

Sierra finished getting dressed then found herself hovering nervously near the end of the bed. "I guess I sort of skipped a step when telling you about my magic—our magic. Jenna, Aura, Brigit, and I, well ..." It felt awkward talking about it, like she was bragging rather than just telling the truth. "We're the most powerful coven currently in existence. Or at least we are when we're working together at full strength."

Andrew's jaw dropped open. "Wait, you're one of the Elementa? I remember my granny telling me about them when I was growing up. It sounded more like a fairy tale than anything else. A powerful group of witches with the sole purpose of protecting the world or some such nonsense."

Sierra flinched but didn't respond.

"Wait, that's true too?" He raked his hand through his hair, making it stick up in every direction.

Sierra rocked her hand side to side. "Possibly? There's a prophecy. We're still trying to figure out what it means."

He leaned back on his hands, but he appeared lost in thought. "I may be able to help with that. I'm pretty sure Granny had a book somewhere that mentioned it."

Hope surged through Sierra. "That would be amazing. That's why I came here tonight. We're facing a magical problem and nothing that we've tried seems to be helping." She described the black marks in the park and in Jenna's woods. "The last time I was here I saw a bunch of magical tomes on your shelves that I'd never seen before. I was hoping I could use them for research."

Andrew stood and moved to stand next to her. "Sierra, you never have to ask to use Granny's supplies. You're welcome to take any of them you might find useful, and it sounds like you could use whatever help you can find. Feel free to grab a stack tonight. I'll dig through the rest and bring you more as soon as I can." He lifted his hands and gently cupped her jaw. "I promise, I'm all in on this. With you and with the magic. I realize there are some things we need to work through—namely that my boss probably wouldn't be super happy we're ... involved—but we'll figure it out. I like you. I find you beautiful and fascinating. Your magic is powerful and amazing to behold."

Warmth spread through her. "You mean I haven't scared you off yet with the earthquakes, the six-year-old, or the general hot mess that is my life and past?" She asked it lightly but couldn't have been more serious. It wasn't easy for a single mom to date, especially not when she had to hide a huge part of her life. With Andrew she didn't need to hide at all. The relief was intense.

"I'm a first-grade teacher. That's a bad choice of profession for someone who's scared of kids." He winked at her. "As to the rest of it, no. You haven't scared me off. You're just you, with all the wonderful and messy things that come along with it. I'm sure I have things in my life and past we'll have to work through too. That's just how relationships go."

She felt a huge smile spread on her face. "So, does that mean we're in a relationship?"

A panicked look crossed his face. "I didn't mean to say that."

Her heart stopped, and she took a step back. "Oh."

He chased her and grabbed her hands, preventing her from fleeing. "I meant that I didn't mean to just blurt it out like that. I would love to be in a relationship with you. But only if that's what you want too."

Her heart resumed its normal rhythm and she sighed in relief. "Yes, Andrew. That's what I want. I can't promise it will be easy though."

"Easy is overrated." He drew her close and gave her a warm kiss.

Things started to heat up, and Sierra reluctantly pulled away. "Not that I don't want to stay and see where that was going, but I really do need to head out. I need to pick up Lucas. I've already been gone longer than I thought I would be."

Andrew placed one more quick peck on her lips. "Of course. Take care of your son." He gestured to his still naked body. "You'll forgive me if I don't walk you to the door?"

Sierra laughed. "Don't want to give the neighbors a show?"

Andrew shook his head and gave her a wink. "It's not the neighbors. It's cold outside. I don't want to freeze off the goods."

She gave him a heated look. "We wouldn't want that. Rain check." She left his house feeling considerably lighter than when she'd come.

As she headed to her minivan, she realized that the formerly dead bushes in front of Andrew's bungalow were now blooming riotously.

Apparently their great sex had caused more than just an earthquake. She smirked to herself then climbed into the driver's seat and headed out. She'd leave that little surprise for Andrew to find later.

Chapter Nineteen

A NDREW WAS SURPRISED, THOUGH very happy, that Holden invited him to what Holden had dubbed "dudes do sports" day at Denver's house. Apparently, Holden, Denver, and Killian were having a guys-only hangout where they ate junk food and fought over the remote, flipping between the Patriots football game and the Bruins hockey game. Andrew wasn't a huge sports nut, but he had nothing against them. It was an amusing enough way to spend a Sunday afternoon.

He was told there would be hamburgers and hot dogs on the grill, but he didn't want to show up empty-handed, so he stopped off and picked up some chips and beer.

It turned out that Denver lived in his neighborhood of tiny bungalow houses, so rather than driving his car, he just hoofed it over on foot. Denver's place had vinyl siding just like Andrew's, though Denver's was white instead of blue. His yard was neatly trimmed, but there were no flowerbeds or a garden to speak of. Lucas would not approve.

There was an older model truck parked in the open garage. Based on the two other cars in the driveway, Andrew was the last to arrive.

The door was wrenched open from the inside before he could even lift his hand to knock. "Andrew! Come on in," Holden said like he owned the place. A loud bark announced the presence of an adorable dog that looked like a chocolate-colored version of a golden retriever. The dog came running up to the door, but Holden grabbed her collar. "Rosie, at least wait until he gets inside before you jump him."

"Offerings to the sports gods," Andrew said solemnly as he showed off his snacks and drinks.

"Oh, Doritos. My favorite." Killian snatched the bag out of his hands and ripped it open before Andrew had made it more than five feet into the house. Andrew used his newly free hand to give Rosie scritches.

Denver's house closely mimicked his own, with a small living room right off the entry and an open concept kitchen in the back. The decorations were limited—giving off strong bachelor pad vibes—but the couch and chairs looked well-used and comfortable, and unlike Andrew's house, Denver's had a back deck.

The big screen TV was already playing the talking heads pre-game show, with Gillette stadium as the backdrop.

"Food should be off the grill in about ten minutes or so. Make yourself at home," Denver said from near the back door. He kept sneaking glances outside at the grill and then back at the TV.

Andrew tucked his beer into the fridge with the multiple other varieties already there.

"Killian's a beer snob," Holden said as he reached past Andrew to snag a Sam Adams.

"Hey, I'm not a snob. I just have good taste in beer," Killian chimed in from his spot on the couch.

Holden rolled his eyes. "Sure, if you say so."

"It seems like it's a useful thing for a pub owner to have good taste in beer," Andrew said as he grabbed one of the Corona Lights he'd brought.

"Thank you, I couldn't agree more. You can stay. Holden can leave." Killian didn't even take his eyes away from the TV as he said it, just chomped on more chips and sipped on a bottle of Emerald Crown Lager.

Holden laughed. "Wait, I'm getting kicked out but you're not even going to comment on Andrew's choice of piss water?"

Andrew froze, the Corona halfway to his mouth.

Killian glanced in Andrew's direction and blanched. "I've changed my mind. You can both leave."

"What did I tell you about not scaring off the new guy?" Denver asked as he grabbed a plate and some tongs and went outside.

The noisy commotion of four guys hanging out, eating food, watching TV, and playing with a dog was exactly the sort of lighthearted day Andrew needed. Not that he didn't like hanging out with Sierra, but this was a totally different vibe. He was just settling in to concentrate on the football game when Holden opened his big mouth.

"What's going on with you and Sierra?" Holden asked, shattering Andrew's peace and bringing the chatter to a screeching halt. Killian even stopped munching on chips to pay attention to the answer.

"Um, what?" Andrew asked dumbly, unable to come up with a better reply.

Holden gave Andrew a sideways glare that spoke louder than any words could have. "Come on. We saw you talking to her at the Copper Lantern. Plus, you were at the flower shop when I stopped by to get Sierra's help."

As much as he enjoyed their company, Andrew wasn't quite sure he was willing to talk with his new friends about the Sierra situation. What they had was so new, and there were still so many things that could go wrong with it. What if he said something and it somehow made it back to Principal Bodrock? Would he get fired?

"Sierra is a lovely woman," he hedged, trying to figure out exactly what to say.

"No shit. We know she's awesome. She also has a kid and hasn't had the easiest go of it in the past, so what are your intentions when it comes to her?" Holden pressed.

Denver smacked Holden in the chest. "Seriously, Holden? Get a grip. Andrew doesn't have to tell us anything. We didn't invite him over just to interrogate him."

Holden scoffed. "Speak for yourself."

The greasy hamburger Andrew had recently finished sat like a lump of lead in his stomach. He thought he'd been making friends with these three, but this wasn't how he'd seen the day going when he arrived. He started to stand. "Maybe I should head out."

Holden's hand landed on his shoulder and forced him back to the couch. "Oh, don't get all huffy about it. I'm sorry for making you uncomfortable. We all just look out for Sierra a little extra, that's all. She's got enough on her plate already, so anything we can do to make it easier feels like the right thing to do."

Andrew's spine straightened as he took offense on Sierra's behalf. "Sierra is more than capable of taking care of herself, Lucas, and anyone else that enters her atmosphere. She's been through much more than most people, and she's come out strong on the other side. I fully believe she's capable of tackling anything she sets her mind to. I would consider myself lucky if she deemed me worthy of her time and effort." A soft grin split Denver's mouth and Killian let out a slight harrumph of agreement before going back to eating chips. "And while we're on the topic of

Sierra, what did you need her help for anyway? What sort of help could a detective need from a florist?" Andrew crossed his arms as his eyes narrowed in Holden's direction.

Holden suddenly looked very uncomfortable that the interrogation had turned back on him and glanced around the room to try to catch the eyes of the other two.

"You're the one that mentioned her," Denver said by way of offering Holden no help whatsoever.

For the first time all afternoon, Holden shifted around and looked uncomfortable in his own skin. He squeezed the back of his neck right at the base of his skull, as if he had a headache. "Um, I'm not sure if I'm allowed to discuss it with you."

Now it was Andrew's turn to roll his eyes. "Let me guess, it wasn't because Sierra is a florist but because she's a witch?"

This time it was Andrew who shocked the room into silence. Denver even grabbed the remote to mute the TV. "You know about that?"

Andrew absently rubbed the tiny scar on his hand. "Let's just say I figured it out when Lucas healed a cut on my hand after I accidentally sliced it open on a piece of glass."

The other three looked shocked by the news. "Lucas is a witch too?" Denver asked, his voice rising with surprise.

"We shouldn't be that surprised, I guess," Holden said. "We know the girls had powers back in high school. Who's to say how old they were when their powers manifested."

Guilt crept over Andrew. If the other three men had known about Sierra but not known about Lucas, maybe there was a reason for that. Had Sierra been trying to keep it a secret? He sincerely hoped he hadn't just betrayed her trust. "Um, can you forget I said anything?"

"Cat's out of the bag now, mate," Killian said. "Plus, what's one more witch when we already have four of them running around?"

"And that's not to mention the rogue witches from the summer," Denver added.

Andrew was lost. There was so much more going on in Rock Cove than he was aware of. "Rogue witches?"

Denver quickly filled him in on a situation that had happened just before he moved to the town. "Jenna thinks their former mentor Roderick is in on it too," Denver concluded.

Andrew sat back against the couch, all food forgotten. "And I thought the fact that my granny could do simple magic tricks was a big deal. What you're describing is a whole new level."

"Mrs. Healy was a witch?" Now it was Holden's turn to be shocked. "I'll be damned."

Andrew nodded. "She was an earth witch. I've already shown Sierra all her supplies in case they could help her. I also dropped off a load of books at her shop a few days ago in case they contained anything interesting."

"Maybe they can help her with the situation in the park," Denver said.

"That's what she was hoping," Andrew said.

"A second black mark appeared in Jenna's forest last weekend," Denver chimed in. "Jenna and Sierra spent hours trying to fix it, but nothing worked. I really hope your grandmother had something special in her supplies, otherwise those two are going to wear themselves out trying to fix it."

Andrew's head was spinning. As a little kid he'd always wished he'd inherited some of Granny's powers, but mostly because he'd thought they were neat and would be fun to show off to his friends. He'd never really processed the destructive side of magic, even after riding out the earthquake Sierra had accidentally caused. Now that he was starting to grasp the bigger picture, he would do anything to have the power to help Sierra figure out what was going on.

Since he didn't have a way to help her magically, he would help in the way he knew he could. Andrew was a scholar and book nerd at heart. He couldn't do spells, but he could read, so he would. Every spare moment when he wasn't teaching or preparing for whatever new hell the Dragon Lady threw at him, he would be spending time with Sierra or studying his granny's books, looking for a solution.

A sudden commotion on the TV drew their eyes. The Patriots had just scored another touchdown, putting their lead at 21–7 going into halftime. By mutual agreement, the four of them let the magic talk drop. Football was so much easier to understand.

Chapter Twenty

S IERRA NEEDED TO CLEAR her head. She'd been cooped up inside for too long. It didn't matter if it was her apartment or her flower shop—both places she loved for obvious reasons—she was sick and tired of staring at the same four walls. She was an earth witch. Her place was in nature.

It was Sunday afternoon, so the store wasn't open. Just yesterday she'd finished a big order for someone's fiftieth anniversary party, so she was clear of her responsibilities at the shop for at least a while. Too bad she couldn't seem to get out from under the magical conundrum as easily. She'd been frantically reading every book that Andrew had dropped off, looking for any clue that could help her heal the scars in the grove and the park. So far, nothing had jumped out at her. The books were interesting, but none of them talked about the type of dark magic it would have taken to steal the amount of energy she suspected the other witch had taken.

Finally, in a fit of frustration, she grabbed a stack of Madelyn's books, shoved them in a bag, and called for Lucas. "Grab your stuff. I want to head to Aunt Jenna's for a while."

Lucas grumbled a bit as he often did when forced to stop playing his video game, but he also knew that Jenna had tons of property, and he was just as much a fan of being outdoors as she was. He would probably load himself up with a bag full of stuff he just "couldn't live without" and then touch exactly none of it. Instead, he would probably lie in the grass and talk to the trees. There was no use putting up a fuss. It was easier to just let him haul half his room into the van than to fight about it.

She texted Jenna that they were on their way over, and as expected, just got a thumbs-up emoji in response. When Sierra pulled her van into Jenna's driveway fifteen minutes later, her friend was standing outside waiting to greet them. "Hey guys. You stopping by for anything in particular? Has something come up?" Jenna glanced significantly at the heavy bag of supplies Sierra was hauling around.

Sierra shook her head. "Sorry, no breakthroughs yet. I wanted to spend some time in the grove practicing, if it's all right with you. Maybe it'll shake something loose in my head."

Jenna was already nodding. "Knock yourself out. Do you want me to come?"

Sierra thought about it for a moment, truly considering her answer. Part of her mind wanted Jenna there. Sierra felt more powerful when Jenna was around and less like she was going to screw things up. The other part of her brain realized she was using Jenna as a crutch. When they'd been training together, Roderick had told Sierra that she wasn't as strong as the rest of her coven, but she was starting to doubt that. She was one of the Elementa. One of the most powerful witches on the planet. It was time she started acting like it.

"No, I'm okay. I think it would be good for me to do this myself." Just saying the words felt empowering. She could do this. She *would* do this.

Jenna sent her a small smile then turned her attention to Lucas. "Come on, champ. I have some bushes in my back yard that could use your attention." Jenna wrapped her arm around Lucas's shoulders and guided him toward her back deck.

"Lucas, stay inside the wards, okay?" Sierra said. She was grateful Jenna had protective barriers around her house and yard that gave an added level of protection to anyone inside them, just like Sierra had put around her building after the break-in.

He turned back around and rolled his eyes at her. "Sure, Mom."

Sierra watched them go for a few seconds then squared her shoulders and marched into the woods. She'd been practicing her magic at home and whenever she could at the shop—as long as there weren't any customers of course. She was ready for this.

The grove was peaceful, even in its largely dormant stage. Almost all the leaves had fallen from the trees, but she could still feel the vital energy of the trees, just buried deeper than it had been previously. The woods were going into hibernation for the winter, but that didn't stop her from connecting with it.

She set down her bag of supplies in the middle of the grass and went over to the stone circle. She took her assigned place and, as was customary, did her call to the goddesses.

> *"Mother, maiden, crone divine,*
> *With your help my gifts align.*
> *I join you in this sacred space,*
> *By your will and with your grace.*
> *Earth shifts and moves through me,*

Dirt and rock, plant and tree.
I call upon this ancient land,
Protect me now at my command."

She closed her eyes as she felt the rush of power enter her system. The rough scratch of stone running through her veins brought her comfort. She waited as the flow of energy spread through her entire body, healing her in a way that she would never fully be able to explain to someone who had never experienced it.

With a sigh of contentment, she opened her eyes. Unfortunately, as soon as she did, she was confronted by the ugly black mark that was still tainting the forest floor. The fact that it was in their grove, their sacred space, bothered her to her core. She had to be able to heal it, to cleanse it. To rid the space of the damage.

Juiced with magical energy, Sierra stepped off the stone circle and crossed to her bag of supplies. She carefully selected four fat candles. White was for healing, gold was for health, indigo was for cleansing, and green was for nature. She placed the candles around the black mark, one in each of the cardinal directions. Between the candles she carefully placed hunks of clear quartz for purification. Lastly, she pulled out the largest bundle of sage she'd ever attempted to use in a spell and held it poised in her hand. If anything called for a powerful cleansing ritual, it was this. With a sweep of her hand, she lit the four candles and then began to chant.

"Ancient Gaia Mother of life,
Help me in this time of strife.
The ground was marked, the damage done,
Magic used, the spell was spun."

The pressure closed in on her, as if the vital energy of the grove knew something was wrong.

"Earth will rumble, crystals shine
Forces surge, essence aligns."

The ground beneath her feet began to tremble. It started low and slowly built until it was stronger than the earthquake she'd accidentally caused at Andrew's house. The quartz crystals blazed into brilliant shining beacons, almost too bright to look at with the naked eye.

"I call upon the rocks and trees,
Heal the land of this disease."

The trees began to sway and creak in their places, responding to her call.

"With sage and fire cleanse this space
By your will and with your grace."

The sage burst into flames so rapidly that it almost burned down to her fingers before she tossed it into the center of the black smudge. The flames on the candles surged until they were several feet tall—far taller than should have been possible on candles and wicks of that size.

The earth's energy flowed through her, and she poured everything she had into the spell. For a moment, it looked like it was starting to work. The black mark started to recede and shrink, slowly collapsing in on itself.

A spark of excitement raced through her. She was doing it. She wasn't useless, or weak, or any of the things she'd convinced herself of over the years. It was her magic—and hers alone—that was fixing the damage.

But then her knees started to buckle. The spell was draining her magical stores too fast. She struggled to hold on as she watched the candle flames shrink, then sputter out. The crystals blinked out one at a time, and the earth beneath her feet stilled.

Unable to keep herself upright for a moment longer, Sierra sank to the ground in a graceless slump. Her heart raced, she couldn't suck in a full breath, and her vision darkened.

"Sierra!"

The shouted voice barely penetrated her exhausted mind. She turned her head as Andrew fell to his knees next to her. Andrew was there? How had that happened? *When* did that happen?

Andrew was frantically running his hands over her, first grasping her wrist to check her pulse then using his other hand to brush her hair away from her face. "Are you hurt? Tell me what's wrong," he demanded.

She was so tired she wasn't sure she could explain everything, but she knew she needed to reassure him that she was fine. Or, at least, that she would be fine. Eventually. "I'm okay."

He scoffed in disbelief.

Sierra struggled to sit up, and Andrew leaned in to support her. "I guess I overdid it a bit."

Andrew's gaze zoomed around the grove, taking in the puddles of melted wax that used to be candles and the crystals that still circled the charred mark on the ground. "Conjuring earthquakes again, I see. Not only that but making the trees dance and the candles melt as fast as ice cubes in the desert."

She sagged against his chest and was secretly pleased when he wrapped his arms around her waist. "You saw?"

He made a humming sound. "Saw. Felt. Experienced. I'm not sure what the right verb is in this situation. And whatever magic you used today was a hell of a lot more intense than the last time you made my world move."

"Yeah well, last time I wasn't even doing it on purpose. This time I had a reason to try." Her arm flailed limply in the direction of the scar a few feet away from them. "Not that I'm complaining or anything, but what exactly are you doing here? How did you find me?"

"I was hanging out with Holden, Killian, and Denver watching football. They happened to mention this," he gestured to the black mark, "and I figured I would swing by with some more books in case they could help you find a cure or whatever. Jenna and Denver were doing the lovey dovey texting thing through the whole second half. She happened to mention that you'd stopped by, so I came here instead of your place. I hope that was all right." He seemed uncertain.

She snuggled her face into the crook of his neck. "It's more than all right. In fact, I might need you to carry me out of here," she joked tiredly.

He seemed to take her seriously. "I can do that, but that means I'd have to come back for the books." She glanced in the direction he'd nodded and saw a bunch of books he appeared to have flung everywhere in his hurry to get to her side.

"We wouldn't want that." She pulled away from him and slowly stood. He jumped to his feet and held his hands out as if to catch her if she fell. Thankfully, she was able to stand on her own two feet. She could use a hot bath and a good night's sleep, but she'd recover eventually.

"Sierra. I know you're a super powerful witch and all that, but can I ask you a favor?" Andrew asked has he grabbed her hand and squeezed it tightly.

"Of course. Anything."

He tipped his head down until their foreheads were touching. "Can you please not scare me like that again?"

"I'll do my best." As much as she wanted to promise Andrew, she wasn't sure she would be able to keep that promise. Something was stirring in Rock Cove. First the situation with Jenna, and now the one Sierra was dealing with. Magic was going awry or someone was abusing it. Neither option looked promising for her and her coven.

Especially not if the Prophecy was true.

They gathered up what was left of Sierra's supplies and stuffed them back in her bag then grabbed the extra books Andrew had brought. It was a lot to haul, but they managed to make it through the woods and back to Jenna's backyard.

"I see you found her," Jenna said to Andrew as they approached where she was sitting, keeping an eye on Lucas.

"Yeah, thanks for the directions." Andrew shifted like he was uncomfortable and glanced between Jenna and Sierra.

"Any luck?" Jenna asked Sierra.

Sierra held her finger and thumb about an inch apart. "A tiny bit, but not so much that you'd notice. I, uh, may have overextended myself a little." She didn't want to confess to Jenna that she'd almost passed out. Jenna wouldn't judge her or anything, but Sierra was still embarrassed. She could feel Andrew's concerned gaze on her, but she didn't think he would say anything.

"Look what I caught, Mom!" Lucas interrupted as he came closer. He held up his hands proudly, which were carefully cupped around a field mouse. "He was destroying Aunt Jenna's bushes."

Well, it could have been worse. At least he hadn't shoved a snake in her face. Being an earth witch came with an affinity for nature in all its forms, but some forms were still more appealing than others. "Good job, bud."

Lucas smiled then shoved the mouse at Andrew. "See, Mr. Knight? Isn't he cool?"

Andrew bent over so he was closer to Lucas's height. "He sure is. But I think Mr. Mouse would probably be happier if he stayed here, don't you think?"

Lucas glanced at Sierra as if asking her opinion. "Mr. Knight is probably right. Do you think you could talk to him like you talk to flowers?"

Lucas seemed to contemplate it for a moment. "Yeah."

"Maybe you could tell the mouse not to harm the bushes anymore and then let him go over by the trees, hm?" Sierra suggested.

"Okay, Mom. But if I can't keep the mouse, can we get a dog?" His eyes turned pleading.

It wasn't the first time he'd asked, and she was sure it wouldn't be the last time. However, she wasn't sure she had the energy for a dog. "We'll see."

"Okay!" He raced off to the woods to deposit the mouse.

Jenna chuckled. "Good luck with that. You know you're going to have a dog sooner rather than later with those baby brown eyes batting in your direction."

"Maybe I can just ask Denver if I can borrow Rosie for a day or two. Maybe that would tide Lucas over for a while." A girl could dream, right?

Sierra walked over to her minivan and started loading up her supplies. Andrew followed and handed her the books. "Thanks for stopping by."

She leaned in to give him a quick kiss, but Lucas came barreling up, and she jumped back. She hadn't told her son that she was dating his teacher yet, and she wasn't sure when it was appropriate to break that news. She didn't want to do it prematurely, just in case something happened and it didn't work out.

She sent Andrew an apologetic look. He sent her back a soft smile of understanding. "Sierra, I'll see you soon. And Lucas, I'll see you tomorrow morning," Andrew said as he waved at her son.

Could he get any more perfect?

Chapter Twenty-One

"SHE'S GETTING STRONGER BY the day."

Roderick didn't need Danika's reminder. He was well aware that Sierra's powers were growing. It was the reason he'd stopped by her shop and tried to tempt her to join him. If he couldn't stop her from using her magic, maybe he could convince her to use it to help him. The more power he had on his side, the more likely he was to succeed in his goal of raising the Harbinger.

Sucking the life force and magic out of the spot in the park had been a nice energy bump and doing the same in Jenna's grove had given him an even bigger boost, but it still wasn't enough. Raising the Harbinger was his raison d'être. If he knew one thing above all else, it was that he was put on this Earth with the end goal of bringing the Harbinger into it.

"I am aware of her growing powers, Danika. But thank you again for pointing out to me what I already know."

She glared at him and crossed her arms in defiance. His timid mouse was getting braver. "Then what are you going to do about it?"

"Clean up your mess, as usual." He was already bored with this conversation.

Danika's stunt at Sierra's apartment had backfired in spectacular fashion. She'd had one directive. Get in, get the talisman, and get out. Unfortunately, she'd been caught. Instead of just vanishing, she'd gone on the offensive and attacked Sierra and her son.

There was no faster way to wake up a mother's protective instincts than to threaten her child. Sierra's decision to study magic again was as understandable as it was unfortunate, and Danika was to blame for it.

"My mess!" she yelled. "How is this my fault? I'm the one that got you Sierra's talisman. You know, one of the key ingredients to your so-called plan to carry out the stupid prophecy. Except we've been trying for weeks, and we've had exactly zero luck trying to tap into her powers. Or Jenna's for that matter."

Fire raced under his skin as he held himself back from incinerating her on the spot for her insubordination. "If you no longer believe in our mission, then there's the door." He gestured to the exit. Not that he would let her get that far. She knew too much. She would be a liability if she ever turned against him. He really should just get rid of her and be done with it. But she might still serve some sort of greater purpose in his scheme.

Danika didn't move, but Roderick refused to break his stare. "I've been planning this for thirty years, studying their powers and subtly manipulating them until they were exactly where I wanted them to be. I spent years sowing the seeds of doubt in Sierra in hopes that she would give up her magic. If there's no earth witch, there's no Elementa. But I didn't stop there. I have two of them eating out of my hand and one willing to do anything I ask her to.

"You, on the other hand, thought it was a good idea to engage one of the Elementa in a public fight in the middle of town. You also attacked a child thereby ensuring that the woman I spent years convincing to give up her magic would come out of retirement and reclaim her position as one of the most powerful witches in the world and one of the only people that can stand in my way. Do you see the problem yet?" He lobbed a fireball at her, close enough to singe her clothing, but not a direct hit.

Danika cringed away from the flames but didn't move from her spot. She slowly dropped her eyes to the floor. "I'm sorry, Architect."

His rage tapered back to a simmer. At least he didn't need to commit murder today. Plus, what he had in mind would be much easier if she was still around. "Now, would you like to hear my plan or not?"

She quickly glanced at his face then dropped her gaze back to the floor. "Yes, Architect."

"Good. Now pay attention, and don't screw this up."

Chapter Twenty-Two

ANDREW WAS RUNNING LATE. He was never late, especially when it came to school and his kids. And the worst part about it was that it was the Dragon Lady's fault. Apparently planning and executing Emergency Services Day wasn't enough of a hoop for him to jump through, because now Principal Bodrock had him planning a school-wide career day. Oh joy.

He didn't mind paying his dues—he was the new guy after all—but this one seemed like it was an extra hassle. While the day with the police, firefighters, and EMTs was a well-run machine, career day needed much more effort. Not only did he have to find and convince a variety of people to volunteer to talk to the students about what they did for a living, but he only had a week to do it.

He was relying heavily on the small network of friends he'd already made. Sierra had even agreed to ask her friends if they would be willing to help. Unfortunately, the Dragon Lady insisted that the mayor was one of the speakers. Andrew wasn't sure if she had the hots for the guy or if she had secret political ambitions to become Mayor Dragon Lady one day. Neither would surprise him. The problem was that the Honorable Virgil Inghram was so busy and so important that he could only squeeze Andrew in for a ten-minute meeting over the lunch hour.

Andrew only got thirty minutes to eat on a good day, so with the short drive each way and the ten-minute meeting, he knew he was going to be cutting it close to get back to his students. But he wasn't sure which would piss off his boss more, being late or not getting the mayor to agree to career day. He had decided to risk it and took the trip to city hall.

Of course, it hadn't gone according to plan. The mayor had been running late, and eventually, his prior meeting had run so long that the mayor's assistant let Andrew know he was going to have to reschedule. Andrew was not only late returning to school, but he still didn't have the mayor on board. He'd texted Jasmine to see if she could cover his classroom, but he hadn't gotten a response. That wasn't good.

Andrew ran up to his classroom gasping for breath. He screeched to a halt when he heard the one thing that could make his day even worse. Principal Bodrock was in his classroom.

"Now children, we're going to be making a pretty craft you can take home and show your parents." There was a cheerfulness to Bodrock's voice Andrew had never heard before. "Today we're going to be pressing flowers. The idea is to take these blooms, press them between some paper, and then put them inside a heavy book and close it tightly. The book will smash the flower and keep it in that shape while it dries. Then, in a few weeks, we'll open the books again, and you can take your dried flowers home to your parents. Won't that be fun? Now everyone, come up to the front of the class and pick out a flower."

A general din started as the students shuffled around to follow her directions, but Andrew's stomach rebelled. What was she thinking? There was no way Lucas was going to be okay taking flowers and smashing them flat. Principal Bodrock knew that Lucas was a sensitive kid and that he had a soft spot for nature. There was no way she hadn't thought about this and knew what it was going to do to him. Was she trying to set him off? Why would she do that?

Andrew stepped into the classroom just as the principal said, "Lucas, come now. Select a flower." The rest of the students were already back at their tables with stacks of newsprint.

"No," Lucas said quietly.

Bodrock's lips twisted into a smirk. "What's wrong, Lucas? Don't you want to do arts and crafts with the class?" The rest of the students had already started. A few of them were carefully laying out their flowers and leaves on the paper, while others were ripping out some of the flower petals to throw at their friends. "Ah, Mr. Knight. So glad you could *finally* join us. I'm just leading your students in an art lesson."

Andrew's eyes narrowed at his principal, but he couldn't help darting glances at Lucas. Lucas was shifting uncomfortably, his small hands gripping the legs of his pants like he never wanted to let go. "I can see that. Can I speak with you, Principal Bodrock?"

She smiled in his direction, but it didn't reach her eyes. "Of course. Let's just get Lucas started on this activity, and then I'll be right with you."

Andrew could see a storm brewing in Lucas's face. He was moments away from having a meltdown. His eyes were frantically darting around the room, watching as his classmate ripped up the flowers or smashed them between the pages of heavy dictionaries.

"Come now, Lucas. I'll even bring you a flower. How would that be?" Bodrock handed him a sunflower. Of all the luck. There was no way Lucas was going to smash his favorite flower in the pages of a book.

"There now, all you need to do is wrap it in paper and slip it between the book pages."

"No!" Lucas yelled. He gripped the stem of the sunflower and bolted from the classroom.

Andrew ran out of the room after him, but Lucas was fast. He was already halfway down the hall and heading into the school nurse's office before Andrew could reach him.

"Mr. Knight, a word," Bodrock's voice stopped him in his tracks.

Andrew was seething. He had no desire to talk to his boss right then. "I should really go check on Lucas." He gestured down the hall.

The principal shrugged. "He's safe enough with the nurse for now."

Andrew tried to take a deep breath, but air was seesawing in and out of his lungs so hard his chest was burning. "What can I do for you then?" he asked through gritted teeth.

"Why were you not in your classroom?" she asked, one eyebrow winging up.

"I went to city hall to try to get the mayor on board for career day, as you requested."

She crossed her arms and stared him down. "And did you succeed?"

"Not yet, he was too busy to see me."

"I see. So not only were you absent when you should have been teaching your students, but you also have nothing to show for it." Her perfectly manicured fingers were tapping on her opposite elbow.

He'd had just about enough of this. "Why were you having the students press flowers?" The question came out far more accusatory than he intended it to, but he was having trouble reining himself in.

Bodrock sniffed. "It's a time-honored craft that I thought the children would enjoy. Plus, they'll have something to take home to their parents to show off their hard work, and you can mix in a science lesson under the guise of art."

Under any other circumstances she was right. There was nothing inherently wrong with the activity of pressing flowers, except when an earth witch was in the room. "I appreciate your perspective, and I thank you for covering for me in my absence. However, you know that Lucas Dalton is sensitive when it comes to plants. This type of activity would be very difficult for him." There, that was reasonable and logical, right? Andrew's heart was breaking for Lucas, but he couldn't let it show.

The corner of Bodrock's mouth ticked. "I'm aware of Mr. Dalton's issues. I was doing my part to help him get past them. He won't be able to get very far in life if he overreacts whenever someone cuts a blade of grass. Heaven forbid someone mow the lawn in front of him."

Was she serious? He knew she disliked people she considered different, but he hadn't thought she was cruel. "Lucas is only six years old. He's got plenty of time in his life to figure out how to deal with unpleasant things. Now is the time to nurture him and support him, not force exposure therapy on him."

She moved closer until she was right up in his face. "What, exactly, are you accusing me of, Mr. Knight?"

Andrew realized he was at a crossroads. He could take a step back, de-escalate the situation, and minimize the damage to his own career. Or he could push the issue—push his boss—and protect the kid he was starting to care about as far more than just another student in his classroom. Every student deserved his devotion and protection, but Lucas was more than that to him. Andrew's emotions were already plenty tangled up about Sierra, and Sierra and Lucas came as a packaged deal. Besides, Lucas was plenty worth it all on his own.

There was no question how he was going to react.

"Principal Bodrock, you need to back the hell off of Lucas Dalton. That kid is going through more than you can possibly know. He's had a lot on his shoulders at such a young age. What does it matter if he likes plants and animals? Pull the bee out of your bonnet. As the principal of this school, you need support *all* the students, not just the ones you approve of."

She sneered at him. "You see a harmless kid that happens to like plants and animals, and I see something more nefarious. I assumed, as Madelyn's grandson, you might be more aware of the dangerous people all around you. I guess I was wrong. I may not have cause to fire you right now, but you can bet that I'll be on your case every minute of every day until I have the evidence to do so." Without another word she spun on her heel and left Andrew gaping after her.

What had he just done?

Chapter Twenty-Three

S IERRA WALKED INTO CINDER & Spice, comforted instantly by the scent of good coffee, pumpkin muffins, and cinnamon rolls. It was still a bit early in the season to have the giant fireplace in the back of the restaurant crackling away, but the decor was appropriately fall themed, with pumpkins scattered on the counters and the tables, garlands of fake leaves draped over the mantle, and even a few hay bales and dried corn stalks out front to lure people in.

It had been too long since she'd hung out with her friends, and she'd asked Aura to meet her here so she could talk to both Aura and Brigit at the same time. She wasn't optimistic enough to invite Jenna—the bad blood between her and Brigit ran deep, and would take time and effort to fix—but Sierra talked to her almost every day anyway.

She snagged a booth in the back of the dining area to wait. The server came and took her pumpkin spice latte order as Sierra took her coat off and put it on the bench next to her. She was just pulling out her phone to flip through social media when the door opened and Aura came strutting in.

Of the four of them, Aura was always the one who was picture-perfect no matter what time of day or night it was. She'd come from a wealthy family, who had certain expectations of her and how she presented herself. On top of that, she could have been a model or an actress, but she'd gone a different route and become a meteorologist. It still put her in front of a camera, but she backed it up with a degree in science.

Today's outfit was a closely fitting dove-gray suit with a pencil skirt and a peplum jacket with a wide belt. It could easily have been worn on the streets of Milan or behind the desk at a fancy New York law firm, and Aura wore it like she owned it.

"Sorry, I'm late," Aura said as she gracefully sank into the seat across from Sierra. She carefully placed her clutch bag on the bench seat and neatly folded her coat to sit on top of it. Aura's fastidiousness was an absolute hallmark of her personality. "Mother had me helping her organize her upcoming holiday gala."

Sierra masked a shudder. "Sounds lovely." Aura's parents were wealthy socialites and hosted an annual gala that drew the upper crust of Boston's elite to their home. Sierra had never been invited and was more than thankful for that.

"The event will be, of course, but dealing with my mother is absolutely not." She tossed her long blonde hair over her shoulder. "That woman wields perfectionism as a blunt instrument."

Sierra laughed. Aura cracked a smile that eventually built into a chuckle. As much as Aura's mother demanded of her, it was good that Aura could separate herself from it. "Now I feel bad about my secret reason for asking you out to lunch."

Aura's eyebrows winged up. "It wasn't just to have lunch and catch up?"

The server stopped by to drop off Sierra's latte, and they placed their lunch orders.

"Well, that too, of course. It's been too long since we've hung out." She carefully blew on her hot drink and took a sip. The creamy pumpkin and cinnamon flavor exploded over her tongue, and she almost hummed in pleasure.

"I've heard through the grapevine there might be someone else taking up your time these days." Aura said as she accepted her steaming cappuccino from the server.

Sierra tried to hold in a blush, but she wasn't sure how successful she was. "You mean Lucas?" she asked innocently.

Aura rolled her eyes. "Don't play coy with me. You know I'm talking about the hottie teacher. I haven't laid eyes on him myself yet, but I've heard he's a snack."

Sierra glanced frantically around the café to make sure no one overheard Aura's loud declaration. It was during lunch on a school day. It's not exactly like Andrew's boss or coworkers would be there to overhear, right? "Shhh," she hissed. "Keep your voice down."

Aura leaned across the table and dropped her voice to a whisper. "Is it a secret? Secrets can be fun too."

Sierra shook her head then changed her mind. "Actually, sort of. Andrew is Lucas's teacher. Strictly speaking we're probably not supposed to be involved."

Aura leaned back against the booth. "Then why are you? Why risk it?" She carefully sipped her cappuccino.

Sierra sighed. She'd been asking herself the same thing. The risk of exposure for him was high. Was it possible he could lose his job over this?

And what about Lucas? What would happen to him if she and Andrew started dating then broke up at some point in the future? Sierra's track record with men wasn't stellar, so it was hard to trust her own judgement.

Except that Andrew was amazing. He was kind, generous, and fabulous with her son. He was already aware of magic and not only was he not afraid of it, but he also actively appreciated it and encouraged her to do more of it. He was everything his jerk of a cousin was not. And honestly, he made her feel good.

"Because I honestly don't know how to stay away." Even Sierra could hear the wistfulness in her own voice.

Aura's perfectly lip-sticked mouth curved into a soft grin. "Then go for it. Work it out together. You deserve some happiness. It's been too long."

That got Sierra's hackles up. "Hey, I've been happy. I have Lucas and my dad. And the shop." It had taken her a while to get over losing Todd, even if he was an ass. But once she had, she never felt like her life was lesser in any way. She thought her life was going great. Yes, it would have been nice to have a partner to share it with, but she'd never felt like there was something missing in her life.

Aura reached across the table and grabbed her hand. "Of course, your son and your business make you happy. I just meant that it would be nice for you to have someone to share both the happiness and the load with."

Wasn't that the truth. As much as she could do everything herself, she did wish she didn't have to. She slumped as the fight went out of her. "You're not wrong."

The door to the kitchen opened with a thud, and Brigit walked out carrying a tray of food. She spotted the two of them in the corner and made her way over. "Salad with grilled chicken and a slice of crusty bread for Aura, and French onion soup in a bread bowl for Sierra." She also plunked a club sandwich with chips on the table next to Aura. "Shove over, I'm joining you."

Aura once again rolled her eyes, but did as demanded. "Nice to see you too, Brigit."

"It's always nice to see me," Brigit said before she bit into her sandwich and chewed.

"Sure, let's go with that," Sierra said as she dug her spoon into the melty, cheesy goodness on top of her soup.

Aura laughed as she carefully drizzled balsamic vinaigrette on her salad and took a bite.

"So, what's this I hear about you dating Lucas's teacher?" Brigit asked between bites.

Sierra froze with her spoon halfway to her mouth. "Do you two have some sort of psychic connection or something? If not, I'd love to know where you get your gossip."

Brigit looked at Aura who helpfully explained. "We were just talking about that. Apparently, they're a thing, but it needs to be kept all hush-hush because of his job."

Brigit mimed zipping her lips. "Got it. But I have to say, go get it, girl. He really is easy on the eyes."

He really was. Just the thought of his blond hair, hazel eyes, and scruffy facial hair had her going weak in the knees. Not that it was all about his looks, obviously, but they certainly didn't hurt.

Brigit smirked. "I know that look. Someone's been getting some. I bet he's good in bed."

Sierra's eyes instantly snapped to Brigit's Cheshire cat grin. "Get that picture out of your head immediately." Images of their time together came flooding back. It came bursting out before she could stop herself. "But he did rock my world enough that I caused a localized earthquake."

She promptly shoved a huge bite of food in her mouth to avoid answering whatever question was coming her way.

Aura's mouth dropped open. "Are you serious?"

"I knew it," Brigit said, her eyes going dreamy. "Where do I find me one of those guys?"

The café door opened abruptly, and Holden walked through. He went straight to the counter to pick up a to-go order. Unfortunately, Brigit's back was to the door, and she couldn't see who had just walked in. As much as Sierra wanted to push them together, it seemed like something they needed to work out between them. "Closer than you'd imagine, I think." Holden glanced around the room like he was looking for something—or someone. He seemed to notice the back of Brigit's head then caught Sierra staring at him. He nodded to her, grabbed his bag of food, and left the café.

"If you didn't invite us here to talk about your suddenly not-so-boring dating life, then why did you? You said you had an ulterior motive," Aura asked as she carefully loaded her fork with the perfect combination of veggies and chicken.

"Right, of course." She couldn't believe she'd almost forgotten. "They're doing career day at the elementary school. Andrew—Lucas's teacher," she quickly corrected herself, "is responsible for lining up local folks with interesting careers to come talk to the kids. I was hoping the both of you would be available."

"I'm in. I love kids," Brigit said.

"Of course, whatever you need," Aura replied.

"Will Jenna also be there?" Brigit asked stiffly.

And there it was. Brigit was so easy-going with everyone else that it was sometimes hard to remember that she had such a horrible relationship with Jenna. "Yes, she will. So play nice." Sierra gave Brigit a pointed look.

Brigit huffed. "I will if she will."

Aura gave Brigit a sidelong glare. "Brigit, come on. You know I love you like a sister, but I'm still going to call you out on your crap when you need it. This is on you, not her. You need to fix it. She's not your enemy. She never was."

"I'll be the judge of that. But fine, I'll behave. For Lucas's sake," Brigit said.

The lunch conversation strayed to other topics, but for the first time in a long time Sierra had hope that the chasm between Jenna and Brigit wasn't quite as insurmountable as it seemed.

Chapter Twenty-Four

ANDREW WAS EXCITED AND nervous at the same time. He was standing outside the shop's back door getting ready to push Sierra's doorbell and found himself wiping his damp palms on his jeans. It wasn't like he hadn't spent time with her before, and he saw Lucas every school day, but this was the first outing he'd planned for the three of them, and he just hoped it didn't turn out to be disappointing.

Dating a single mom meant that there were very few opportunities for them to spend time together that didn't also involve her son. Yes, she could obviously get babysitters or whatever, but he didn't want her to think that he liked her *despite* Lucas. He enjoyed hanging out with Lucas almost as much as he enjoyed Sierra. He understood Sierra and Lucas were a packaged deal, and he wanted her to know it.

He'd already checked with her that they were free for the day, but he had wanted the activity to be a surprise. He was suddenly second-guessing that instinct.

Oh well, too late now. He smashed his finger on the buzzer and waited.

The thunder of feet pounding down stairs announced Lucas's arrival—no way would Sierra have made that ruckus. The door was ripped open and, as expected, Lucas was standing there with a huge grin on his face and clutching a stuffed animal. "Hi, Mr. Knight!"

Andrew crouched down to his eye level. "Hi, Lucas. Who do we have here?" Andrew tapped the stuffed animal with his finger.

"Oh, this is Siren. She's a whale. Aunt Jenna bought this for me at the aquarium. Jenna saw her being born, isn't that awesome?"

That rush of information was a lot to unpack. Jenna had seen a stuffed animal being born? Thankfully Sierra walked up behind her son and filled in the blanks. "Jenna studies right whales for the aquarium. This spring she was lucky enough to witness a calf being born and she named it Siren. Lucas thought the story was cool, so she was generous enough to buy him the toy."

"That sounds amazing, bud. I'll have to get her to tell me more about her job someday."

The little boy squeezed the toy in a tight hug. "Where are we going? And can Siren come?"

Andrew stood up, let out a self-deprecating laugh, and shoved his hands in his pockets. "How does apple picking sound?" He addressed the question to Lucas but glanced at Sierra to make sure his choice of activity was also mom-approved. Her brilliant smile assured him it was.

"Yes!" Lucas spun excitedly in place. "Can we also pick out pumpkins? And get donuts and cider?" He directed these questions to Sierra.

"Of course, buddy." She reached out and tapped the tip of his nose. "It wouldn't be apple picking without cider and donuts."

"I'm gonna get my coat." Just like that Lucas was off like a shot, storming back up the steps.

Sierra watched him go with a fond, if exasperated, smile. She took a step away from the door and invited Andrew inside the back of her shop, which was overflowing with coolers, worktables, and buckets of flowers on every available surface. "I'm going to need to grab my coat too."

She turned to head back upstairs, but Andrew snaked out a hand and grabbed her wrist. "Did I do okay?" he asked, unable to hold in his uncertainty a second longer.

Sierra sent him a brilliant smile that lit him up inside like finally seeing the sun after a long, dark winter. "You did great. Apple picking just so happens to be one of Lucas's favorite fall activities, and we haven't had a chance to go yet this year." She leaned closer and gave him a quick peck on the lips before she drew back.

Andrew let out a sigh of relief. "Then I can't wait to experience it with you both. Turning two earth witches loose on an orchard full of fruit trees? Who knows what might happen."

She laughed. "Hopefully nothing too dramatic. I'll be right back."

Minutes later they were loaded up in Andrew's small SUV and headed west. There was a locally famous family-owned farm about forty-five minutes away. Lucas kept up a steady stream of chatter the entire drive, which saved Andrew from having to come up with topics of conversation.

He knew he needed to tell Sierra about his confrontation with Principal Bodrock, but he didn't know where to start. She probably knew at least some of what had happened since she would have had to come pick Lucas up from school the day he'd run to the nurse's office. She almost assuredly didn't realize that the principal had done it on purpose.

She also had no idea that Andrew had not only confronted Bodrock about it but that his job was now on the line because of it. If the principal ever found out about his relationship with Sierra, it might give her exactly the evidence she needed to fire him. Logically he knew that, but here he was, unable to stay away. This was probably a really bad idea, but he couldn't make himself stop seeing Sierra, and he would *never* stop defending Lucas.

Andrew pulled into the dirt parking lot facing a cheerful red building with wood siding and a large welcome sign. The entire front of the shop was covered in potted mums in reds, oranges and yellows, and enormous piles of pumpkins and gourds.

As soon as the car stopped, Lucas scrambled out. He raced across the parking lot to the pumpkins and started digging through the piles.

"He never slows down, does he?" Andrew asked as he and Sierra climbed out of the car at a more normal speed.

"Not unless he's asleep or you stick a video game in front of his face."

"I vaguely recall being the same way when I was a kid, but now it just seems so exhausting," Andrew said with a chuckle.

"Yeah, there are definitely days I can barely keep up with him." They finally reached the spot where Lucas was digging for gourd-related treasure. "Lucas, come on. Let's do apples first. We can get pumpkins on the way out."

The little boy reluctantly stopped his search. "Okay, but I want to find the ugliest one to bring home."

"I wouldn't have it any other way," Sierra replied with a smile.

They headed inside the building to purchase a bag and then followed the directions to the apple orchards. The farm had multiple varieties of trees. Lucas apparently favored Macintosh while Sierra preferred Cortland. Andrew liked almost all varieties, so he went with whatever they seemed to like the best.

"Thank you for this," Sierra said as they strolled next to one another, their hands not quite touching. Lucas was racing around in front of them ducking and weaving between the trees and haphazardly grabbing whatever fruit seemed to strike his fancy.

Andrew reached his pinky finger out to brush against hers. "It's my pleasure, though there's really no need to thank me. I get to spend a beautiful fall afternoon doing something fun with two people who are rapidly becoming my favorite people to hang out with. What's not to love?"

She blushed prettily. "I guess I'm just not used to guys that understand the kid thing. Lucas comes first. He always will. A lot of guys can't accept that."

He grabbed her wrist and tugged her to a stop, bringing her to face him. "You never have to worry about that with me. I understand how precious kids are. There are too many kids in this world who have absentee or abusive parents. Having loving parents who put them first is the best indicator of a happy and healthy child. I would never take that away from a young person." He reached up and tucked a lock of her gorgeous brown hair behind her ear. "You are an amazing mother, and you're raising a terrific kid."

She sucked in a deep breath and let it out slowly. "Thank you for saying that. It means a lot."

Now was the time. As much as he didn't want to, he had to tell her. "There's something else I wanted to tell you."

They slowly started walking again, doing their best to keep Lucas in sight. "Me too. I got Aura, Brigit, and Jenna on board for career day."

And there she was again, helping him out and being amazing. Too bad his news was far less happy. "That's amazing! I can't thank you enough for helping me find people on such short notice. But, um," he paused and ran his hands through his hair. "Did Lucas happen to mention the flower pressing activity?"

Sierra's cut him a look out of the side of her eye. "Yes, he mentioned it. He wasn't happy about it, obviously. Was that something you planned for the kids?" Her voice was curious rather than accusatory, but he still jumped in to defend himself.

"No, I would never have planned something that I knew would make Lucas uncomfortable. It was, uh, Principal Bodrock. She knows about Lucas's sensitivity to plants and thought it might help him work through it."

This time it was Sierra that stopped walking. "Are you telling me that the school principal deliberately planned an activity that she knew would upset my son?" Sierra's voice practically had frost on it.

"I think so. I confronted her about it—after Lucas had already run to the nurse's office—and she basically admitted it." Sierra crossed her arms and was getting ready to speak, but Andrew cut her off. "That's not all. She made a comment that makes me think she not only knows that witches exist but also that she might suspect Lucas. Then she threatened to fire me. Well, she said she couldn't fire me yet, but she would be looking for any reason to do so."

Sierra opened her mouth to say something, but was once again interrupted, this time by Lucas. He came running up, screeched to a stop, and shoved a red fruit in front of her face. "Hey, look at this apple, Mom! Isn't it weird? It sorta looks like an old woman all hunched over."

Sierra turned her attention to her son and gave the apple its due praise and then sent Lucas back on his way to pick more fruit. "If she's looking for any excuse to let you go, is this wise?" she asked, gesturing between them to indicate whatever budding relationship they had forming.

"Is it smart? No, probably not. But I can't seem to tear myself away from you, Sierra. I know what we're doing isn't a good idea while I'm still Lucas's teacher, but I can't stop thinking about you." He lightly grasped her chin and stared into her warm brown eyes. "You make me feel at home."

"If something happens to you and you wind up having to leave Rock Cove, it's not just the two of us that are at risk here. We're both adults, and we know what we're risking. Lucas is still a kid, and he's growing more attached to you every day in your classroom and every time we hang out like this."

His heart lurched in his chest. He knew he'd done the right thing by telling her what had happened but was really hoping that she wasn't going to give up on them yet, not when things were barely getting started between them. "What are you saying? Do you want to stop?" *Please, no.*

She hesitated as her eyes searched the field for Lucas. She found him excitedly talking to a tree as he picked apples and added them to their almost overflowing bag. "He's so happy. He doesn't have a lot of good male role models in his life, apart from my father. I don't want to take that away from him just because I'm scared things could fall apart."

"Then let's not think about the bad things or all the ways things could go wrong. Let's go stuff our faces with cider and donuts and pick out the ugliest pumpkin to put in a place of honor. We'll take everything else as it comes."

A small smile crept across her face. "I think I can do that."

"Good. Now, race you back to the car." And with that, he called for Lucas and the two of them bolted down the orchard rows, racing through the fields like wild men and leaving Sierra in their dust.

Chapter Twenty-Five

S IERRA WAS LOST IN thought throughout the entire drive back to her apartment. She managed to make appropriate noises and responses to Lucas's never-ending chatter, but she had a lot to think about.

She was furious about what Andrew had told her about the principal. Sierra had never had a close relationship with the woman, but it hadn't been antagonistic either. There was only one elementary school in the area, so it wasn't a good idea to get on the principal's bad side. Not when Lucas still had years to go at the school.

That being said, there was no way she could condone what the principal had done. Lucas was more sensitive than other kids, but it still wasn't acceptable for Principal Bodrock to push him into doing something he wasn't comfortable doing. And if what Andrew suspected was true and Bodrock somehow suspected Lucas was a witch, that made things even more dangerous. Was there a way to report her? Who would that sort of complaint even go to, the superintendent? And what would Sierra say,

"I think the school principal is discriminating against my son for being a witch"? Not exactly the easiest sell in the world.

Then there was the situation with Andrew. She was touched that he was willing to go to bat for Lucas. She was both proud and mildly horrified with the way he'd stood up to his boss. As a parent of a young kid, she was incredibly grateful that he was willing to fight for what was right for his students. However, as someone who had growing feelings for him, she was worried about his job.

What would happen to them if he were fired? Since there weren't any other schools in the area, he would probably have to move to find a new one. She couldn't easily pick up and move her flower shop even if she *wanted* to leave Rock Cove, which she didn't. Plus, it was far too early in their relationship for her to think of picking up and following him anyway.

She glanced at Andrew out of the corner of her eye. He was happily keeping up the conversation with Lucas as he expertly navigated the roads back to town. He had wormed his way into their lives, and he fit there so naturally, much better than his asshole of a cousin.

Andrew had said they would take it a day at a time, and it made sense. They could keep their relationship on the down low for the rest of the school year and then maybe next summer they could date more publicly. It wasn't like she didn't have enough going on in other areas of her life to keep her occupied. Between Lucas, the store, and the magical damage she was trying to fix, she felt a bit like her life was in overdrive.

But that was even more reason why she didn't want to give up on her relationship with Andrew. He was the calm in the storm. A place where she could be herself and maybe even lay some of her burdens at his feet and not feel like she was failing. She knew he would support her in whatever way he could, be that emotionally, magically, or otherwise. He was like a pressure relief valve on an otherwise hectic life.

Which is exactly why she didn't want to let this perfect day end. He pulled up behind her store and threw the car in park. "Do you want to come inside and have dinner with us?" she asked before she could overthink it.

His brilliant smile told her she'd said the right thing. "I would love to."

Between the three of them, they grabbed the bags of apples, the ugly pumpkin, and Lucas's stuffed whale and made it inside the store and up the stairs to the second floor. It had been a long time—years in fact—since Sierra had invited a man up to her place. She reminded herself that it was just dinner. Nothing else had to happen—not that she didn't *want* it to happen. They'd already slept together, and he had pretty much rocked her world. But letting someone into her. It probably didn't make sense to anyone but her, but sex could easily just be about the physical release that came naturally. Opening her home was like giving someone a peek into her heart.

She unlocked the door at the top of the steps. "Welcome to the mayhem," she said as she pushed the door open.

The small apartment wasn't as messy as it could have been. She and Lucas had gotten into a bit of a disagreement the week before about the real definition of the word clean. She'd mostly won the argument, so most of his toys were either put away where they belonged or at least in semi-neat piles.

"Do you want to see my room, Mr. Knight?" Lucas asked as he stood in the entryway hugging his whale.

Andrew glanced her way as if to check if she was okay with it, which she appreciated. She gave him a subtle nod of assent.

"I would love to, buddy."

Lucas tore down the short hallway—which was completely unnecessary considering it was less than ten feet—and threw open the door to his bedroom. Andrew followed him at a more reasonable pace, and Sierra brought up the rear.

"This is amazing," Andrew said as he glanced around the cozy space, and it didn't sound like the sort of placating tone adults tended to use on kids. It sounded like he meant it.

Sierra tried to picture her son's room through the eyes of an outsider. It probably looked like other boys' rooms his own age, though maybe with more plant themes than would be typical. The walls were painted sage green, and he had white shelves all along one wall that were overflowing with books, various stuffed animals, and almost the complete set of the Legos Botanicals editions. His twin bed was messy, with the pine-tree-patterned comforter and sheets hanging off the mattress and dangling on the floor.

Andrew stepped inside the room, carefully stepping around the blankets and handful of stuffies on the carpet, and went to the shelves to inspect the various flowers and trees made from Legos. "Did you make these yourself?" he asked Lucas.

Lucas shrugged. "Mom helped on some of them. But those ones," he pointed at a jar containing Lego sunflowers, "I did myself." His little chest puffed with pride.

"That's awesome. I haven't built anything out of Legos in years." Andrew leaned closer to inspect a Japanese red maple bonsai tree that had taken Sierra and Lucas a week to construct.

"I can help you sometime, if you want," Lucas offered.

Sierra sucked in a quick breath, hoping that Andrew didn't hear it. Her son was such an amazing person and so generous. And he was absolutely falling in love with his teacher. Not that she could blame him. There was a lot to love about Andrew.

"I would love that, Lucas," Andrew responded before ruffling Lucas's hair.

"I'm going to go start dinner," Sierra blurted before she fled to the kitchen. She took a few deep breaths to slow her racing heart. All the reasons why she and Andrew shouldn't be involved seemed to disintegrate before her eyes. The honest affection and caring between Andrew and Lucas was enough to squeeze her heart and almost bring tears to her eyes. She swallowed them down and yanked open the fridge to distract herself from what she was starting to think was an slow slide toward love.

It had been a long day, so that called for a quick and easy dinner. She pulled out some ground hamburger, tomato sauce, spaghetti, and frozen garlic bread and started throwing together a fast meal. It was also Lucas's favorite food, which meant fewer chances of him putting up a fuss.

The scent of the garlic bread inevitably lured her son into the kitchen with Andrew in tow. "Wow, this looks delicious," Andrew said as he sat down at their small kitchen table and gave her a smile.

"My mom is the best cook," Lucas confided as he grabbed his chair and moved it a few inches closer to Andrew. "And spaghetti is my favorite."

"Only the best for you, bud." Sierra grinned at her son as she scooped him a pile of pasta and then smothered it in sauce. She filled Andrew's plate and her own then sat down next to them to enjoy. Mealtime was one of the only times that Lucas wasn't constantly chattering, since he took a break to stuff his face.

"Thanks for including me in your dinner," Andrew said as he dunked a slice of garlic bread into the tomato sauce and took a bite.

She wanted to say that it was no big deal, since she'd been cooking for her and Lucas anyway, and it wasn't that much hassle to feed one extra mouth. Except she knew that wasn't really what he was saying. It wasn't about the food itself, but about being included in their ritual.

"You're welcome. Anytime." She probably shouldn't have opened the door on that quite as wide as she had, but she couldn't stop herself. She was tired of overthinking.

"I just might take you up on that," he said with a brilliant smile that did rude things to her libido.

She desperately needed to find some way to occupy her son so she could jump this man.

Chapter Twenty-Six

ANDREW HADN'T PICTURED HIMSELF with an instant family, but that's exactly what it felt like sitting in Sierra's cozy kitchen, tucking into a hearty meal with her and her son. Their apartment wasn't huge, with a living room, an eat-in kitchen, two bedrooms, and a bathroom, but it felt like a *home*. It was warm, lived in, and had nothing that was picture-perfect or that belonged on a magazine cover. It was a comfortable place for a real family and where Lucas could grow and thrive.

Lucas's room had been a perfect encapsulation of everything Andrew had grown to know about the boy. It was overflowing with things about animals and plants. He also had books on geology and minerals and had proudly shown off some crack-your-own geodes he'd done with his mom. The crystals inside sparkled as they refracted the overhead lights.

Now he sat across from Sierra at the table, watching her delicately spin the pasta around her fork and place it in her mouth with the minimal amount of mess. Lucas, on the other hand, was slurping his pasta and getting red sauce all over his face. To each their own, he guessed.

Conversation flowed easily over dinner as they slowly filled their bellies, and when the last plate was empty, Lucas asked, "Mr. Knight, do you want to play video games with me?"

Lucas's eyes had the pleading appeal of a tiny puppy, and Andrew was tempted to give in, but before he could answer either way, Sierra beat him to the punch. "No, sir. You need to take a bath. And after that, it's off to bed with you. School tomorrow, remember? It's career day."

"Aww, mom. But I want to see if I can beat Mr. Knight in Mario Kart." Lucas turned his baby browns on his mother and even batted his eyelashes.

Andrew had to hold in a grin. Now was not the time to give in. This was Sierra's domain. Whatever she said went. Andrew was just the lucky outsider who got to experience it with her. "Not today. You got to hang out with Mr. Knight plenty. Plus, you'll see him again at school tomorrow."

Lucas grumbled, but it was mostly good-natured. He carried his plate to the sink—even rinsed it to Andrew's shock—and then headed down the hall. Sierra followed him, and the sound of water filling the tub reached his ears. After a quick admonishment for Lucas to be careful in the tub, Sierra came back to the kitchen.

"He's such a great kid," Andrew said.

Sierra started clearing the table. "Thanks, I happen to think so too."

"Let me help," he said as he joined her in bringing the leftovers to the counter and scraping food into the trash. He rinsed the rest of the plates and carefully loaded them into the dishwasher as she finished packing up the food.

Next thing he knew, everything was done, the dishwasher was swishing away silently, and it was just the two of them in the kitchen with no six-year-old in sight.

"Sierra, I ..." he started to talk, but she cut him off by slamming her mouth against his with a claiming kiss.

He spun her around until her back was against the counter then crowded into her, his tongue tangling with hers. Her arms wound around his neck and her hands sunk into his hair, keeping his mouth against hers as they shared drugging kisses. Andrew's arms banded around her waist, pressing her even closer to his chest so that not even a breath of air could fit between them.

Time seemed to disappear. His hands started to wander, sliding up her sides and then cupping her breasts through her lightweight sweater. She moaned into his mouth and arched into his hands as her hips pressed firmly against his own. She had to feel how hard he was, even through the layers of fabric, but he couldn't bring himself to feel embarrassed about wanting her. Sierra was everything, and he wanted to do whatever he could to prove it to her.

The slam of a door had them breaking apart. Andrew suddenly found himself across the room with no memory of moving.

"Mom, I'm ready for bed," Lucas said as he wandered into the kitchen wearing pajamas with teddy bears all over them. If he thought it was strange how not-casually Andrew was leaning against the kitchen table while Sierra busied herself unnecessarily wiping down the already clean counters, he didn't say anything.

"Did you brush your teeth?" Sierra asked as she dropped her towel to the counter and faced her son.

"Yep!"

Sierra pulled Lucas against her in a tight squeeze. "I love you, bud. Sleep well."

Lucas hugged his mom back and then wriggled free. "I love you too, Mom." He turned to face Andrew. "Night, Mr. Knight. See you tomorrow." With that, the ball of energy disappeared down the hall, and his bedroom door clunked shut.

Andrew stood frozen in place. He had no idea what came next. Was he supposed to offer to leave? Did she want him to stay? What was the protocol here? "That was close." Nothing like almost getting caught making out by a kid.

A sly grin crept across Sierra's face. "Indeed it was. But luckily for us, once he crashes, he's down for the count. Not even a marching band drumline could wake him up."

A tiny spark of hope bloomed in Andrew's gut. Was she saying what he thought she was saying? "So," he prompted her.

"Race you to my bedroom?" She took off, mocking his earlier actions in the orchard.

As much as he wanted to race after her, he forced himself to slow down. This wasn't a race, despite her taunt. He needed just that extra moment to get himself under control before he faced her again. He didn't want to be on such a hair trigger that he couldn't last once they finally came together. He wanted to take his time with her, at least as much as she could give him.

By the time he made it to her bedroom, she was already lying on the bed staring at him out of heavily lidded eyes. He glanced around her space for the first time. The walls of her bedroom were painted a soft lilac color, which matched the floral printed duvet that looked as soft as a cloud. A long, low dresser covered in knickknacks sat beneath walls covered in floral art prints.

None of that mattered right now. Not when she looked like she wanted to devour him.

Andrew stepped into her private sanctuary and closed the door, flipping the lock behind him. Better safe than sorry. And then he just stood and stared at her. She looked like some sort of wood nymph come to life. The very embodiment of earth and life. And, for now at least, she was all his.

"You just going to stand there?" she teased him.

"Just taking my time and enjoying the view. Don't worry though, we'll get there." He stalked closer until he was inches from her.

"Are we going to get there any time in this century?" she asked as she raked his body from head to toes with her scorching gaze.

"Well, when you put it that way," he said, then gripped the collar of his sweater and yanked it over his head. He dropped it on the floor as his hands went to the button on his pants. "You going to join in on this?" He arched an eyebrow at her.

"Just enjoying the view," she repeated his own words back to him with a smirk. She took the hint and pulled her sweater off and shimmied out of her snug jeans.

Andrew lost track of what he was doing with his own clothes as she slowly revealed her incredible body. God, she was amazing. He still couldn't believe his luck that he was there with her. With a soft plop, his pants and boxer briefs hit the floor, his cock standing proudly in front of him.

Sierra licked her lips as she took him in. "Get over here." She crooked her finger in his direction.

He didn't hesitate. He crawled on top of her and pressed her gently into the mattress. "Sierra, I ..." He didn't even know what he wanted to say to her.

But somehow, she knew. "I know. Me too." She surged up to meet him, fusing their mouths together.

Andrew groaned and slipped his tongue between her lips and traced her teeth then swept through her mouth. She tasted like heaven. One of his hands cupped her jaw lovingly as the other started at her waist and slowly traced the path he'd started earlier to her breasts. This time, however, they were bare to him. He cupped one reverently, then broke their kiss to swoop down and take her peak into his mouth and suckled on it.

Sierra let out a hiss of breath as her hands dove into his hair, neither pulling him away nor forcing him to do anything, just making a connection.

Andrew's tongue traced a path from the first nipple over to her other one, showering it with the same attention. Her hips started to move restlessly beneath him. He felt a shove to his shoulder, and he went with it as she rolled him to his back. He found he didn't mind at all that she was suddenly on top of him and taking control.

She squirmed on top of him for a moment before she pushed away and reached for her bedside table. She grabbed a condom and, within seconds, rolled it onto his straining dick. He had to squeeze his eyes shut to cover exactly what her touch did to him.

"You still with me down there?" she asked lightly.

"Oh, yeah. More than. Just give me a second." There was no way he was going to be some sort of two-pump-chump. As soon as the immediate need to come had abated, he gave her a nod.

She rose up above him like some sort of avenging Amazon. She used one hand to guide his cock to her entrance then slowly slid down his length. They let out simultaneous groans at the sensation. She took a moment to adjust to the sensation then started to move. She slowly lifted her hips then dropped back down. Then she did it again. And again.

It was like the very best type of torture. She was perfect. Her long, brown hair hung loosely over her shoulders, occasionally obscuring the sight of her breasts before she moved and they were once again revealed to him. She pumped up and down then swiveled her hips in a figure eight motion that practically had him levitating off the bed.

"Sierra, baby," he couldn't even put into words what this meant to him or what he wanted.

"I'm right here, Andrew." She leaned down, pressing her breasts to his chest as she pressed her lips to his.

The rhythm of her hips slowly increased and eventually she broke their kiss on a long moan. She rode him in earnest. "I'm almost there," she said.

"Me too."

She seemed determined to get him across the finish line first, but he wouldn't let her. He reached between them and slid his thumb across her clitoris, pressing and flicking the sensitive bud.

She shattered.

It was about time, since he came seconds after she did. He collapsed, all energy gone from his body.

Several minutes—or was it hours?—passed as they lay there just breathing and sharing the same air. Eventually she stirred on top of him and rolled to her side with a slight groan that shouldn't have been as adorable as it was. She draped her arm over his torso and threw one of her legs over his. He brought his hand up to the back of her head and slowly ran his fingers through her long hair.

Contentment filled him. He wished this could be his everyday life. That they could each go off to their respective jobs during the day, but then in the evening, they would come home to one another. They could take turns cooking and hanging out with Lucas. And then at night, he could sleep with her wrapped around him.

Unfortunately, they weren't there yet. "I should probably go." He forced himself to say the words even though they were the last thing he wanted.

"Already?" she asked.

"I don't want to, but we probably shouldn't risk me staying over. What if Lucas needs you?"

Mentioning her son sealed the deal. "I guess you're right."

He leaned over and gave her a lingering kiss. "Don't worry. This won't be the last time we do this."

"You promise me?" she asked with a mischievous grin.

"I promise." He kissed her again then pulled himself away from her. He quickly disposed of the condom and pulled on his clothes. "I'll see you tomorrow at career day."

"You certainly will."

Chapter Twenty-Seven

SIERRA HAD BEEN TO Rock Cove Elementary School countless times, but usually it was to pick up Lucas either after school, or from the nurse's office. It was rare to be there for a school-wide event like career day.

Sierra arrived at the parking lot just as Aura was stepping out of her BMW in sky-high heels and a pale blue skirt suit. "Has hell frozen over?" Aura asked as she pulled her peacoat more snuggly around her waist.

"What do you mean?"

Aura tipped her head in the direction of the school's entrance, where Brigit and Jenna were standing. They weren't talking—they weren't even looking at one another—but honestly, it was probably the best they could hope for, at least for now. Sierra would take silence and civility over talking and arguing any day.

"Thank you all for doing this," Sierra said as she and Aura approached the other two.

"Are we the only ones talking?" Jenna asked.

"I don't think so." Andrew had mentioned something about the mayor, but beyond that Sierra wasn't sure who else to expect.

"There you are." Andrew appeared next to them. Sierra's heart fluttered a little at his gorgeous smile. "Everyone else is already inside, so let's head to the gym."

They dutifully followed him through the doors and down the hall into the gym. Sierra watched his ass as he walked down the hallway and was having a hard time keeping her attention on the school and her reason for being there.

A sudden smack on her arm made her look at Jenna, who was smirking at her. Jenna used her fingers to gesture to Sierra's eyes, then from Andrew's feet to his head, and then waggled one left and right in a clear *uh-uh* gesture. Sierra blushed furiously at being caught, which just made Jenna smirk even harder.

"Here we are," Andrew said as he opened the doors to the gym.

Principal Bodrock was already inside talking to the mayor. There appeared to be at least two others milling around the front of the gym as well, a man in light blue scrubs and one wearing a lab coat. A nurse and doctor maybe?

This was the first time Sierra had been in the same place as the principal since she'd heard about the flower-pressing incident. She felt the shifting and scraping of her power beneath her skin just begging to come out, but she swallowed it down. She still didn't know what to do about the principal's actions, but she was damn sure the answer wasn't to attack her right before a school assembly.

"Right, so the kids will be here in a few minutes," Andrew raised his voice to get everyone's attention. The principal, the mayor, and the folks in scrubs wandered over to hear better. "We're going to start with the mayor, then move on to our nurse," he gestured to the man in the light blue scrubs, "and our veterinarian. Then we'll have our meteorologist, chef, marine biologist, and florist." He pointed to them each in turn. "You'll each have about five minutes to talk about what you do for a living. I'm sure I don't need to remind you of this, but these are elementary school kids, so keep it high-level and easy to understand. There will be time for the kids to ask questions at the end. Sound good?"

They all nodded their agreement. Sierra briefly thought about asking Andrew to swap her with Jenna so that she and Brigit didn't have to sit next to one another. But she couldn't help but wonder if there was a reason he'd put her last in the lineup and then decided she was overthinking it. Andrew was just doing his job. Right now, they were teacher and parent and not boyfriend and girlfriend. Not that they had talked about labels yet or anything. Was she jumping the gun? She was probably jumping the gun.

Andrew sent her a brilliant smile that made her mind go blank. Before her mind had a chance to reboot, the doors to the gymnasium were thrown open, and kids started filing in. The lineup started with the littlest ones, the kindergarteners, who were led by their teacher to the front row of chairs. Next up were the first graders. Lucas was near the front of the line, and he waved enthusiastically as soon as he saw her. Sierra smiled and waved back. Out of the corner of her eye she saw the principal scowl in her direction, but she tuned it out. She was not letting the Dragon Lady get to her today.

As soon as the remainder of the kids were seated, the principal kicked off the festivities. Sierra couldn't help noticing that while she'd forced Andrew to plan the entire event, she didn't even bother acknowledging his contributions. In fact, Andrew was leaning against the wall of the gym, not even on stage with the rest of them. Even more reason to hate the woman.

The principal introduced the mayor—whom she seemed to have a weird obsession with—then turned it over to him for his prepared spiel. One by one, each of the presenters stood at the mic and gave their talks. The kids clapped politely for each of them, but based on the enthusiasm for Jenna and the vet, there were quite a few animal lovers in the audience.

The kids asked several good, and a few hilarious, questions like "do whales eat sharks?", "where do hurricanes come from?", and if the mayor had his own castle like the ones in England. They patiently answered each question until the principal cleared her throat and took the mic back.

"Okay, kids. Why don't we give our guests one more round of applause as a thank you for coming today." The kids clapped enthusiastically before the teachers in the back of the room gestured for the older students to start filing back out of the gym.

"That went well," Andrew said as he materialized next to them. "Thanks to you, Sierra. And all of you, of course. Thanks for agreeing to speak today." Andrew turned to her friends and gave them each a nod in turn.

"Mom, that was awesome! You were the best one." Lucas came running up and threw his arms around her.

Sierra hugged him back with a chuckle. "I was, was I? Not Aunt Jenna or the mayor?"

Lucas looked at Jenna but didn't let go of Sierra. "You were good too. I love learning about whales."

Jenna ruffled his hair. "I'll tell you about whales any time you want, champ."

"I introduced Mr. Knight to Siren yesterday. We took her apple picking."

Sierra's mouth dropped open, and Andrew froze, a look of horror plastered on his face. It had never occurred to her that she would need to warn Lucas not to say anything about her and Andrew. It should have, though. Lucas could talk anyone under the table. He was also just a kid, so he wouldn't understand the reason he shouldn't have brought it up.

This was totally Sierra's fault. She should have seen this coming.

"What's this I hear about going apple picking? Mr. Knight, do you care to explain what he's talking about?" Principal Bodrock's stern voice cut through the din of the kids' excited chatter as they waited for their turn to head back to their classrooms.

"Lucas, why don't you join the rest of your classmates. Ms. Fell is going to take you back to the room. I'll be there in a little bit," Andrew said stiffly.

Lucas seemed aware of the sudden tension. He gave Andrew a questioning look, then glanced at Sierra, but didn't release her.

"It's all right Lucas. Have a good rest of your day at school. I'll see you in a few hours." Lucas reluctantly left their little huddle and rejoined his place in line. He gave her one last wave as the other teacher, Ms. Fell, led them from the gym.

"Um, do you want us to stick around?" Jenna asked.

Sierra glanced at her friends. They had various expressions that ranged from pinched nervousness to defensive. Jenna shifted so she was standing slightly between Bodrock and Sierra.

"No, that won't be necessary. Thank you for volunteering to present today, ladies, but Mr. Knight and I can take it from here." Bodrock straightened her shoulders and rose to her full height, which couldn't have been more than five feet, four inches. Even though Sierra was taller than the other woman by several inches, she couldn't help feeling like Bodrock was looking down on her.

Jenna, Aura, and Brigit didn't move. Sierra wasn't sure what to do. Her eyes frantically moved between her friends and then settled on Andrew. She knew that part of this was her fault. She wanted to be there to support him and do whatever she could to make this better.

"It isn't what it sounded like, Principal Bodrock," Andrew finally said. His eyes were as wide as saucers, and he licked his lips nervously. "We didn't go apple picking together, we just happened to run into each other at the apple orchard. It was a coincidence, nothing more."

Despite knowing that denial was the best course of action for everyone involved, Sierra couldn't help feeling a little like it was a slap in the face. Yesterday had been one of the best days of her life. Spending that time with Andrew and Lucas had felt so natural and amazing, and yet here they were less than twenty-four hours later, having to deny everything about it. It sucked.

Her mouth felt like it was filled with sawdust. "Yes, it was a fluke. I take Lucas to the same orchard every year. We just so happened to run into Mr. Knight there yesterday." The lie tasted bitter on her tongue, not to mention having to call him by his last name.

Principal Bodrock tugged at the bottom of her cardigan sweater then adjusted one of her perfectly placed pearl earrings. "You really need to learn to lie better, Ms. Dalton." She turned her laser stare on Andrew. "Mr. Knight, I'm sure you remember the conflict of interest and ethics policy you signed at the start of this school year."

Andrew swallowed thickly and wouldn't meet Sierra's eyes. "Yes, of course."

Bodrock smiled, showing far more teeth than was considered polite. "Wonderful. Please stop by my office at the end of the day to discuss this." She turned to Sierra and her friends, who were the only remaining people left in the gym. "Ladies." She nodded at them and left.

As soon as the door shut behind her, Sierra reached out to grab Andrew's hand. He took a step back so she couldn't reach him. "I need to get back to my classroom. I'll walk you out." And with that, he shadowed the principal's footsteps and trusted that they would follow.

Chapter Twenty-Eight

W HAT IN THE HELL had he been thinking?

Andrew walked into his house feeling like he'd gone ten rounds with Conor McGregor. How one small, gray-haired woman could have the same impact as a mixed marital artist was anyone's guess, but Andrew had no desire to deal with the Dragon Lady ever again. He didn't even bother to take off his jacket or shoes, just plopped himself on his couch and threw his hand over his eyes to block the light.

Bodrock had very professionally and almost politely torn him a new one as she pointed out line by line all the policies he would be breaking if he were involved with one of his students' parents. He knew what he was doing with Sierra wasn't allowed. Well, allowed wasn't really the right word. Highly discouraged. Inappropriate. Fucking stupid. Take your pick.

For the first time since meeting Sierra and being taken in by her beauty, charm, and amazing personality, he needed to take a step back and reevaluate this situation. Maybe even his life. He loved being a teacher. He'd gone into teaching largely because of his granny, but he loved working with kids. They were a constant surprise and, as frustrating as they could be, a continual joy. He loved working with them and watching them grow and learn new things.

Being with Sierra, no matter how amazing she was, was putting that entire future at risk. If he was fired from Rock Cove Elementary, the best-case scenario was that he'd have to leave the city and find another school where he could teach. The worst-case scenario, however, was that Bodrock would find a way to bad-mouth him and make it hard for him to find another teaching job.

His cellphone buzzed in his pocket, and he let out a pained groan. He didn't want to talk to anyone. He just wanted to wallow in his misery. He sighed when it finally stopped. Good.

It immediately started ringing again. There was only one person who would be calling him that incessantly. Well, it was possible it could be Sierra, but his gut was telling him it wasn't. With a sigh, he fished his phone out of his pocket and sure enough, Jasmine's name flashed on his screen.

"You rang?" he answered.

"I heard about what happened. What did that witch say to you?"

Andrew sat bolt upright, immediately squeezing the bridge of his nose to stave off the instantaneous headache. What did Jasmine know? How was it possible she knew that Sierra was a witch? This was bad. Worse than bad.

"I can't believe she pulled a stunt like that. And in front of Sierra and her friends no less." Jasmine continued her rant.

Andrew let out a sigh of relief and rubbed his forehead as the facts realigned themselves in his head. "Yeah, it wasn't great." He could still picture the slack-jawed look on Sierra's face when Lucas had so innocently blurted out the details of their apple picking date in front of his boss. That wasn't as painful as the hurt and betrayed expression she'd gotten when he'd immediately denied it and called it a coincidence.

But what was he supposed to do? They didn't have a lot of options. They hadn't really talked about keeping their relationship quiet, but she had to know that was best for both of them, right?

"What did she say?" Jasmine prompted.

"What do you think she said, Jas? She practically read me the riot act and told me all the ways I was fucking up by being involved with Sierra. I tried to play it off like we weren't really involved and that we ran into each other at the orchard on accident, but I'm pretty sure she didn't buy it. This damn woman holds my career in her hands. I said what I thought I needed to in order to save my job." He yanked on his short hair and the slight pain helped ground him a bit and kept him from completely flying off the handle.

Jasmine didn't respond right away. "I meant Sierra. What did Sierra say?"

Oh, crap. He had no idea what Sierra was thinking. He'd been so panicked about his own situation, with good reason, that he hadn't taken the time to think about what Sierra might be going through. Her son had basically outed her relationship in front of not only her friends, but his coworkers and boss. Was she okay with that? Was she embarrassed?

"I haven't talked to her," he finally admitted.

"Andrew!" she scolded. "Don't be a dick. You care for her, right?"

Of course he did. He might even *more* than care for her. She and Lucas each had their own spot in his heart that was uniquely their own. He swallowed thickly. "Yes. I do."

"Then you need to talk to her. To fix this."

He flopped back on the couch and stared at the ceiling. "Fix it how, Jas? Is me talking to her suddenly going to make it so that my job is no longer on the line? Does me telling her that I might be falling in love with her create a situation where what we're doing is okay and somehow not against the rules?"

"No, obviously. It's not great timing that you found her now, but that doesn't mean your relationship isn't worth fighting for."

Sierra and Lucas were absolutely worth fighting for, but so was his job. He didn't want to be forced to pick between them, but he didn't see any other solution here. Was there a way they could pause their relationship until June? It sounded ridiculous even in his own head. She deserved to find love with someone who could fully be there for her and wouldn't make her wait for eight months before he could take her out on a date.

It was probably better for both of them if they just broke it off. He would do what he needed to salvage his career, and she could find someone who could be there for her and didn't have to hide their relationship.

"Earth to Andrew, are you listening to me?" Jasmine asked, bringing him back to the present.

"Sorry, I zoned out for minute. What were you saying?"

She let out an exasperated huff. "Just talk to her. I'm sure you can work something out. The way that woman was looking at you, I'm surprised she didn't have little heart emojis for eyes or something."

A sudden knock on his door startled him. He wasn't expecting a delivery or anything, but who else just came over to someone's house without texting first?

"I don't know, Jas. I feel like this relationship is sort of doomed. Principal Bodrock isn't wrong. What we're doing isn't okay. It was a mistake to get involved with her," he said as he yanked the door open and watched for the second time that day as Sierra's face crumpled. "Gotta go, Jasmine." He smashed his finger on the screen to end the call and shoved the phone in his pocket. It immediately started ringing again, so he silenced it.

For long moments he and Sierra just stared at one another. Finally, she broke the silence. "Doomed, huh? I guess that answers my question."

Damn it. "That's not what I meant." He tried to backpedal.

"Oh no? How else am I supposed to take it? Especially since '*what we're doing isn't okay*' and '*it was a mistake to get involved*,'" she quoted him once again.

He ran his hand through his already disheveled hair and yanked again. Hard. How had things gone sideways so quickly?

"Why don't you come in? We can talk this through." He stepped back, opened the door wider, and gestured for her to enter.

She stayed exactly where she was. "Is there really much else to say?" She crossed her arms over her chest, and he refused to look at the way it plumped her breasts.

"Why don't you start with why you came over tonight?"

She let out a humorless laugh. "I wanted to see if you were all right. I assume you met with the principal, and since she seems like a nasty piece of work, I wanted to check on you."

Sierra was nothing if not kind and generous. She cared about others and would have wanted to make sure he was okay. "I can't lie. It wasn't a pleasant conversation."

"What did she say to you?"

"Nothing I didn't already know. While it's not officially against policy for a teacher to date a parent, it is highly discouraged and generally only allowed when the student in question isn't assigned to that teacher's classroom." He felt like a drone repeating back the words that Bodrock had used with him earlier.

"Right and has that policy changed during the time that we've been ... involved?" she asked.

He blanched. "No. It's always been the policy."

Storms brewed in her eyes. "If that policy has existed since we first met, then why did you think it was okay to get involved in the first place?"

It was a great question, and honestly one he didn't have a good answer for. "I ..."

She cut him off. "Is this policy more important than what we were building together?"

He didn't know what she expected him to say. "No, but the policies exist for a reason. There's a conflict of interest when it comes to grading and discipline when a teacher is involved with a student's parent. Not to mention that it opens the school up to legal or ethical complaints from other parents if they were to find out about the relationship."

"I see. It was fun while it lasted and thanks for the roll in the hay, but when there are serious obstacles, this house of cards collapses. At least I know what promises mean to you." She stormed back toward her car.

"Sierra," he called after her, but she didn't stop. She slammed her door and took off into the night. "FUCK!" He slammed his door closed. This day couldn't get any worse.

Chapter Twenty-Nine

THERE WAS NOTHING IN life Sierra wanted more than to play hooky and spend the day in bed. Her alarm had gone off at six-thirty, the same as every other day. But today, for the first day in a long time, she wanted to shove her pillow over her head and call in sick.

Not that she could exactly call in sick to her life. Lucas would be up at any moment and ask for breakfast. She still needed to get him to school on time, even if she never wanted to see that place—or at least one specific teacher—ever again. And yes, she could call in Zachary to cover the store front, but she had a series of orders for flower arrangements that had come in the night before that he wasn't ready to handle.

No rest for the wicked.

With a sigh, she dragged herself out of bed and jumped in the shower. The hot water and the scent of the herbal bath products woke her up and jump-started her energy.

She could do this. Just because she and Andrew had exploded spec-tacularly right when she thought she might be falling in love with him was no excuse to freak out. She'd been on her own before—well, her and Lucas—and she could do it again. She didn't need a man, even if he was sweet, caring, and not only didn't mind her being a witch, but actually seemed to think it was amazing. He was also a jerk. Boy, she really knew how to pick 'em. Maybe there was something about her that only attracted men who were wrong for her.

Not that she could blame him for being worried about his job and his future. She'd had the exact same fear. She would have just expected that he would have come to her, and they would have worked through it together. She had no idea who he'd been talking to on the phone, but it sounded as if he'd already unilaterally decided that their relationship wasn't going to work.

Fine. She had other things to deal with.

She rousted Lucas and got some cereal into him before loading him up in the van and dropping him at school. When she got back to the Petal Patch, Zachary was already there. She let him run the register while she dove into making the arrangements and placing them in the cooler. A few walk-ins came by the shop to pick up bouquets or, in one case, a lucky bamboo plant. Killian even stopped by to pick up some mums for the planters outside the Copper Lantern.

It was after lunch before she finally got a break. The busy morning had kept her from spiraling when her mind inevitably wandered back to Andrew. Now that things were slowing down, her brain was starting to get in her own way again. She needed a distraction. Something else to think about.

She needed to solve the magical mystery and restore the grove and the park. There had to be something she was missing. She'd combed through what felt like hundreds of books looking for a clue but hadn't found anything useful. There were still several stacks that Andrew—not that she was thinking about him—had brought over. She would call Jenna and maybe even Aura and Brigit and see if they wanted to get together and dig through them. A girl's night sounded just about perfect.

Since it was her idea, it was only fitting that Sierra offer to host. The problem was that her apartment wasn't big enough for all four of them to hang out comfortably. Jenna's house was plenty big enough, but it was just a matter of getting her to agree.

Hoping that her friend wasn't on a boat in the middle of Massachusetts Bay, Sierra tapped Jenna's contact in her phone and waited while it rang.

"Hey, Sierra. You don't normally call during the workday," Jenna greeted her pleasantly.

"What, I can't just have the sudden urge to talk to the bestest best friend in the world?"

"Definitely not when you start the conversation off that way." Jenna laughed. "What's up?"

"I think it's time we have another magic summit at your place. I haven't gotten anywhere with the magical damage to the park or the grove, so I think we need to put our heads together." Maybe if Sierra eased Jenna into it, she wouldn't freak out when Sierra got around to the actual ask.

"I'm down for that. Since Denver helped us out last time, do you want me to invite him? And you can feel free to invite Andrew. He's apparently making friends with the boys."

"I was thinking more of a girl's night." She didn't really want to get into what had happened. She'd save that for when she could tell Jenna in person.

"That works too. Cookie dough and PJs?"

That sounded amazing. "Sure, but, um ..." she trailed off, then just blurted it out, "I think we should invite Aura and Brigit too."

Several seconds went by before Jenna sighed and responded, "Maybe this is more of a liquor situation."

"I'll bring the daiquiri mix and rum," Sierra vowed. "Besides, don't you think we should bring them into the loop on the whole prophecy situation? It involves them too, you know."

"I know. You're not wrong, but what's to stop her from *accidentally* setting my house on fire or something?"

"She was perfectly polite yesterday at career day," Sierra pointed out as she tapped her fingers on the counter.

Jenna sighed. "I suppose so, but that's because she didn't say two words to me the entire day."

"Which is progress from being a bitch, right?" Sierra prompted.

"Ugh, fine. But you're inviting them, not me. It's up to them if they choose to come."

It was as good as Sierra could hope for. "That's fair. And thanks, Jenna. I could really use some good news for a change."

"Anytime. You know that. You and me."

Sierra did know that. Even when Jenna had lived halfway across the country, Sierra had still known that she could rely on Jenna no matter what. "You and me." Sierra repeated the words back to her and then hung up to make plans.

At 6:00 p.m. sharp she was knocking on Jenna's door with alcohol, cookie dough, magic books, and Lucas in tow. Jenna yanked the door open and, when she saw how much stuff Sierra was trying to balance, immediately grabbed the bag from the store. "Sure, go for the alcohol first, I see how it is," Sierra said with a smile. "My dad was busy tonight, so Lucas is going to hang out in the other room and keep himself entertained, isn't that right, Lucas?" Sierra gave her son an eagle-eyed stare, but he just rolled his eyes.

"Yes, Mom."

"Lucas is always welcome. Without him, my bushes would still be overrun with mice, isn't that right?" Jenna said as she wrapped her arm around his much smaller frame and ushered him into the kitchen.

"You just gotta know how to talk to 'em, Aunt Jenna. They'll listen if you ask 'em nice." And he was off, telling Jenna all about the various conversations he'd had with animals and bugs. It reminded Sierra of the additional research she wanted to do on Lucas's powers. Unfortunately, she hadn't had a spare second to think about it in weeks.

Sierra watched them go with a little pang. She couldn't wait for Jenna to be a mother—assuming that's what she wanted. She'd be a natural at it. It was too bad that their kids couldn't grow up together, but maybe Lucas could be the protective older "cousin" or something.

She had almost closed the door when a sudden, "Knock, knock!" came from the porch. She pulled it back open again and saw, with no small amount of satisfaction, both Aura and Brigit.

"You know you don't actually have to *say* knock-knock, you know? That's what this is for." Sierra teased Aura as she demonstrated how to properly knock on the door. She stepped back and made space for them to join her in the entryway.

Aura joined her without hesitation, but Brigit looked around as if bracing herself. "Jenna put wards around the property?" she asked lightly, though it was obviously a serious question.

Sierra shrugged. "She added them a few months ago after the Circle of Thirteen tried to arrest her. Plus, they came in handy when that rogue witch, Danika, attacked her and Denver in the front yard."

"The Circle tried to arrest her?" Aura shrieked just as Brigit simultaneously asked, "She was attacked at her house?"

"You've missed a bit." Jenna had silently appeared behind Sierra. "You might as well come all the way in the house. The wards wouldn't have let you get this far if you intended to harm me. Plus, there's rum in the kitchen. I have a feeling we're going to need it." She turned and padded back down the hall.

Sierra turned back to Brigit and raised her eyebrows.

Brigit gave one final nod that looked like she was coming to some decision and stepped into the house. "Point me to the rum."

Sierra took over blender duty as soon as she walked into the kitchen. Lucas was nowhere to be seen, and Jenna helpfully explained that she'd set him up in the den with his portable gaming system. One less thing to think about.

"Tell me about the Circle," Aura demanded before Sierra had even finished pouring the first batch of drinks.

Sierra nodded at Jenna. It was her story to tell.

"Do you remember that video of me that went viral on YouTube in June? It showed me doing magic at the zoo in front of a bunch of ordinaries." Jenna waited until she got nods from both Aura and Brigit. "A rogue witch named Danika—the same woman who attacked me outside of Cinder & Spice—was the one that broke the glass gorilla enclosure. I did use my magic, but only to stop the gorilla from escaping. Unfortunately, Mabel Hexley showed up on my doorstep a few days later and accused me of causing the damage and letting the gorilla out. She tried to throw me in some nullifying cuffs and cart me away."

"Mabel Hexley? The woman that did our initiation ceremony?" Aura asked.

"The very same," Jenna answered.

"Is she still as terrifying as she was back then?" Aura asked with a laugh.

"Yes." Jenna said.

"Absolutely," Sierra said at the same time.

"Tell us about the attack," Brigit demanded. Despite her claims of wanting rum, she hadn't even taken a sip of her strawberry deliciousness yet.

Jenna shrugged and took a healthy swallow of her own drink. "She seems to be working with someone else." Jenna's eyes cut to Sierra, but Sierra gave her a subtle head shake. It wasn't a good time to bring up Jenna's suspicions about Roderick. Not when Brigit was so close to him. "She attacked Denver and me one night after work. We battled it out in the grove. Thankfully neither Denver nor I were seriously injured."

"Who is she working for? And what on earth is going on? We've lived in Rock Cove our entire lives and nothing like this has ever happened before. Why now?" Aura asked as she grabbed the tub of cookie dough and a spoon. She took a giant scoop of the chocolate chip concoction and proceeded to nibble on it.

Jenna set her drink down and grabbed a thick, leather-bound book from her kitchen table. She brought it over to the kitchen island where they were all standing and placed it in the middle. "Your mother's spell book?" Brigit asked.

Jenna nodded. "I found this among her things after my parents' funeral." She flipped the book open to a page in the middle and unfolded the paper containing the Prophecy.

The day shall come when storms will rise,
Evil comes in friendship's guise.
Chaos reigns to ill effect,

Giving rise to an Architect.
While lives are lost and costs incurred,
He shall raise the harbinger.
Yet hope remains while bonds stay strong,
Friendship rules and all belong.
Fire, Air, Earth and Water,
Must stand against the endless slaughter.

"Fire, Air, Earth and Water," Aura read aloud.

Jenna nodded. "It means us. The Elementa. Or at least so the Circle of Thirteen thinks."

"Because one fated destiny wasn't enough," Brigit scoffed.

"You always did want to be special," Aura said.

"Not this special," Brigit grumped.

Sierra couldn't help it. She burst out laughing. Jenna glanced at her like she was losing her marbles, but soon enough she broke into a grin and then let out a chuckle. Aura and Brigit joined in, and it was *almost* like they were back to their old selves. They laughed until their stomachs hurt.

Eventually, the laughter died down. Sierra poured them each another drink. "Let's move this into the living room. The couches are way more comfortable."

"Oh, what happened with Andrew?" Jenna asked as they gathered their snacks and drinks and carted everything into the other room.

Sierra blanched. She had almost forgotten about the Andrew situation. She sighed and dropped her pile of magic books on the coffee table. "He broke things off last night, but can we not talk about that right now? We have more important things to discuss." She tapped one of the books for emphasis.

Jenna gave her a shoulder a squeeze and then nodded. "Later then."

"What's more important than boy trouble?" Aura asked as she sipped her drink. The chinos and sweater she wore were far more casual than her usual attire but still looked too formal for hanging out and eating cookie dough.

Sierra crossed her legs and sat sideways on the couch so she could see everyone better. She pulled the sleeves of her enormous hoodie over her hands to form mittens. "Someone's been doing spells all over town. I think they're somehow stealing power and stockpiling it for something. It could even be the Architect from the Prophecy." She went on to explain the black marks in the park and in the grove in Jenna's woods. "No matter what I've tried, nothing works. I haven't been able to fix it."

"What's all this then?" Brigit gestured to the books Sierra had spread all over the table.

"I've been through all my own books and most of Jenna's with no success. These are from Andrew. His grandmother was an earth witch. I was hoping you could help me comb through them, and maybe together we could come up with something?" Even she could hear the hopeful note in her voice.

"No one told me this was going to be a book club," Brigit snarked.

Sierra fluttered her lashes at her. "Pretty please? I brought you daiquiris and cookie dough."

Without bothering to say anything, Jenna grabbed a book and started reading. Aura shrugged and did the same.

"Fine," Brigit said. "But only because you brought cookie dough."

They pored over the books for hours. Occasionally someone would find something interesting and read it out loud to the rest of them and they would dissect it together. Finally, at almost 11:00 p.m., Sierra stumbled across a promising passage. "Um, guys?" Her voice was loud after the long silence. "I think I found something."

"One of the darkest magics is that of stealing the life force of another living thing. It is possible to use a witch's own magic as a conduit to suck the essence out of living things around them. The easiest objects are those of the simplest forms of life, such as plants. From there it gets progressively more difficult the more complex the life-form the witch is trying to drain. An insect is more difficult than a plant, and a mouse even moreso than the insect. Draining the life essence of a human is a grave offense and can be punishable by death if caught.

"Only those with the purist of hearts can heal such damage. The witch who hopes to cure such ails must tap into the love in their heart and all the power at their fingertips. Only then will they be able to heal what hatred has stolen."

Jenna was still wide awake—having put on a pot of coffee an hour ago—but Brigit and Aura—who had to get up early for their jobs—were suddenly blinking back to awareness.

"Do you think this is it?" she asked them, searching from one confused expression to the next.

"Maybe?" Aura said gamely. "It seems relevant, but I don't really know what to do with it. How exactly do you 'tap into the love in your heart and all the power at your fingertips'?"

"I don't know, but you can be damn sure I'm going to figure it out." Sierra glanced at the clock and realized exactly how late it was. "I'm sorry for keeping you all so late. Jenna, let me just grab Lucas and we'll get out of your hair."

Jenna waved her off. "You know I don't mind." She started cleaning up the empty drink glasses and mugs. Sierra grabbed the half-eaten tub of cookie dough.

"Lucas?" she called loudly as she entered the kitchen. Jenna's den was on the other end of the house from the living room, so he would probably have had a hard time hearing her. "Lucas, baby. It's time to head home." She wandered down the hall. Had he fallen asleep? It was several hours after his bedtime, and he didn't wake up easily.

She opened the door to the den. The light was on and Lucas's backpack was there, but he wasn't anywhere to be found. "Lucas?" she called again, her voice getting louder with each call.

Her son didn't come running.

"Lucas?" she said again as she checked the downstairs bathroom.

"What's wrong?" Jenna asked as Sierra came back into the kitchen.

"I can't find Lucas," Sierra said, panic starting to set in.

"He's probably upstairs passed out in one of the spare bedrooms."

Yes. That was probably it. Sierra and Jenna went upstairs and opened every bedroom door. There was no sign of him anywhere.

Lucas was gone.

Chapter Thirty

ANDREW WOULD NORMALLY NEVER go to the Copper Lantern on a weeknight. His mornings started way too early for him to even think about drinking a beer the night before unless he wanted the next day to be pure hell on his poor head. Tonight, however, he was cursing himself. He couldn't believe how things had gone down the night before with Sierra. Now that he'd had a day to think about it, he was sure that he and Sierra could have come up with a solution. But no, he'd had to run his mouth, and she'd overheard the worst possible thing she could have heard him say.

No part of him thought what he and Sierra had shared was a mistake. He would do anything to take those words back, but it was too late for that. They were already out in the world and Sierra had heard them. He'd immediately wanted to call her and apologize, but with the way she'd stormed off, he didn't think she would have taken his call. He could have texted her, but that just seemed far too impersonal for the groveling exercise he knew he was going to have to engage in.

Which led him to why he was sitting in the pub on a Tuesday night stewing over his mistakes and trying to figure out how to fix them. He'd been staring into the same pint for close to an hour when a hand slammed down on his shoulder and he was immediately flanked by Denver and Holden.

"'Sup, man," Holden said as he flagged Killian down behind the bar and waved for two pints.

"Uh," Andrew said as he took a tiny sip of his lager. "Nothing?" He didn't really want to dump all his crap on Holden and Denver's heads. This was his fuck up. He would figure out how to fix it.

"Nothing, huh?" Denver said as he took a drink from the glass Killian had just dropped in front of him. "That's not what Killian said when he texted us. He said you've been sitting here looking like a lost puppy and nursing a single beer for the entire night."

Andrew's gaze flew to Killian, but the other man just shrugged, unrepentant. "You weren't opening up to me about whatever's wrong, so I figured maybe you would talk to these two bozos." With that he turned around and went to the other end of the bar to fill someone else's drink order.

"Guys, it's fine, really. I'll figure it out. Somehow." He grabbed a basket of peanuts from farther down the bar and started shelling them and shoving them into his mouth.

Holden leaned around Andrew to talk to Denver. "Does it sound fine to you?" he asked, tongue in cheek.

"No, Detective, it does not. What did you do, get into a fight with Sierra? She didn't put a whammy on you, did she?" Denver asked as he peeled a peanut and popped it into his mouth.

Andrew glanced at him sharply. "She would never—"

Denver raised his hand in a stop gesture. "I was joking with you, man. I know they're not like that. Believe me, I know. They could do some scary-ass shit if they wanted to. Jenna has more power in her pinky finger than I have in my entire body."

Andrew's shoulders dropped and some of his instant anger seeped out of him.

"You didn't deny it, though," Holden pointed out. Damn his cop instincts to keep digging. "You did get into a fight with her. Tell daddy Holden all about it. We'll help you fix it."

"Yeah, it's not exactly like you can just buy a florist a bouquet of flowers to apologize," Denver mused. "We'll help you think of something better. Don't worry."

Holden's phone started ringing. He pulled it out of his pocket and glanced at the screen. "Shit, it's the station. I guess it's a good thing I haven't taken a drink yet." He shoved his beer across the polished wood bar. "Kay," he answered.

Andrew was debating how much he wanted to tell Denver about what he had said to Sierra when Holden stilled beside him as he listened.

Andrew's stomach dropped. He had no idea how he knew, but nothing that was going to come out of Holden's mouth was going to be good.

"Has an AMBER alert already gone out?" Holden's question was clipped. Andrew didn't know much cop speak, but that was a term that Andrew was more than familiar with. AMBER alerts were for abducted children. "10–4. I'm en route now."

"AMBER alert?" Andrew couldn't help but ask as soon as Holden ended the call. Before the words even came out of Holden's mouth, Andrew knew what he was going to say.

"Lucas is missing."

Andrew was off his stool and across the bar before his brain even kicked in. He needed to get to Sierra. She would be terrified. She needed someone to stay with her. To comfort her. He knew she was pissed at him, but he wasn't going to leave her alone at a time like this. She needed all the support she could get, and Andrew would do whatever he could to get Lucas back.

Holden's meaty paw landed on his shoulder for the second time that night. "Hold on there, champ. You don't even know where you're going."

Andrew tried to pull away, but Holden had thirty pounds of muscle on him easily. "I'm going to Sierra's house, and you're not stopping me."

Holden nodded and then said, "Except Sierra isn't at her house. She's at Jenna's."

"Right," Andrew had only been there once before, but he was pretty confident he could find it again, even though it was pitch black outside.

Oh god, it was so dark out. If Lucas was lost outside, he must be terrified. And cold. Night had long since fallen, and it was late fall in New England. The temperatures could easily fall into the fifties if not the forties. That was cold for most people, not to mention a kid his size.

He tried to head to his car again, but Holden still hadn't let go of him. "You're not driving there."

Andrew slapped Holden's arm off his shoulder. "The hell I'm not. Sierra might be pissed at me, but I'm going to be there for her regardless. She can go back to being pissed at me after we find Lucas."

Holden crossed his arms across his chest, emphasizing how many muscles he had. *Damn he was big.* "I didn't say you couldn't go. I said you're not driving. You're practically vibrating with anxiety and in no shape to get behind the wheel. Denver will take you. Now, we're wasting time." Holden strode to his hulking black SUV without another word.

"Come on, man," Denver said slightly more gently. "I'm over here." He gestured to his truck.

They rode in silence until they reached Jenna's house. Andrew was grateful for it, since there was no way he would be able to keep up any sort of conversation with his mind whirling all over the place. He wished he'd tried to pump Holden for more information. Had Lucas gotten lost? Had he been kidnapped? How long had he been missing? Where was the last place he'd been seen?

Jenna's house was buzzing with activity. It looked like every police car in Rock Cove—not that they had many, it was a tiny town after all—was already in the driveway. Uniformed officers were carrying flashlights and setting up battery-operated work lamps to illuminate as much of the surrounding yard as possible.

Andrew's heart skipped a beat when he saw Sierra standing on the front porch, surrounded by Jenna, Aura, and Brigit. Jenna had her arms around Sierra, who appeared to be crying on her friend's shoulder.

"Folks, you can't be here," a uniformed officer approached the car as Denver and Andrew tried to get out of the vehicle. "This is an active investigation."

"The hell I can't," Denver said. "This is my girlfriend's house."

Jenna glanced up at the sound of Denver's voice, which made Sierra look up too. "Andrew?" she asked, her voice watery.

Andrew stood frozen in shock, unsure what to do. As soon as he'd heard about Lucas, his sole goal had been to get to Sierra's side and support her. He would do anything for the woman he loved, even if she wasn't so sure about him.

Oh god, he loved her. He was only just realizing how much he loved her, but this wasn't the time for him to process that.

Now he was wondering how wise his plan was. The last thing he wanted to do was cause her more pain when she was already dealing with so much. "Sierra," his voice was so low that there was no way she could have possibly heard him.

Except somehow, she did. She raced down the steps and threw her arms around him. His own arms banded around her and clenched her close, never intending to let her go. "I can't believe you're here," she whispered in his ear.

"Of course, I am. Where else would I be?" He put his hands on the back of her thighs and lifted. She easily wrapped her legs around his waist and let him carry her back to the house.

"Fine. If you're staying, then at least stay out of our way." The cop huffed and went back to whatever it was they were doing.

Jenna was already opening the door by the time Andrew reached it. She gestured in the direction of the living room, and Andrew slowly sat on the couch and arranged Sierra across his lap. "What happened, baby?"

Sierra sniffed as she lifted her head off his shoulder. She glanced around the room. Denver and the rest of Sierra's friends had followed them, but there were no cops. "The four of us, were doing research into the black marks. You know the one in the grove?" Andrew nodded. "I thought I finally found something, and we were calling it quits for the night. I went to find Lucas in the other room. He was supposed to be hanging out in the den. He had a bag full of books and toys and his portable gaming system ..." She trailed off like she was getting lost in her head. "But he wasn't there. We searched the entire house from top to bottom. He's not here. He's not anywhere. This is like my worst nightmare come to life." She dropped her head back to his shoulder, and Andrew rubbed her back consolingly.

"Can you do, you know, anything?" Denver asked Jenna, making a weird twirling motion with his hand.

Jenna was already shaking her head. "We've tried everything already. We've searched as much of the property as we could by ourselves, though the police are obviously doing it again. We also tried a locator spell, but nothing. It's like it just fizzles out and doesn't go anywhere. The only way that would be possible was if—"

"Someone has him behind a ward." Brigit's voice was as hard as steel. Andrew didn't really know the woman, other than meeting her for career day, but her reaction immediately raised his opinion of her. She was clearly pissed. And a pissed-off witch could only help their situation.

"What do we do?" Andrew asked the room at large. He hated feeling powerless, but he was just a teacher. Holden was a cop, and the four women surrounding him were the most powerful coven in the world. What could he do that would even make a difference?

"We let the police do their job," Jenna said, and when multiple people tried to interrupt her, she lifted her hand to cut them off. "And in the meantime, we do ours."

Chapter Thirty-One

RODERICK HAD THOUGHT HIS idea was brilliant a few days ago, but staring down at the sullen child in front of him, he realized that he'd underestimated the stubbornness of six-year-old boys. He'd expected Lucas to be terrified and willing to do anything to get back to his mother, but so far, the boy hadn't said a word. Which, according to everything Sierra had ever told him about her son, really wasn't like him.

Roderick and Danika had been taking turns stalking Sierra and Lucas and waiting for their opportunity, except Sierra never let Lucas out of her sight. She was annoyingly perceptive and attentive.

A few days ago, Roderick had sent Danika to use her gifts to walk through the walls of Sierra's apartment and snatch Lucas while he was sleeping, but sometime after Danika's last attack, Sierra had warded her whole building—the shop and the apartment—and Danika could no longer just let herself in.

Then tonight Sierra and Lucas had gone over to Jenna's house, which was also warded. Her wards expanded beyond the boundaries of the building itself, and included much of the immediate yard, which meant Roderick couldn't even get close enough to the house to look through the windows and see what the coven and Lucas were up to.

Roderick had just about given up for the night and assumed that they would have to try again another day, when the back door opened, and the young boy slipped outside. For a while, Lucas just sat there on the back porch staring into the night, but eventually he seemed to get bored with that and went to search through the bushes in the garden. He spoke to them, keeping up a steady flow of one-sided conversation, but it was low enough that Roderick couldn't make out what he was saying.

Eventually, Lucas emerged from the bushes, his hands cupped around something small. "Hey, Mr. Mouse. I told your friend this last time, but you really shouldn't be destroying Aunt Jenna's bushes. I'll take you to where I let him go, and maybe you two can find each other again. But you can't come back, okay? Aunt Jenna doesn't like it when her garden gets destroyed." Lucas had marched across the yard, left the protection of the wards, and stopped at the edge of the forest to release the mouse.

It was like fate had shone down on Roderick for the first time in months. He said a quick spell under his breath and stole Lucas's voice. With another flick of his fingers, Roderick had bound Lucas as surely as if he'd tied him up with rope. The poor kid had wiggled and squirmed in place so hard that he'd fallen over on the grass with a thud, but since he was magically bound and gagged, there was nothing he could do. With a third wave of his hand, Roderick sent him to sleep. It would make it easier to transport him.

It was still surprising to him that Jenna had no idea how often he visited her property without her knowledge. He would have assumed she'd at least have some sort of detection mechanism in place for other witches if not one for him in particular. But apparently, she didn't, because he was able to teleport in and out of her land freely. Which was amazingly useful when he had to transport an unconscious six-year-old boy undetected in the pitch black and without a vehicle.

Teleportation was a newer gift that Roderick had been cultivating. It wasn't something just any witch could do. He'd slowly amassed additional power over the years until he'd been able to accomplish it. Doing it took a lot out of him, and generally he could only travel short distances. The more he tried to take with him through the portal, the more it drained him. He'd never tried to take another human with him before, but at least the kid was small.

They'd landed in his warehouse as intended, but Roderick had immediately collapsed, unable to move a single muscle. His magical stores had been completely drained. Danika had been at the warehouse waiting for him, which had both been a blessing and a curse. She'd once again witnessed his weakness, which he despised. However, she'd taken one look at the kid, shoved him—still magically bound and asleep—into a chair, and then helped Roderick make his way to the couch.

Which is where he'd been ever since. It took several hours to recover his energy and his magic. By then, dawn had already peeked through the eastern-facing windows. Presumably Sierra was more than aware that her son was missing. While his intention with snatching Lucas hadn't been to torment Sierra, he couldn't say he minded that side effect. She was getting too powerful. She needed to be taken down a peg and be reminded of how weak she truly was.

It had been hours since Roderick had removed the gag spell and the sleeping spell from Lucas, and he still hadn't said a single word. Roderick and Danika had both tried talking to him, but all the kid did was glance at Danika in fear and remain stubbornly silent.

"Do you know who I am?" Roderick asked. When Lucas didn't respond, Roderick continued. "I am a very powerful witch known as the Architect. I'm happy to finally be meeting you, Lucas. I've heard so much about you." He waited for an acknowledgement, but when one didn't come, he continued, "Do you know what this is?" Roderick asked again, as he dangled a metal charm in front of Lucas's face.

The boy's eyes widened in recognition, but he kept his mouth shut.

"I see from your face that you do." Roderick ran the silver chain slowly through his fingers until he was touching the charm, forged in the shape of a witch's knot. He could feel a low hum of energy coming from the talisman, but it was blocked from him. He couldn't tap into it, no matter what he tried. "This particular talisman belonged to your mother, but I have your Aunt Jenna's too," he placed Jenna's talisman on the table in front of the boy. "I'm holding them for safekeeping. Did you know that I was the one who gave them their talismans when they were younger?"

Lucas's soft brown eyes went even wider.

Roderick slowly pulled the chain through his fingers in a constant loop. Every time he reached the charm, he gave it a slight squeeze of frustration and then kept going once more.

Lucas's eyes tracked his every move.

"You see, Lucas, when a witch reaches the age of sixteen, they're assigned a mentor and their mentor provides them with their talisman. I am Jenna and your mom's mentor, and I gave them these talismans. One day, when you turn sixteen, you'll get your own mentor who will give you your very own talisman. Wouldn't you like that?"

It was obvious that Lucas had inherited his mother's gift of magic. If the talking to mice situation hadn't clued Roderick in, just being in Lucas's presence for more than a few minutes would have done the trick.

The kid practically oozed power, even at his young age. He'd never met a kid that young with that much manifested power.

Lucas Dalton was definitely a curiosity, and it just might make him perfect for what Roderick was trying to do.

"Your symbol wouldn't be the witch's knot like this one," Roderick continued as if Lucas was actively participating in the conversation. "This symbol represents the Elementa. Your mom's coven. Your talisman would represent your power in some way that was meaningful to you. Let me guess, you're an earth witch like your mother?"

Lucas's barely perceptible nod was enough of an answer.

"There are lots of aspects of earth magic. There's the earth itself, the dirt, the rocks, and the planet on which we exist. There are crystals and gems, which can be quite lovely and powerful in the right hands. And then there's the gift of attunement to living things. Being in touch with animals and plants." Roderick's sharp vision caught Lucas's sharp swallow. *Bingo.*

"What's your favorite animal, Lucas? Do you have a pet at home? A dog or a gerbil perhaps?" Roderick knew for a fact that Sierra and Lucas did not have a pet, since Danika had thoroughly searched their apartment.

Lucas licked his lips. "No. We don't have a pet. But I want a dog," he confessed.

The quiet voice was music to Roderick's ears. Finally, he was getting through to the boy. He masked his excitement. "Every little boy deserves a dog. We'll have to convince your mom to get you one when you go home." Lucas may never get back home to his mother, but no need to tell him that. "And what about plants, do you like them too? They were always your mother's favorite. That's why she owns a flower shop."

Lucas nodded. "I like sunflowers."

"And who wouldn't?" Roderick asked good-naturedly. "They're so cheerful and bright."

"Uh-huh."

Good thing Roderick had planned for this. "I don't have any sunflowers for you, but we do have a few plants around here. Would you like to see them?" Before Lucas could even answer, Roderick was gesturing to Danika to bring him a wilted plant that he'd acquired for exactly this purpose. "As you can tell, neither Danika nor I are earth witches. We couldn't keep this poor flower alive, and it wilted on us. Do you think maybe you could fix it?"

He set the potted plant—still in its wrapping from the store, price tag included—on the coffee table between him and Lucas. To his credit, the kid stared at him with suspicion, but eventually his instincts won out. He leaned forward and touched his hand to the dirt. He concentrated for a few seconds, and Roderick watched in delight as the Gerbera daisy slowly came back to life.

"You're a natural," Roderick praised, and for once he wasn't just trying to get on the kid's good side. To have that much control at that young an age was extremely rare. "You want to see if you can manage something a bit trickier? It's something I haven't been able to figure out myself, and I could really use another witch's help." He heard Danika scoff but hoped that Lucas ignored her.

Lucas glanced at the bright orange flowers he'd just brought back from the dead. "Okay. What is it?"

Roderick laid the necklace he'd been fiddling with down on the table next to the plant. "This talisman was your mother's. After years of using it, it is attuned to her magic, and hers alone. I've been trying to do a spell that will help the whole world, your mother included. But unfortunately, I don't seem to have enough magic to pull it off. I'm trying to borrow, *just borrow,*" he clarified when he saw Lucas's widened eyes, "the power from this talisman to help me accomplish my goal."

"What are you trying to do?" Lucas asked, staring at the necklace lying in front of him.

How to explain his lifelong mission to a small child? "I think you're old enough to know that there are bad people in the world. There are good people too, of course, and they try to stop the bad people, but sometimes the bad people can't be stopped. Sometimes they get away with it. Those bad people need to be dealt with. That's all I'm trying to do. I'm trying to stop bad people from doing bad things."

Lucas seemed to be thinking about what Roderick had said. His knee started bouncing, and he kept glancing from Roderick to the talisman and back again. "If I help you use the magic, you'll stop bad guys?" Lucas's eyes narrowed and his forehead wrinkled.

"Exactly."

Lucas hesitated, then slowly reached for the talisman. As soon as it touched the boy's skin, a powerful hum filled the air that Roderick could feel from several feet away—far more intense than the faint buzz Roderick felt whenever he'd touched the metal. Roderick smiled. *Oh yes, this just might work after all.*

"Can you feel the power, Lucas?" Roderick asked quietly.

The little boy nodded as he squeezed his eyes shut. "Yeah."

"Good, that's very good," Roderick coached. "Now see if you can tap into that power. Pull it out of the talisman and give it to me." He held his hand out, palm facing up.

Lucas inched closer to him and placed his much smaller hand on top of Roderick's larger, rougher one. The boy's face scrunched up in concentration. Roderick could feel the push and pull of Lucas's magic as he tried to do what Roderick asked.

A buzz started in the center of Roderick's palm as he felt the first dribbles of earth magic enter his body. He'd taken enough energy from other sources through the years that the sensation was no longer foreign to him, though it was still uncomfortable. He was as fire witch. Earth magic was not intended to live in his skin.

Seconds later, the flow of magic cut off. Lucas slumped sideways, panting heavily.

Damn it. Lucas's magic, as advanced as it was for a six-year-old, was still nascent. He didn't have the oomph to carry out what Roderick was asking of him.

The grove might help Lucas. It amplified a witch's powers, which was why Roderick kept sneaking back onto Jenna's property despite the risk of being caught. Perhaps if he took Lucas there it would give the boy the extra push he needed to complete the transfer. They would just need to get in and out quickly, without alerting the girls.

Unfortunately, given the gentle snores coming from the boy, that wasn't going to be possible any time soon. They were going to have to let him sleep and eat to recover the magic he'd already drained with the first attempt.

That was fine. Roderick had been planning this for decades. He could wait a few more hours.

Chapter Thirty-Two

Sierra was hunched over Jenna's dining room table the way she'd been the entire night. Each of her friends, and Andrew, had tried to convince her to get some sleep at one point or another since Lucas had vanished, but there was absolutely no way that she was going to be able to close her eyes. Not while her son was missing. He was out there somewhere. Likely terrified out of his mind. She didn't think he would have wandered off. No, someone had gotten to him.

She wouldn't rest until she found him.

There was an enormous map of Rock Cove and the surrounding regions spread out on the table in front of her. The morning sun glinted off a quartz crystal dangling from a chain, which Sierra was slowly waving back and forth over the map. She concentrated on Lucas with every fiber of her being and channeled her magic into the crystal, hoping it would drop and point her to wherever Lucas was.

"Anything?" Jenna asked quietly.

Sierra threw the crystal down on the map and grunted in disgust. "Nothing. He's nowhere. How is that possible?"

Jenna handed her a fresh cup of coffee. Sierra didn't even want to contemplate how many she'd had since last night. Coffee wasn't even her drink of choice, but she would mainline the stuff if it kept her awake and functioning enough to search for her son.

"As much as I hate to agree with Brigit on anything," Jenna said.

"I heard that!" Brigit yelled from the kitchen.

Jenna winced but kept going. "Someone probably has him behind wards. It's the only thing that would prevent us from being able to magically locate him."

Brigit entered the room with her own mug of coffee. Everyone except Aura had called in sick to their jobs today. None of them had felt up to going to work with Lucas missing. Aura had only gone in because she worked the morning news, and it had been too late to find a replacement. "Have you tried scrying for him?" Brigit asked as she sipped her drink.

"What's scrying?" Andrew asked groggily from the couch.

"It's a way to see things you otherwise wouldn't be able to see. Sometimes even the future," Jenna explained.

"Jenna, do you have a ..." Sierra started to ask her.

"On it." Jenna dashed away and up the stairs. Her attic was full of everything a witch could possibly need. A scrying vessel would be no problem. Jenna returned a few minutes later and handed Sierra a piece of black velvet and a crystal ball. Some witches used a bowl of water or even a picture frame with a piece of black paper inside it, but trust Jenna to have the best of everything.

Sierra shoved the map aside and carefully placed the black fabric and the crystal ball on the table. Now came the hard part. Scrying required relaxing the mind and letting it open to the energy around it. Sierra was anything but relaxed. But for Lucas, she could do anything.

She sat at the table and stared at the crystal ball, taking deep breaths and letting her mind wander. She sucked in cleansing air and let out negative thoughts. She tuned out all the noise and distractions around her, focused intently on the crystal, and willed it to show her anything she could use.

It stayed stubbornly empty.

"Damn it!" she yelled as she stormed away from the table. She wanted to throw the crystal ball out the window but respected her friend enough not to destroy her house or her witch supplies.

Her rage consumed her, and she began to pace the living room. Who had her son? Where had they taken him? How could she find him and get him back? With each unanswered question she felt her power welling higher inside of her, just asking to burst out of her skin. She needed to direct it somewhere. Somewhere she wouldn't hurt anyone.

"Baby," Andrew said tentatively.

She didn't stop pacing. "What?" she spat out. She was not in the mood to be interrupted or to be placated.

"Um, can you stop the shaking?" he asked tentatively.

What was he talking about? She wasn't shaking. She *wanted* to shake someone, but since she didn't know who had her kid, she didn't know who to go after.

"Please. You're going to damage something."

Sierra came back to herself and looked around. Jenna and Brigit were both standing in the doorway to the kitchen as the house shook on its foundation. Books were falling off Jenna's bookshelves, and the shattering of glass in the direction of the kitchen meant a glass or vase had probably met its demise. For some reason, Andrew was brave enough, or stupid enough, to try to get close to her in the middle of another earthquake.

"Shit, I'm sorry," she wailed as she pulled back the power she didn't realize she'd been letting out. The earthquake finally stopped, and Sierra assessed the damage. A handful of things had fallen on the floor, but at least in the living room, it looked like nothing had broken. "I'm so sorry, Jenna. I'll help you fix it, I swear."

Jenna came back to her side and wrapped her in a huge hug. "Don't even think about it. No one could blame you if your feelings are a bit out of control. It's understandable."

"Uh, guys?" Brigit asked. When they all looked in her direction, Brigit pointed back to the dining room table. The quartz crystal was moving of its own accord, floating a few inches above the map. "Sierra, are you doing that?"

Sierra was tempted to immediately say no, but since she had so recently been unaware of the earthquake she'd been causing, she stopped to really contemplate it. "No. It's not me."

The crystal circled the map in confusion, as if it couldn't quite pin down where it wanted to land. Then, with sudden certainty, it dropped heavily on the map, its pointed tip aimed at a very familiar stretch of woods.

"Are you kidding me?" Jenna screeched.

Sierra didn't wait for the others. She bolted out the back door of Jenna's house and straight into the trees. Her pulse was thrumming in her ears as her feet pounded on the ground. Without even meaning to do so, she used her power to clear any branches and rocks that were in her path, anything that might slow her down or trip her.

She thought she heard someone's voice behind her calling for her, but she tuned them out. No way in hell was she stopping when Lucas was so close.

The grove came up abruptly as Sierra burst through the last remaining trees into the clearing beyond. What she saw didn't even make sense.

Lucas was standing in the middle of the stone circle, his arm out in front of him and something small and shiny dangling from his fist. That bitch Danika was standing off to the side of the circle. She wasn't close enough to touch Lucas but wasn't far either.

"Take me with you!" Danika screamed in panic as what appeared to be a black portal snapped shut next to her. Danika's wide eyes circled in panic as her gaze landed on Sierra.

Sierra had never seen a portal like that before, but she didn't have time to figure it out. They could research it later. The woman in front of her had been responsible for kidnapping her son. That's all she needed to know. Sierra flung her hand out and grabbed the tree nearest to Danika and yanked. With an ear-shattering crack, the trunk snapped, and the heavy fir tree toppled toward Danika.

With a shriek, Danika dove sideways. Unfortunately, she moved toward the stone circle. She rolled to safety, but when she recovered her balance, she had her arm around Lucas's throat.

"Lucas!" Sierra called.

"Mom?!" Lucas called back.

"Don't worry, buddy. I'll get you out of this," she told him. She needed to find a way to get Lucas away from Danika, because as it was, any spell she sent Danika's direction would also hit Lucas. "Let him go, Danika. Now!"

Sierra felt someone come to a stop next to her. Out of the corner of her eye she saw Andrew gasping for breath, leaning forward with his hands on his thighs as he tried to recover from their mad dash. As grateful as she was that Andrew had come to help, Sierra now had two people she needed to worry about and protect. She couldn't let anything happen to Andrew any more than she could let something happen to Lucas. Her job had just become twice as difficult.

The most important thing was making sure Danika was stopped. No way was she getting away again. When Danika attacked them in her apartment, Sierra had been unprepared and out of practice. That wasn't the case anymore.

Sierra silently called to the ground beneath her feet and drew the power into herself. With a wave of her hand, she threw up a magical shield that covered the grove. It was similar to a ward, but hers wouldn't let *anyone* in or out. Danika wouldn't be escaping.

Danika watched Sierra's green magic spread around the grove. "Lucas, do it. Do what the Architect asked you to do," Danika said even as her arm tightened around his throat.

Sierra froze. The Architect had told Lucas to do something? What would he even want with a six-year-old boy?

Lucas's small hands latched onto Danika's arm where it pressed into his neck. "How?" he started to cry in fear. "How can I do it? He's not even here anymore."

"Then give it to me. He may be gone, but I'm still here. Give me the power."

Power? What was she talking about?

Lucas was still crying but trying his best to stop. His terrified brown eyes met Sierra's as he lifted one of his shaking hands in front of him. Only then did it become obvious what he was holding.

Her talisman.

"Lucas, no! Whatever this Architect person asked you to do, you don't have to do it. I'm going to get you out of this, I promise." Sierra said as she stalked closer to the stone circle. "Get behind me and stay there," she whispered to Andrew. She felt him comply, her mind always attuned to his presence. Now at least Sierra was standing between Danika and the man Sierra loved.

"He said it was going to stop the bad guys," Lucas said, clearly torn as he glanced from Sierra to Danika.

"And it will. The bad guys need to be punished. And you're going to help us do that," Danika said almost soothingly.

Sierra had no idea what poison Danika and the Architect had been pouring into Lucas's ears, but she needed to get him away from them before he did something they would all regret. "No, Lucas. Listen to Mommy. You don't have to do anything they told you to do. We're going to stop the bad guys. That's what Jenna, Aura, Brigit, and I are here for. It's our whole reason for being. To stop the bad guys." Sierra's eyes narrowed in on Danika, wishing with every fiber of her being that she could stop her heart for kidnapping Lucas.

Danika was slowly backing herself and Lucas across the stone circle. Her feet reached the edge of the slightly raised platform, and she stopped. As soon as Danika and Lucas stepped off the platform, the magical energy they could channel would greatly diminish. The panic in Danika's eyes as she surveyed the grove meant she likely knew it too. If ever there was someone looking for an exit strategy, it was her.

"Come on now, Lucas. You heard what the Architect said. You can give the power to me. I'll take good care of it until I can give it to him."

Sierra was trying to tune out Danika's ranting. She needed a plan. Her eyes narrowed as her gaze landed on the thing that could solve this standoff. She surreptitiously wiggled her fingers, and the vine that was growing up the tree behind Danika slowly came to life. Without the leaves, it was impossible to tell if it was Virginia creeper or poison ivy, but Sierra was pulling for the second one. Every extra bit of suffering she could cause Danika made Sierra happier, even if it was twisted.

The vine released the tree it was clinging to and slithered down the trunk and across the ground. As fast as a whip crack, the vine wrapped around Danika's ankle and yanked hard. With an undignified yelp, Danika crashed to the ground.

Unfortunately, since Danika's arm was around Lucas's neck, she pulled him down with her. Lucas's cry of pain as he crashed into the hard stone circle went straight to Sierra's heart, but she couldn't think about what it meant. As long as Danika was away from Lucas.

Sierra curled her power around the vine and yanked hard, pulling Danika as far away from Lucas as she could. Andrew ran across the grove and crashed down on his knees next to Lucas, his much larger frame surrounding the little boy and doing his best to shield him.

Sierra turned her focus away from her son and back to Danika. Now, the bitch would pay.

Chapter Thirty-Three

THE BOY'S SCREAM OF pain when he'd hit the ground had sent chills through Andrew, and he needed to figure out what was wrong.

"Mr. Knight?" Lucas asked weakly through his sobs. "My arm hurts." He carefully brought his left arm to hug his body, yelping in pain. His right arm cupped his left forearm, which Andrew could tell was quite broken.

"Shhh, shh. Don't worry, Lucas. I've got you." Lucas needed to go to the hospital, but that wasn't currently possible. Andrew did his best to comfort him in the meantime.

A motion off to Andrew's left drew his eye. Danika made a slashing motion with her hand, and a blade that appeared to be made of smoke seemed to materialize out of nowhere and slashed through the vine. He had no idea what sort of magic that was, but it was like nothing he'd ever seen before.

Danika struggled to her feet, her entire focus on Sierra, who was standing halfway across the grove. That meant Danika didn't notice the giant tree branch that Sierra pulled from god-knows-where and—using her magic—swung right at Danika's head.

Danika dodged sideways at the last second, turning her fall into an awkward tuck and roll. She came up spitting mad. She sent the smoky blade flying directly at Sierra's neck.

Before Andrew could even think of calling out a warning, Sierra waved her hand and must have done something, because the blade clanged against an invisible wall and dropped to the ground. Seconds later, a boulder was flying through the air, aimed at Danika.

He looked around desperately, hoping to find some way to help Sierra. A frantic waving motion snagged his attention, and he realized that both Brigit and Jenna were standing no more than ten feet behind him waving their arms to get his attention. He had no idea why they weren't rushing in to help.

"You have to help Lucas. His arm is broken," Andrew yelled at them.

He saw Jenna's mouth move, but he couldn't hear what she said. She let out a silent scream as she slammed her hand against another invisible barrier and then pointed to her ears.

Andrew pointed at Lucas's broken arm and then mimed the motion of snapping an invisible stick. Brigit smacked the wall again before she threw her hands up in frustration.

A flash of light drew Andrew's attention back to the fight. Whatever spell Danika had just cast had briefly lit up the grove like New York City at Christmas, but Sierra waved her hand, and the multicolored sparks dropped to the ground and instantly fizzled out.

With a yell of rage, Danika's arm lashed out not toward Sierra, but toward Andrew and Lucas, who was still whimpering in pain. A second smoky blade flew toward Lucas, and Andrew didn't think twice. He lunged in front of the boy and was rewarded with the sharp stab of the conjured blade sinking into his shoulder. Andrew collapsed across the stone circle with a groan as he groped for the blade he couldn't reach. He maneuvered himself as much as he could through the searing pain until he was between Lucas and the fight, but he didn't take his eyes off Danika. No telling what she would do next.

"Not my family, you fucking bitch!" Sierra yelled. She put her palms together and speared her arms out in front of her, parallel to the ground. A low rumbling started as Sierra slowly spread her hands. A tiny fissure opened beneath Danika's feet. The wider Sierra's hands spread, the larger the gap grew beneath the other woman.

Danika danced sideways but the fissure followed her. She stepped on the edge of it and wrenched her ankle and went down hard. With a swipe of her arm, she conjured a sledgehammer and walloped Sierra across the arm. The swing not only snapped Sierra's upper arm audibly enough that Andrew could hear it from dozens of feet away, but it shoved Sierra sideways until her hand brushed up against the giant black dead zone in the middle of the grove. Sierra yelped a second time as her hand instantly turned red and blistered. She twisted out of the way so that she didn't fall into the black area, but the motion threw her off balance and she collapsed on her already broken arm with a sharp cry.

"This is why he came after you, you know," Danika taunted as she crawled across the dead leaves to get away from the gaping hole in the ground that hadn't closed. "You were always the weakest of them all. You gave up your powers because you knew you couldn't hack it. You failed to protect your son, not once, but twice. You're not fit to be his mother, and you're definitely not fit to be part of the Elementa. The fates made a mistake with you. You never should have been chosen."

Holy crap, the lies that woman was spewing. Sierra wasn't weak. She was immensely powerful. The few spells Andrew had seen her work over the time that he'd known her were a thousand times more powerful than anything his granny could have done.

"The only mistake here is you." Sierra pushed herself to a sitting position using her unbroken arm. "I am one of the Elementa, one of the most powerful witches of the age." Slowly, awkwardly, she rose to her feet and stumbled to where Danika was still on the ground, panting and holding her injured leg. Sierra waved her hands and Danika's body locked up like it was frozen. "Each of us alone is no stronger or weaker than the rest, but together we are greater than the sum of our parts."

Sierra made a slashing motion with her hands, and the noise from the world outside the bubble of the grove returned. Jenna rushed to Sierra's side to stand watch over Danika, while Brigit dropped down next to Andrew and Lucas.

"It doesn't matter!" Danika spat at them, even as she struggled impotently to get away. "The Architect is going to find a way to raise the Harbinger, one way or another. It is destiny."

"Well, your destiny sucks. I think we'll take it from here," Sierra said.

"Did anyone call for some handcuffs?" A new voice joined the fray. Denver picked his way across the mess of rocks, sticks, and cracks in the ground to reach Jenna's side. He held out a box that was covered in runes and inscriptions. Jenna traced a finger over it in a complicated pattern, and it suddenly cracked open to reveal the strangest set of handcuffs Andrew had ever seen. They were pewter bands, each probably two inches wide, and they were inscribed with yet more symbols. Andrew had no idea what they were, but Danika clearly did.

"No! Please don't." She tried to wriggle away, but she didn't get far.

"You kidnapped my son. You deserve much worse than this." Sierra used her magic to float the cuffs until they were right in front of Danika's hands. They snapped into place with a satisfying clank.

The stabbing sensation in Andrew's shoulder changed as soon as the metal cuffs closed around Danika's wrists. It was like someone had pulled the knife out of his shoulder, but no one had touched it.

"Shit, the bleeding is getting worse! Andrew needs help," Brigit called.

Jenna came running over and dropped down next to him. "Using the nullifiers on Danika must have ended all her active spells."

"Should we call 911?" Denver asked. "I thought you weren't supposed to pull a blade out because it would stanch the flow of blood."

"Too late for that," Jenna said.

Andrew was starting to feel lightheaded. He tried to pay attention to the conversation going on around him, but between the pain and the blood loss, it was getting increasingly difficult.

"Sorry about this. It's going to hurt," Jenna said to Andrew. "Prop him up."

Brigit and Denver moved him into a seated position. He was very grateful that someone was supporting him, because there was no way he would have been able to do it himself. Jenna gently touched his arm, and then her hand pressed hard on his wound.

It was like fire racing through his body as she pushed on the damaged skin. He groaned, unable to keep the pain to himself. Jenna closed her eyes and started chanting under her breath. The searing pain was replaced by the soothing sensation of water gently splashing against his skin. The pain surged again, though less than before, then it was replaced by the waves. Over and over again, Andrew felt the odd rhythm of the searing pain followed by the soothing water. Each time it got lighter and closer to the surface.

He started to come back to himself, no longer floating on a haze of pain and lightheadedness. With one final zap, he felt the magic seal the wound on his back.

Jenna let him go, her arms falling to their sides as she panted.

Everything came back to him instantly. "Sierra, Lucas!" He yelped and frantically looked around the grove. Lucas was sitting a few feet away being snuggled by Brigit, who was carefully and gently running her finger down Lucas's broken arm. Denver had picked up Sierra and brought her over to the stone circle. He was sitting with her as she lay in front of Denver, her hand splayed on the stone.

Andrew glared at Jenna. "Why did you heal me first? They're clearly both badly injured. You should have saved your energy for them."

Jenna's icy blue eyes narrowed. "I'm going to ignore the fact that you said that because I realize you've been through a lot, and you just lost a lot of blood. But when someone is bleeding out right in front of my eyes, they take priority over a few broken bones, got it?"

He couldn't stand to see Sierra or Lucas in so much pain. He crawled across the stone until he could gather Sierra in his arms, holding her snugly across his lap.

"Are you okay? Of course you're not okay. That was a stupid question. I'm sorry." He ran his fingers through Sierra's messy mop of brown waves. "Jenna, Sierra needs you to heal her."

"Andrew," Sierra said, interrupting his rambling. "Slow down."

"No. I heard your arm snap from all the way over here." Sweat was pouring off him, despite the fall chill.

"Take a deep breath. Then look at my arm again." Her voice was far too calm for the current situation.

He sent a frustrated hand through his own hair then did as she asked. Her arm didn't even look broken. He tentatively reached out to inspect it, hesitant to touch it because he didn't want to cause her any more pain than she was already in.

"What? How?" He didn't even know how to phrase his question. He turned his wide-eyed stare on her beautiful brown eyes. "Jenna hasn't had a chance to heal you yet."

"With enough power, witches can heal themselves. It's not easy, or fast, and most witches don't have enough in their magical stores to heal something big like this. But we're not most witches. And we have a secret weapon."

Andrew glanced down to where Sierra's hand was still splayed widely on the stone circle. He glanced at Lucas, where he sat in Brigit's lap, and realized that his hand was also touching the stone circle. "So, you're both okay?" he asked.

Sierra lifted the hand that wasn't currently plastered to the stone beneath them and waved it back and forth. "More or less. Or at least, we will be eventually, given enough time."

"Holy crap." He could barely wrap his mind around everything that had just happened. His pulse rate was slowly coming down as he realized that the woman he loved and the child he adored were both safe. Finally. "What about Danika?" His blood pressure shot up once more. His eyes flew across the grove, but the other witch was exactly where she'd fallen. She wasn't even bothering to struggle anymore.

"She's fine for now. With the nullifying cuffs on she can't do any magic of her own. Plus, we have her bound and gagged so we don't have to listen to her whine," Sierra said.

"But what do we do with her?" Denver asked. "It's not like we can keep her locked up or anything. Jenna's house isn't exactly a prison."

Jenna let out a sigh. "I think we really only have one option, as much as I'm loath to admit it." She glanced from Denver to Sierra and then over to the prone witch across the grove. "We need to notify the Circle of Thirteen. They're the only people equipped to deal with a rogue witch."

"Are you sure about that? After everything that went down back in June?" Sierra asked as she nibbled on her lips.

Jenna shrugged. "Even if I do want to hold a grudge against them forever for trying to arrest me, it's our only move here." She glanced at Denver. "I think it's time we call your friend Derrek."

"On it," Denver said as he fished his phone out of the back pocket of his jeans. He clicked a few buttons and then waited for someone to answer.

He glanced at Sierra for an explanation. "A few months ago, Denver tracked down a man named Derrek Cox. He's a lawyer, but he's also a sort of hired muscle for the Circle of Thirteen. Derrek can notify the Circle that we need them."

Denver hung up the phone and glanced at them. "He said it would probably be a few hours, so I guess we wait."

Sierra pushed away from Andrew. He was about to complain, but she turned to her son. "Lucas, come here buddy." She opened her arms and Lucas crawled out of Brigit's lap and into Sierra's. "Are you okay? I'm so sorry this happened to you. I was so scared for you."

Lucas, finally back in his mother's embrace, wrapped his arms tightly around her neck and let out a sob. His whole body started shaking with it. Sierra ran her hand up and down his back soothingly but didn't stop him or shush him. She just let him get it all out.

Andrew suddenly felt like a bit of an outsider. He started to inch away to give Sierra some privacy with her son, but her arm flashed out and grabbed his. "Don't you dare go anywhere."

He froze in place, unsure how to proceed. He'd never even fully cleared the air with Sierra after their fight and his awful words. Now didn't seem like the time, but he also couldn't stop himself from saying *something*. "Sierra, I'm sorry for how things happened the other night. I never would have said any of that if I'd been in my right mind."

She grabbed his hand and squeezed it. "There's nothing to forgive. You were freaked out, and no one could blame you." She glanced down at Lucas's head where it was buried against her neck. "You jumped in front of a blade for Lucas."

"Anyone would have done that." Anyone who wouldn't do everything possible to save a small kid was a monster.

"No, Andrew. Not everyone would have done that. I owe you my son's life. I'm hoping that you'll accept us both." For the first time, her eyes took on a look of uncertainty.

Was she serious? Did she really not know how he felt about them? "Of course I'll accept you. I love you, Sierra. And I love Lucas. I would be the most honored person in the world if you agree to spend your life with me." A thought suddenly occurred to him. "Wait, you said family."

"What?" She cocked her head.

"When Danika threw the knife at us, you said 'Not my family.'" He hadn't processed it at the time, but now that they had a moment to catch their breath, he distinctly remembered her saying it.

She sent him a wide smile. "Of course you're part of my family. I love you, Andrew Knight. I'd love to spend the rest of our lives with you." She grabbed his face and planted a kiss on his lips.

"Did they just get engaged? What the hell did I miss?" A new voice broke them apart. Aura was standing in the trees looking around as if she was walking into a different dimension.

"Not engaged, not yet," Sierra was saying, and Andrew was in total agreement. They were still trying to figure out how things were going to work between them, but he had no doubt in his mind that that *would* figure it out. Together.

"But maybe someday," he sent Sierra a loving look.

"Someday," she agreed with a nod.

Chapter Thirty-Four

SIERRA NEVER WANTED TO let Lucas out of her sight again. The last twenty-four hours had been the longest of her life. It was still sinking in that not only was Lucas back with her, but safe and sound. His broken arm was already healed. She still had questions, though. She didn't want to traumatize him even more, but she needed answers and he was the only one that could give them.

"Lucas, can I see the talisman you were holding?" At the word talisman, Jenna, Aura, and Brigit all snapped to attention.

Lucas nodded, held out his hand, and opened his fist. There, nestled inside, was a witch's knot talisman. Sierra could feel her own energy humming from the small metal charm and wanted to sigh in relief at having it back. "What did they want you to do with Mommy's talisman?" she asked lightly as she lifted the grubby charm from her son's sweaty palm. She quickly put it around her neck and fastened the clasp. An immediate sense of rightness and calm settled over her.

"Aunt Jenna, you can have yours too if you want it." Lucas dug a second talisman out of the pocket of his pants and handed it to a slack-jawed Jenna. Lucas wiggled in Sierra's lap, so she let him go. He sat next to her on the stone circle, but he wouldn't meet her eyes. "He wanted me to tap into the magic. To give it to him. He said he was trying to use the magic to stop bad guys."

Sierra's hands flexed and clenched as she glanced at her friends. "And did you do it?" she asked gently. She wasn't even sure if it was possible or not. A witch's talisman was supposed to be unique to them, but she and Lucas shared more than a magical affinity, they shared DNA. Maybe that made a difference.

Lucas buried his face in his hands and mumbled something she couldn't hear.

She leaned over until she was closer to him. "I promise you won't get in trouble, no matter what happened. I just need to know."

He pulled his hands away from his face, but his eyes were red from crying. "I tried to. He told me I was a natural and he needed my help."

Sierra felt Andrew's arm squeeze her and knew that he was just as horrified by what they were hearing as she was. "It's okay, baby. I promise. Did it work? Did you give him anything?"

Lucas sniffed. "I think a little, but then I got tired. I couldn't make it work." He buried his face in his hands and started crying again.

Sierra gave him a fierce hug. "You were so brave, Lucas. Thank you for telling me what happened. You didn't do anything wrong."

The seven of them sat in the grove for hours talking and waiting for the Circle representative to show up. Sierra could feel that once her arm had finished healing, the magic of the stone circle then topped off her depleted magic stores.

It was going to take a lot of time to figure out the ramifications of Lucas's kidnapping. As she had suspected, the Architect was going after power in any form that he could get it. He'd gotten both Jenna's and Sierra's talismans but likely hadn't been able to tap into either of them. Otherwise, he wouldn't have needed Lucas.

And then there were the dead zones, like the one a few dozen feet from her. What Sierra had read in that book confirmed it was possible for a witch to pull the life essence out of living things, including plants, animals, and even humans. Her theory about the Architect had been right.

She slowly rose to her feet, dusted off the back of her pants, and approached the black smudge. She reached her arm out, but Andrew grabbed her wrist before she could touch the dead area.

"What are you doing? That thing hurt you the last time you accidentally touched it."

Had it? Honestly, so much had been going on during the fight that she hadn't even realized it. "I'll be careful, I promise." She looked at Andrew with all the love in her heart. "I know what I'm doing." Or at least she thought she did.

With a reluctant nod, Andrew released her wrist. More carefully this time, she reached out and used one finger to touch the dead zone. She was instantly rewarded with something that felt like a chemical burn. She pulled her finger back to inspect the damage.

Leaves rustled around her as the rest of her friends and Lucas joined her in a ring around the black mark. Lucas slipped his small hand into hers and clung tightly.

"What are you trying to do, Mom?"

The word from the book rattled around in her head once more.

Only those with the purist of hearts can reverse such damage.
The witch who hopes to cure such ails must tap into the love in
their heart and all the power at their fingertips. Only then
will they be able to heal what hatred has stolen.

Sierra hoped that the magic agreed that she had a pure heart, because she suddenly knew what the rest of it meant. She looked at Lucas and gave him a small smile. "Do you trust me?"

"Yes." A simple answer and given unquestioningly.

Sierra held her other hand out to Andrew. "Do you trust me?"

"Unconditionally." He placed his palm in hers.

Sierra centered herself, finding the core of her own magical energy. She felt it shifting and moving beneath her skin, even more intense than it used to be now that she had her talisman. However, she already knew that still wouldn't be enough. Slowly, carefully, her magic reached out through her hand where she held Lucas's and mingled with his magic. He gasped loudly, but to his credit, he didn't let go. Once she felt like there was an even flow between her and Lucas, she magically reached out to Andrew and did the same thing.

"What the hell?" Andrew said, his eyes going wide. "What is that?" He whispered.

"It's magic." She winked at him then began to chant.

"Pure of heart and with intent,
Love inside with power lent."

Sierra filled her heart to the brim with all the love she felt for the men at her sides. She pushed it their way while simultaneously siphoning their power and combining it with her own. She was full to bursting with more magic than she had ever felt in her entire life.

> *"To this ground so dead and black,*
> *Essence and life I shall bring back."*

She could practically feel the *lack* of energy that existed in the black smudge in front of her. It was hungry, but she finally knew what to do for it.

> *"Mother Earth I am your chalice,*
> *Save us from this evil malice."*

Sierra carefully shaped and crafted the energy flowing through her and fed it into the dead zone. It took, and took, but eventually the flow of energy started to slow down. The black mark receded inch by inch until it finally vanished as if it had never been there in the first place.

"Wow! It disappeared!" Lucas's eager voice almost caught her attention, but she refused to be distracted before she did what she needed to do.

She said a silent thank you to the mother goddess and released her power. The flow between her, Lucas, and Andrew evened out and settled into a new normal. Not the same as it had been before, but better.

"What just happened?" Andrew said when she finally dropped his hand.

"I'd say it was some of the most impressive magic I've ever seen." An older Asian man stood across the grove next to Danika. Next to him was a hulking man with black hair who, incongruously, was wearing a suit in the middle of the woods. That had to be Derrek Cox.

"Mr. Shen, thank you for coming," Jenna said.

"Please, call me Kai." He smiled warmly then looked down at Danika, who was staring at him in fear. "Presumably this is who you called me about?"

Anger once again welled inside Sierra. "Yes, she kidnapped my son." She grabbed Lucas and tucked him in front of her, his back to her front, and wrapped her arms around him.

"It was the man who took me," Lucas piped up.

Sierra froze for a moment before she leaned down to catch Lucas's eye. "The man? Which man?"

"The Architect. The one who gave you your talismans." Lucas looked from Sierra to Jenna.

"You mean the man who *took* our talismans?" Sierra tried to clarify.

Lucas immediately shook his head. "He said he was the one that gave them to you. When you were sixteen."

Silence spread across the grove for the span of several heartbeats, and then Jenna said, "I knew it!"

"You're going to take the word of a six-year-old?" Brigit scoffed and started pacing around the grove, clearly agitated.

Kai crossed the distance to stand in front of Sierra and Lucas, his expression tight and pinched. "Lucas, is it?" Kai glanced at Sierra, who nodded in confirmation. "This is very important, so I want to make extra sure I understand you. You're saying that the man who kidnapped you identified himself as the Architect, and that he claimed he gave your mother and her friends their talismans?"

Lucas glanced uncertainly at Sierra but nodded. "Yes."

"And was this woman involved?" Kai pointed at Danika, who had started to struggle again in earnest. Derrek placed his foot gently, but firmly, on her shoulder, and she stilled.

Lucas nodded again. "She was there too. They brought me here together."

Kai nodded grimly at Lucas. "Thank you, son. I appreciate your honesty." Kai glanced over his shoulder at Derrek and then pointed at Danika with his chin. With a wave of his hand, Derrek released the binding and silencing spells Sierra had placed on Danika and hauled her to her feet. "We'll take her for questioning. Hopefully we can get to the bottom of this and locate Mr. Mccann. In the meantime, I suggest you stay sharp and keep that little boy close." He tapped the brim of an invisible hat and then followed Derrek out of the woods.

"Well, that was ... abrupt," Aura said as her eyes followed Kai.

"And to think, he's the nice Circle member," Jenna said.

"Um, not that I'm not happy the psychotic kidnapper is gone, but what happened back there with the black spot?" Andrew asked Sierra. "I felt you inside of me somehow."

Sierra turned to face him, grabbing both his hands in hers. "I found something in one of the books you gave me." She explained the passage about witches stealing powers from other living things and how to fix it.

"Wait, you were stealing my life force?" He tried to pull away from her, but she wouldn't let him go.

"No, not at all. I was borrowing your magic."

That stopped him cold. "What do you mean? I don't have magic. I never have."

She reached up and cupped his jaw. "But you do. You're a latent, just like Todd must have been."

"I'm not following."

Sierra needed to explain, and she wanted everyone to understand. She turned to the bigger group around her, who were all looking at her expectantly. "Andrew's grandmother was Madelyn Healy, an earth witch. So was Todd's—they're cousins." Aura let out a gasp. "I've always wondered why Lucas's powers manifested so early. He's far more powerful than he should be for a kid his age." Sierra ran her hand down Lucas's hair and pulled him against her side. "It wasn't until I realized he was related to Madelyn that it clicked. He got his earth witch powers from two distinct lines of earth witches. The only way for that to have happened is if—"

"Todd had latent magic," Andrew said, somewhat in awe.

Sierra nodded. "Which is ironic given his hatred of witches."

"Right, that makes sense, but what about me?" Andrew asked quietly. "Just because Todd has latent magic doesn't mean I do."

Sierra shrugged. "It seemed logical. Plus, I've never met someone who is as tuned in to magic before who wasn't a witch."

Andrew smiled softly. "If only Granny could see me now."

Sierra cupped his jaw gently. "Who knows? Maybe she still can."

"So, now what?" Denver asked. "The last twenty-four hours have been pretty intense."

"Do you still have that bottle of rum?" Brigit asked. The tension broke and Sierra, Jenna, Aura, and Brigit laughed.

"Daiquiris for the adults and cookies for everyone. Coming right up," Jenna said as she ushered them out of the woods and back to her house.

Chapter Thirty-Five

ANDREW COULD HARDLY BELIEVE that he'd only missed one day of school. Everything that had happened since the last time he'd been at the school made it seem like he hadn't been there in at least a week.

He knew for a fact that the Dragon Lady would be pissed at him for taking the day off. Everyone who worked for the school would know by now that Lucas had been missing. Things like that didn't stay quiet, nor should they. Bodrock was going to guess, quite correctly of course, that he'd taken the day off not because he was sick, but because of Lucas's disappearance. It was only going to make the situation with his job more tenuous.

Luckily, they had a plan. He just crossed his fingers that it worked and didn't blow up spectacularly.

He went through the motions of a normal teaching day. Sierra had decided to keep Lucas home for a few days to help him cope and recover from his ordeal, but other than that, everything else about his day was the same as it always was.

Toward the end of the day, he got an email from Bodrock asking him to stop by her office before he left for the day. Since he'd been planning on doing exactly that anyway, he easily agreed.

He'd never liked her office. It was a relatively small room, and her decor was a mix of spartan and fussy old lady, which somehow combined to be the worst of both aesthetics.

"Mr. Knight, sit down." It wasn't a request and Andrew didn't treat it as such. He sat in the cramped chair opposite her utilitarian desk.

"What can I do for you?"

She looked down on him over top of the reading glasses that were still perched on the tip of her nose. "Just two days ago you and I were in this very same office. Do you recall the conversation we had?"

"Of course."

"Then you'll recall that I told you that here at Rock Cove Elementary School it is unacceptable for teachers to get involved with their student's parents. And yet, it has come to my attention that you spent all day yesterday in the company of Ms. Sierra Dalton, Lucas's mother."

Andrew leaned back in his chair and crossed his arms. "You are aware that Lucas had been kidnapped, right?"

Bodrock shifting minutely in her seat. "Be that as it may, there are fifteen other students in your class that could have used your teaching and guidance yesterday. Let Lucas's *parent* worry about Lucas. If you really aren't involved with her, as you claimed two days ago, then there was no reason for you to miss work. Besides, with the strange goings on that seem to follow that boy and his mother, it's probably best for everyone to just stay away from them. If I could keep him out of this school I would, but as a public institution, I'm not legally allowed to do that, so here we are."

"By 'strange goings on' do you mean witchcraft?" Andrew asked bluntly.

The Dragon Lady clutched her pearls. "I don't know what you're talking about." She sniffed and turned up her nose, but it wasn't convincing. She didn't show any of the shock or surprise he would have expected if she was truly ignorant.

"Are you sure about that?" Sierra said as she opened the principal's office door and stepped inside.

Bodrock rolled her chair back so she was as far away from the door to her office as possible. "Ms. Dalton, you shouldn't be here. I'm going to have to ask you to step outside."

"I'm pretty sure this conversation involves both my son and the man I'm romantically involved with, so I'm not going anywhere." Sierra came to stand behind Andrew's chair.

Bodrock stood, her short stature not intimidating anyone. She pointed her finger at Andrew. "So you are involved. She just admitted it." Bodrock flicked a dismissive glance at Sierra.

Andrew huffed. "Yes, we are involved. I would like to formally declare our relationship to the school and request that Lucas be transferred from my class to Jasmine Fell's class for the remainder of the school year. That should clear up any conflicts of interest or potential ethical violations, should it not?"

Bodrock sputtered, clearly not ready for him to have a readily available solution to the problem. "That's not the point."

Andrew snapped like he'd just thought of something. "I'm sorry, you're right. We've strayed from the topic. The topic of witches. That is why you don't particularly like Sierra or Lucas, correct? Because they're witches?" He stood so he was no longer the only one sitting. Sierra came to stand next to him, a united front. "It's the same reason you didn't like my grandmother. She was a witch too."

"You know what I want to know?" Sierra asked conversationally. "Do you not like witches because you're a terrified bigot? Or is it because you secretly wish you had powers yourself, but you don't, so now you're bitter?" Sierra used her magic to float a shiny rock from one of Bodrock's bookshelves over to where she was standing, then plucked the rock from the air and held it up to inspect it more closely. "Black tourmaline. Nice. Now what could you possibly be seeking protection from?"

Bodrock's jaw dropped open as she stared in shock at the rock now clutched in Sierra's hands. It only lasted for a few seconds though, before the older woman's eyes narrowed and her hands went to her hips. "You know, ever since last year when Lucas was in kindergarten, I suspected there was something off about you, but I was never able to confirm it. Thank you for proving to me that you're exactly the freak I thought you were. Now I can go talk to Superintendent Sandoval about getting Lucas removed from school. For safety reasons, of course."

Sierra tossed the rock up in the air and caught it again. "Tell Eric hi, from me. We got to know each other so well when I made the flowers for his daughter Tansy's wedding last month. He's such a sweetheart."

"Plus, are you sure you want to be tossing around accusations of witchcraft in public? First, this isn't Salem, nor is it 1692. Second, what's the likelihood that you'll ever achieve your goal of getting elected mayor if you start talking about nonsense and make-believe? I mean, there's no way witches could be real, right?" Andrew gave her a cheeky wink.

Bodrock's eyes seemed fixated on the rock that Sierra was casually throwing and manipulating. "Oh, I'm so sorry, you probably want this back, don't you?" Sierra asked sweetly as she used her power to casually float it back to the exact same spot on the shelf she'd gotten it from in the first place. As soon as it landed, Sierra's eyes hardened, and she took a few steps closer to the principal.

Bodrock tried to back up but hit the wall behind her.

"Here's what's going to happen. You're going to drop this ill-advised witch hunt against my son and me. You're going to transfer him to Ms. Fell's class. You're never going to force him to do anything with plants or animals ever again. And you're going to leave Andrew, Lucas, and me the hell alone for the rest of the time we're stuck at Rock Cove Elementary. If you don't, well," Sierra shrugged. "I'm not the only witch in town."

Sierra turned and left the office as quickly as she arrived. God, Andrew couldn't love her more. That had been magnificent.

"Will there be anything else, Principal Bodrock?" Andrew asked politely.

Bodrock's face was ashen, and her chin was trembling. Nevertheless, she squared her shoulders and turned to face him more fully. "No. That will be all, Mr. Knight."

Andrew acknowledged her with a brief head bob and left the office.

He was free. The sword had been removed from the back of his neck. He'd fought the dragon, and not only had he survived, but he'd come out of the fight with Sierra and Lucas, which was more than he could have possibly asked for.

Sierra was waiting for him when he got to his car. Without waiting another second, he cupped the sides of her jaw and pulled her closer for a claiming kiss. His tongue traced her soft and inviting lips, and she gasped. He took advantage and dove inside. His tongue darted and danced with hers. It was heaven. It was home.

"Maybe keep it in your pants in the school parking lot," an amused voice broke them apart. Jasmine was standing a few feet away by her car, a huge grin on her face.

Andrew blushed. He'd almost forgotten where they were. "Jas, I'd like you to meet Sierra Dalton. Sierra, this is my friend, Jasmine."

Jasmine stuck her hand out to Sierra who shook it. "Nice to meet you, Jasmine."

Jasmine's grin didn't diminish. "Oh, I've heard *all* about you. Nice to see that you two have gotten your act together."

Oh god, the last thing he needed was Jasmine spilling all his angsty secrets to Sierra. He interrupted before things got carried away. "Please consider this your first parent-teacher conference. Lucas is going to be transferring to your class when he gets back to school next week."

Jasmine's eyebrows rose, but she stayed professional. "Happy to have him. He seems like a bright kid."

Sierra's chin went up and her shoulders back. "He is."

Thankfully, Jasmine could read body language because her smirk softened into a pleased smile. "I'll leave you two to whatever it was you were about to get up to. Just not in public." She smirked, climbed in her car, and drove off.

For the first time in what felt like forever, Andrew wasn't sure what to do. His job was safe. Lucas was safe and recovering with the help of a loving grandfather and a host of witchy aunts. He and Sierra were free to be together. There was nothing standing in their way. "What's next? Where do we go from here?"

Sierra interlaced their fingers and kissed the back of his hand. "Roderick is still out there. I won't rest until that man is stopped. I don't care who he used to be to us. He threatened Lucas. Nothing will get in my way."

"And I'll be there every step of the way."

Epilogue

R ODERICK THREW ANOTHER FIREBALL. He had no idea how long he'd been at it, but one cement wall of his warehouse was covered in black soot. "God fucking damn it!" he screamed again. Throwing fireballs wasn't proving to be as cathartic as he had hoped it would be.

His plan was in ruins. He was further from his goal than he'd been in years.

He'd known it was a risk to take Lucas to the grove, but he'd hoped they would have slightly more time than they'd had. He'd been on Jenna's property dozens of times, and she'd never once caught him. He'd been hoping they could slip in undetected, have Lucas use the stone circle to access the magic in the talisman, and transfer it to him.

Instead, Sierra had shown up within minutes. He'd barely had time to teleport himself out of there before he'd been seen or caught, and he'd been forced to leave Danika and the boy behind.

Based on his spying, Danika had been slapped in nullifiers and was now in the hands of the Circle of Thirteen. He had to hold out hope that the binding spell he'd cast to silence her would stop her from spilling his secrets long enough to shut her up more permanently.

The boy was back with his mother, and he'd taken not just one, but *both* talismans with him.

Roderick threw another fireball, this one at his workbench. It wasn't like it was getting him anywhere anyway. The potions swooshed into flame, magnifying the original fireball until it reached the metal roof of the warehouse. That wouldn't do. He didn't want to burn the place down. Not when he'd taken such precautions to protect it and keep it safe from prying magical eyes.

He reached his hand out toward the inferno and used his magic to pull it back inside. The flames slowly dwindled as he drew the fire back into himself. Eventually, it snuffed out with a tiny puff of smoke.

He threw himself on the couch. It was time to go back to the drawing board. He needed to figure out what he wanted to happen, what he needed to accomplish that, and what obstacles could get in his way.

What did he want? Simple. He wanted to raise the Harbinger.

What did he need to accomplish that? He needed more power. His own wasn't enough, not even with the help of the stone circle. He'd tried getting power from the talismans, and it had failed miserably. He'd pulled power directly from the plants and the earth, and while that had given him a boost, it still hadn't been enough. He needed more. Always more.

What obstacles could prevent him from raising the Harbinger? The Elementa. They were the only things standing in his way. He'd tried to derail them by taking their talismans, but it hadn't worked. In fact, it seemed to have driven them closer together. "Damn it!" He sent a fireball flying at the potted plant that Lucas had brought back to life, instantly incinerating it.

He needed to either split the girls apart so they could never come together and stop him, or he needed to get one or more of them to join him.

Brigit was a shoo-in. He would save her for last. But Aura might need a push. Luckily, he had just the thing.

Thank you from Elizabeth

I F YOU MADE IT this far, THANK YOU for reading *Gaia's Temptation!* I hope you enjoyed reading this book as much as I enjoyed writing it, and I hope you'll stick around to find out what happens to Aura and Brigit in books three and four.

Reviews and ratings are the life blood of independent authors. If you liked *Gaia's Temptation*, I hope you'll consider leaving a review.

If you want to be the first to hear announcements and updates about future books, please consider joining my newsletter. As an added bonus, you'll get exclusive content and other short stories by yours truly!

http://www.elizabethsalo.com/newsletter/

Acknowledgements

This book would not have been possible without a host of people who believed in me and made it happen. Among those I should thank are my editor Chris from CK Editorial Services, Amy Teel from Steel Bear Editing, and my cover designer GraphicSoulArt. I also want to thank the constant support of my write-in buddies Elizabeth Meyette, Brynn Paulin, Anne Stone, and Stephanie Michels.

Also by Elizabeth

The Witches of Rock Cove Series

Siren's Song

The Amazons of Themyscira Series

Amazon in Exile

Amazon in Darkness

Amazon in Hiding

About the author

Elizabeth Salo is a Michigan native who loves magic, myths, and mayhem. She writes paranormal romance, romantic suspense, and urban fantasy books and is a sucker for a strong female lead. She firmly believes she should have been born with superpowers, but since she wasn't, she'll have to make do with writing about people who do.

She currently lives in Michigan with her family and more fur babies (and feathered babies, and scaly babies...) than is probably wise.

http://www.elizabethsalo.com/

www.ingramcontent.com/pod-product-compliance
Lightning Source LLC
Chambersburg PA
CBHW020918060726
47591CB00004B/1304